# NANNY FOR THE PROTECTOR

A Billionaire Boss Romance

EMMA BLAKE

# Chapter 1

## Cara

*Deep breath, Cara. You got this.*

As I stepped out of my car, it really felt like the first day of the rest of my life. I was about to do a walk through of a building that might be the perfect place for my daycare center. *My daycare center.* The words made me giddy. Not even the January chill could ruin my mood.

I had been working in childcare as long as I could remember. Babysitting, aftercare, daycare, nannying. And now, at twenty-four, I was ready to step out on my own. Some might say I was a little too young, but I was ready and hungry to take this huge step. I had a business plan, courtesy of my kid sister Katie who was a top-notch business student at Fordham, a meaningful amount of savings, and grit.

Still, my heart beat fast as I walked up to the two-story building on a quiet corner in Brooklyn. *Building* was a generous way to describe it: most of the windows were boarded up and some of the bricks looked less than sturdy.

I saw the potential, though; nothing some TLC couldn't fix.

Katie's voice rang out in my head, *Don't forget to take pictures!* Duly noted. I pulled out my phone and started snapping pictures of the building. I needed to get a clear shot of the whole thing, so I backed up onto the street just a bit to get the full shot.

*This is going to be perfect.*

Just then, a car turned onto the street and parked just behind mine. At first, I thought it might be my realtor, but the car was way too nice to be his. Like, really, *really* nice. A *small fortune* kind of nice.

A man wearing a well-tailored, camel-colored coat stepped out of the car. His blonde hair was well-styled — think Ryan Gosling — and his face was freshly shaved.

*Who's that? He's gorgeous.*

I didn't have long to admire his good looks before a little girl hopped out of the back seat. She was his doppelgänger, clearly his daughter, and she had a spirited smile on her face.

I couldn't help but smile at her. Kids always brought that out in me. I briefly wondered what they were doing here. Surely a man driving a car like that didn't have business on a nearly empty street in the not-so-nice part of Brooklyn. And there was certainly no reason to drag his young daughter all the way out here, too. Hmm…

I shook off the distraction and went back to framing the shot. Just before I could take it, though, my phone rang. My boss. *Goddammit.*

"Hello?"

"Cara? It's Jenny." Jenny was the mother of the twin boys I was nannying. They were definitely rambunctious but loved me to bits. Jenny, on the other hand, was a pain in my ass. "I need you to come pick up the boys *now*. They're driving me crazy."

I frowned. "I'm sorry, Jenny, but I told you I'm not available until the afternoon today."

Jenny laughed dryly. "You can't be serious."

"I told you about this five weeks ago. It's on the calendar."

"But this is an emergency!"

She always thought her mere annoyance with her children was "an emergency." You would think she hadn't chosen to have them and that they'd been a burden forced upon her. "I'm sorry, Jenny. But I can't."

Jenny let out an angry growl. "You know what, Cara? I think we're done here."

"What?"

"This isn't working out. You're never available when I need you. What's the point of a nanny who's so distracted by other things?"

I held my tongue, but I could have listed for her all the times I had gone out of my way to do my job. The nights she and her husband came home hours later than they said they would. The weekends I stayed with the boys. The times I had run all over town to find the type of bagels she wanted. "I've been more than clear about my schedule, Jenny. I don't think it's fair that you —"

"No. We'll find someone else. Goodbye, Cara."

Then she hung up.

I stood there, staring at my phone, wide-eyed, and my mouth hanging open in disbelief. I'd been with that family for nearly a whole year. I had banked on staying with them at least another year to get all the capital I needed for the daycare. And that was the bare minimum. What the hell was I going to do now?

As if the day could get any worse, another car came

flying around the corner, barreling toward me at an ungodly speed for a residential street. However, in my shock, I didn't notice until it was nearly too late.

"Watch out!"

Two big hands grabbed my arms and yanked me into a wall of muscle, out of the way of the car. I gasped as we fell to the ground, but I was kept safe by my protector's strong arms. I could smell his cologne, a musky scent of sandalwood and spice. I wanted to bury my head in his neck and breathe deeply for a minute — or thirty.

"Are you okay?"

I looked up into the face of my savior. It was the man I had watched get out of the luxury car with the little girl. His brown eyes examined my face with intensity. I couldn't find any words to reply. He was too beautiful for words.

"Are you hurt?"

"Um…"

His eyes widened. Clearly, he thought something was really wrong with me. He pulled me closer and ran a hand over my head, checking to see if I had been wounded. I fought the urge to purr like a cat and snuggle in. "Did you hit your head? What's your name?"

I knew I hadn't hit my head, but I was in shock. Almost hit by a car, saved by an insanely handsome man. It felt like some weird dream. "Cara."

"Date of birth?"

"September twenty-third."

"Do you know what year it is?"

I finally gained my senses and sat up, drawing away from him. "I'm fine, I didn't hit my head."

The man got to his feet and helped me up. "Are you sure?"

His hand engulfed mine almost completely and his height made me feel petite and feminine. "Positive. I promise." I smiled sheepishly. What an embarrassment. "Are you okay? You're the one who landed on your back."

He shook his head, adjusting a button on his coat. "I'm fine."

The little girl sprinted over and threw her arms around the man. "Daddy! Are you okay?"

"Fine, I'm fine."

"Are *you* okay?" she then asked me shyly.

My heart grew two sizes. What a sweet girl. "I'm fine. Thanks to your daddy."

She smiled and hid behind his leg.

The man tenderly stroked his daughter's hair. "That was a little scary for all of us, huh?"

I started dusting off the front of my coat. "You're telling me. My whole life flashed before my eyes."

The three of us were quiet for a moment. This was quite an awkward situation.

"Oh! Thank you. Thank you so much. Sorry, I'm an idiot. I haven't even thanked you yet."

The man's lips quirked, soft-looking and oh, so kissable. It was a crime for a man to have such lush-looking lips. I couldn't help but imagine what they would feel like sliding across my mouth, down my neck, onto my…

"It was nothing."

I shook my head slightly to clear it from my dirty fantasies. "Are you kidding? I could have —" I remembered the little girl at his side. "It could have been a bad situation and you just —"

I was interrupted by the grating sound of my realtor's voice.

"Jesus Christ, Cara! What were you doing loitering in the street?"

My entire body braced. *Danny Morden*. Danny was much more than my realtor, though. He was the son of friends of my parents from their church. We had known each other since we were kids, although Danny was about four years older than me. I never understood how his sweet mom and dad created such a jackass like Danny. But that's what he was and what he had always been.

Unfortunately, he had everyone snowed. My parents never shut up about him and his successes in commercial real estate. And how *handsome* he was. "Cara, you and Danny would make *such* a cute pair." That was a phrase to which I'd become numb.

I usually tuned them out until one day, my mother hinted at talking to Danny's parents about maybe getting his help in my search for a building. I had laughed it off, but a day later, I received a phone call from Danny *fucking* Morden saying how happy he'd be to help me find a place for "my school."

That was the type of guy he was. Unable to listen to anyone but his own ego. But he was willing to help me for zero commission. "Come on, Cara. We're practically family. Let me help you out."

Given my financial status, I really couldn't refuse. And maybe I hadn't given Danny a fair shake all these years.

But nearly running me over wasn't a great way to start our working relationship.

Danny walked over to me from his car, a smirk on his lips. "God, can you imagine how awkward it would have been if I had to tell your parents I hit you when you walked out in front of my car?"

I took one look at his greased-up dark hair and his aviator sunglasses shielding his beady eyes and I just knew.

*I'm gonna have to give this asshole a piece of my mind.*

# Chapter 2

## Wesley

I don't think I'd ever seen a woman so small and sweet-looking full of so much piss and vinegar. It was sexy as hell.

"What is wrong with you?!" the young woman, Cara, growled at the aviator-sunglasses-wearing douchebag. "You could have killed me! Or some innocent child! Who do you think you are, driving God knows how fast on a residential street?"

The man who I assumed was the realtor showing us the place, Mr. Morden, laughed awkwardly. "I'm sorry, Cara. Maybe you should learn not to stand in the middle of the street."

Cara's brown eyes filled with fire. I was mesmerized by her. Mr. Morden, on the other hand, got himself in hot water with that one. "You will *not* victim blame me after nearly *hitting me with your car.*"

Mr. Morden looked to me apologetically. We'd never worked together, but Jenson had given me his name when the time had come to start scoping out a location for my company's newest office. "Alright, Cara. I'm sorry, okay? Don't castrate me in front of —"

"There's a child present, so I think you should watch your language, Danny."

I had to stifle a laugh. I'd known Cara barely a few minutes, including saving her life from a speeding car, and I already knew she was a firecracker. I loved it.

Mr. Morden set eyes on Lucy. "Forgive me, Mr. Taves —"

"It's no trouble," I interrupted. "Lucy is wise beyond her years."

Lucy smiled. "Sometimes I hear Daddy's phone calls."

Mr. Morden seemed to grimace. "Uh-huh. Well, it's an honor to meet you, Mr. Taves."

We clapped hands in a manly handshake. "Thanks for meeting with me today."

Cara suddenly looked uncomfortable. "Danny, I thought you were showing *me* this building."

Mr. Morden — or *Danny* — smiled smoothly. "I am. I'm showing it to both of you."

Her face flickered again with anger, but she held it back this time. "I thought…"

Danny didn't wait for her response. He pulled a set of keys out of his pocket and went to the door. "If you two will follow me inside, we can begin the tour. And Mr. Taves, please keep your daughter close. I can't have her going off and poking around. This building is very decrepit."

I looked up at the facade of the brick building. The pictures didn't do it justice, and I didn't mean that in a good way. "Yes, it seems that way." I took Lucy's hand and pulled her close to me. "Don't worry, she's not a wanderer."

Danny opened the door into the building. I gestured for Cara to go in front of us. "After you."

She nodded her head as she walked past me. It required effort not to stare as I walked behind her. And the poor thing clearly thought she had a lock on the property from the jump. She was so young I couldn't imagine what she was even *doing* looking at a commercial property like this.

Me? I was a pro at scoping out buildings. After all, being the CEO and founder of a company poised to over-take Meta took some knowledge. We were growing so fast, taking old formulas, and improving them while also managing to stay a bit further from controversy — just a *bit*. We had our flagship in Midtown, an outpost in Chelsea, and we were looking to expand into Brooklyn. We needed a home for Readly, our social platform inspired by Goodreads. I always preferred buying properties that needed a complete gutting and face-lift, as opposed to newer office buildings. That way I could tailor a building exactly to my company's needs.

I knew what it looked like. What was a businessman doing lugging his six-year-old daughter to property walk throughs? Well, I was all Lucy had. Her mother had left me, *us*, before Lucy had even turned one. Lisbeth was "not cut out for motherhood." At least, that's what she said. Though we were once in love, Lucy's birth seemed to push us away from one another. I was completely enamored with and in awe of our little girl. But Lisbeth always seemed to be somewhere else, thinking about getting back to her work as a corporate lawyer, disinterested in all the things that went into raising a child.

So I stepped up. What else could I do? Lucy was my life. I would have done anything for her. And I did.

During the week, Lucy spent her time at school and

then in various activities until I was done with work. On the weekends, she tagged along for any business obligations I had. I'd tried to get help before in the form of nannies, but they always seemed detached and had their own lives to attend to. None of them really formed a bond with Lucy. And no one could replace her having a mother.

Lucky for me, Lucy was an angel and always made a good companion on trips like this.

"Daddy. It stinks in here."

I glanced around the first floor of the building. It was dingy and dusty beyond belief. There was glass on the floor from a recently broken window, which Danny was trying hard to clean up. And Lucy was right. The smell was terrible. Musty with a hint of rotting garbage.

"Sorry about the mess here. It's a recent addition to our roster, so we haven't been able to bring the cleaning crew through."

I heard Cara grumble to herself, "That's why I thought I was able to see it before the rest of your clients."

So here I was, high-powered CEO, doing a walk through with a naive, inexperienced young woman. She was adorable with her wavy brown hair and freckles to boot all over her nose and cheeks. But what business did she have buying a building like this?

Danny stepped into the center of the room. "What I love about this building is how much potential it has."

*Heard that one before.*

"Just picture it. A reception desk right here. Conference rooms to the left, offices upstairs —"

"Is this loadbearing?"

We turned to find Cara standing against a column in the middle of the room.

Danny scratched the back of his head. "I'm not sure. I'll have to check the property notes."

"Because this would get in the way of the playroom."

I raised an eyebrow.

Lucy perked up. "A playroom?"

Cara smiled at my daughter brightly. "I'm opening a daycare. So there'll be lots of playing."

My daughter squeezed my hand and looked up at me excitedly.

"A daycare, huh?"

Cara flushed prettily as she looked my way. "Yes. I have plans to open a daycare that specializes in high-quality, comprehensive educational opportunities that focuses on low-income families."

That was a big undertaking. An admirable one, but still. *Big.* How could she possibly have the capital for something like that? "That's an honorable thing to want to do."

She flinched at the word *honorable*. "Um. Thank you."

Danny physically put himself in the middle of our conversation and patted me on the back. "Let me show you upstairs."

Upstairs was more of the same. Dingy and dank. But the windows let in enormous amounts of light. I could imagine that would be a good morale booster to the employees of Readly. Danny explained more of the details of what the building boasted, but I didn't hear much of it. I was focused on Cara. Though she seemed very green at this, she was intent and interested in everything Danny talked about. She took notes in a little notebook, scribbling quickly with excitement and determination.

I admired her spirit. It was clear she really wanted this and had the gumption to see the project through. All that tenacity would take her far. And I couldn't help but notice Lucy seemed enraptured of Cara as well. She watched her and tried to follow her around, asking questions about her daycare. Cara must have some experience with children to be taking on such an endeavor; it was obvious she had an ease with children just from the way she spoke to Lucy, like she was a full-fledged person. I appreciated that.

And I had to admit, I was also watching her just because I wanted to. Cara was a beautiful girl. I had the urge to peel off her heavy winter coat so I could get a better look at her voluptuous curves.

*Shake it off. Don't think with your dick.*

Finally, I stopped. "Okay, let's get down to specifics, shall we?"

Danny smiled. *Yes, the price.* "Let's walk and talk, Mr. Taves."

It was obvious how much he wanted to sell to me over Cara. I felt sort of bad as she followed behind at our heels.

"This building is a steal for Brooklyn. Just shy of one million."

"A million?!" Cara blustered.

Danny glared back at her. "Yes. Nine hundred ninety-five, to be exact."

Cara wriggled in between us to face Danny. "But what about all the damage? Surely there's some way that takes away from the price."

He glanced at me with a condescending air, as if to say, *Are you hearing this?* "You're paying for location, Cara. Brooklyn is prime real estate."

"But you said —"

"I'm just showing you what I've got. And if it's not in your budget, I'd be happy to continue this discussion with Mr. Taves, if he's interested." Danny smiled at me. It made me want to punch him.

I pursed my lips. I didn't want to buy anything from this guy. He seemed like a money-hungry jerk. "Nah, I think I'm good. Thanks, Mr. Morden. Come on, Luce."

As we walked toward the front door, I heard Cara and Danny squabble for a minute.

"Listen, Cara, I'm not looking to make you mad. How about we grab dinner tonight and we can smooth things over? Start fresh."

That sounded like more than just a business meeting to me.

"No, thank you. I'm seeing my parents tonight, anyway."

"Some other time, then." Good for her. For some inexplicable reason, it caused me to bristle just thinking of her going out with a greaseball like Morden.

"Uh…sure."

We all made our way outside. The gray January sky reflected the mood of the group. Danny said goodbye to both of us, assuring me that he'd find a property just perfect for my new venture. As soon as he was out of earshot in his little black sports car, I looked to Cara who was tip-tapping on her phone at breakneck pace. "Uh, Luce, head to the car, will you?"

I unlocked the car with the fob and watched Lucy skip down the block, waiting until she was safely inside to converse with Cara. "You know, if you're going to get through to a guy like that, you need to be a bit savvier."

Her head shot up, brown eyes blazing. *Uh-oh*. It looked like I would be on the receiving end of her next dress down. If I hadn't been struck by her exquisite beauty, I might have been terrified. "Excuse me? What makes you think I'm looking for advice from you?"

I took a deep breath and smiled. "Just in negotiation. It's an art form. It can be tough if you haven't cut your teeth in the corporate world."

Cara's sour face mellowed. "Right. Maybe. I'm — I'm sorry. I was rude."

"It's alright."

"I just…" She looked down at her phone and then sighed. "I just lost my nannying gig because the mother is a complete tyrant, and it was going to be the difference between me affording a down payment on the property loan or…"

*Ding, ding, ding* — a bell went off in my head. With Readly needing so much attention, I'd been starting to worry about Lucy. Though I didn't like leaving her with other people, I couldn't have her sitting in my office every night while I worked late on the project. "You're a nanny?"

Cara wilted like a dying flower. "Yeah. Or was. I'm not sure anymore." She looked up at the building. "I just felt so good about this place. I could really picture it all."

She looked hopeful and determined all at once. The combination showed me she was more mature than I originally understood. It also stirred something in me that caught me by surprise.

I glanced over my shoulder at the car and then back to Cara. "Let's meet for coffee." I reached into my coat and pulled out one of my business cards. "Say, Monday morning."

Cara took the card, her fingers brushing mine. I shivered involuntarily. I could chalk it up to the cold, but in reality, Cara's slightest touch had electrified me. She stared at the card and then looked up at me, blinking her big brown eyes. "What for?"

I smiled. "Maybe we can help each other."

# Chapter 3

### Cara

"So, Cara. How'd the showing go?"

I looked over at my sister and then at my parents. We were all sitting on the porch, bundled up in blankets and sipping red wine. It was enclosed in glass, protecting us from the cold and rainy January night.

Mom clapped her hands together. "Yes, Cara, we've been dying to hear! How was Danny?"

Katie glared. "I didn't ask about *Danny*. I asked about *the showing*."

"Same difference!"

I chewed on my lower lip. I'd managed to avoid the subject during dinner. I didn't know where to begin with the showing. The more I thought about it on the way over, the more surreal it felt. Losing my job, a near-death experience, a sexy DILF, and a mysterious proposition, all in the span of half an hour? I didn't know where to begin. "It was good, I think."

Katie laughed. "You think?"

"Well, I loved the building. It's just perfect. I mean, it needs a lot of work, but I knew that going in. I was ready to try and make a deal today, but there was another buyer there. Danny didn't tell me about that."

Dad shrugged. "That's the way it works, kiddo."

"Right, but from our conversations, he made it seem like it was a *private* showing. So imagine my surprise when another guy showed up. And not just like a normal person. Someone with money."

Katie leaned in. "How'd you know he has money?"

I thought about the man who'd saved my life. His whole being screamed the word *expensive*. From his car to the scent of his cologne to the cut of his coat, it was obvious. "I could just tell. The rest of the time, I was just stumbling over myself and didn't know what to say. I looked pathetic."

"Oh, honey…" Mom wrapped her arm around me and squeezed me close to her. "I'm sure it wasn't all that bad."

"It was bad enough that the guy offered to teach me the art of negotiation."

Katie's expression turned with disgust. "That's *so* condescending!"

"Maybe. I don't know. He wasn't a total jerk about it. He actually suggested we get coffee on Monday."

Dad frowned. "To teach you how to negotiate?"

To be honest, I didn't know exactly what the man wanted from me. I hadn't had an opportunity to ask any questions before he waltzed off to his car, leaving me completely bewildered.

*Maybe we can help each other? What the hell does that mean?*

If this guy thought I was going to do some kinky sexual favors for him in exchange for…well, I didn't even know what, he had another thing coming.

"I guess?"

"What's his name?" Katie whipped out her phone. *Here she goes with the googling.* She was a quintessential twentysomething, eager to do FBI level investigation on anyone with just a first name and a few keywords.

"Gosh. You know, I've forgotten. Something with a *T*, maybe?" From the moment I left the showing, the business card felt heavy in my pocket. "Wait. I've got his business card right here." I reached into my jeans and whipped it out.

Katie snatched it from me and read. Her eyes went wide. "Holy shit, Car."

"Language, Katie," Dad scolded.

"You met *Wesley Taves?*"

I looked around. I didn't know the name, but it was clear everyone else did. "Should I know who that is?"

"Um, yeah! He's only, like, one of the biggest business moguls of the twenty-first century! Look!" She quickly tapped something out on her phone and then held it up to me.

There I was, face-to-face with the man who had saved me, except he was on the cover of *Time* magazine. His sandy hair was coiffed perfectly, like it had been effortlessly tousled by a beachy breeze, and his dark brown eyes intrigued me in a way I'd never experienced. He was captivating. The title read, "Wesley Taves: The World's Best Billionaire."

I couldn't believe what I was reading. "Billionaire?! He's a —"

"*Huge*. He's bigger than Zuckerberg and has a bigger net worth than Musk. How haven't you heard of him?"

I shrugged. I guess I had been too busy working on my life to notice much of anything else.

"He's been in *Forbes* and *Time*; he's always in *The New*

*York Times.*" Of course, Katie knew everything about him. She was always trolling for news in the business world. "Plus, he's like, super-hot."

I resisted any agreement. But the truth was, I hadn't been able to get Wesley out of my head all day. The feeling of his arms around me continued to raise goose bumps on my skin, and his masculine scent still tickled my nose.

Mom snatched the phone. "Let me see."

Katie snickered, looking to Dad who seemed uncomfortable with the idea of his wife thinking any other man was hot.

"Hmm. Yes. He's certainly handsome. But way too old for Cara."

I gasped. "I'm not going on a *date* with him! It's a business meeting. Probably something to do with his daughter. He seemed really interested when I said I was a nanny."

"But you have a job, pumpkin."

I looked to my dad sheepishly. "Um. Actually, I'm no longer working with the Nolans."

His eyebrows jumped. "As of when?"

"As of today. The details don't matter." I waved that part of the conversation away. I didn't need my parents prying into my life any more than they already did. They were constantly hovering, asking questions, wondering when I was going to do X, Y, or Z.

Katie giggled. "This is so exciting, Cara. You're going to be so close to brilliance. I have a ton of questions for him. Can I give you a list and maybe you could —"

"Easy, Katie. I haven't even decided whether I'm going yet."

"You have to!"

My parents exchanged a look. Dad took a deep breath. "Pumpkin…"

I knew that tone of voice. The we-know-what's-best-for-you tone of voice. It had been haunting me for years. For a long time, I had trusted my parents' opinions on nearly everything, from what career I should pursue to what shampoo I should buy. I was getting sick of it.

"I don't think this is such a good idea."

*Fine. I'll humor them*. "Why not?"

"People like that…well, they have different morals than people like us. You understand?"

*Us* Smiths were staunchly middle class. Katie and I grew up in the same house my father grew up in here on Long Island. My mother was a teacher and Dad ran a small landscaping business. They worked hard, but we were also comfortable.

"They do whatever they need to get what they want," Mom followed up with a look to Dad who nodded in agreement. "We don't want you getting into a situation you can't get out of."

"You're talking about him like he's a horror movie villain or something. I'll be *fine*. Besides, I haven't even met with him. Who knows what he really wants."

"Exactly. Who knows? That's the issue." Dad took a sip of wine. "We just don't want anyone taking advantage of you, pumpkin."

I chewed on my lower lip. "Yeah. Maybe you're right."

Katie audibly sighed. I hated disappointing her. But I hated disappointing my parents more.

"There'll be plenty of opportunities with people who aren't going to use you up. Just you wait. Now —" Mom cleared her throat "— tell me about Danny. How did he look?"

I rolled my eyes. "The same as he always does."

"Was he wearing those stupid glasses?"

"Katie!"

"What?! They're stupid!"

I laughed. "Yeah, he was wearing the glasses."

"Eww."

"Girls, girls. Danny's *very* handsome."

We both looked at our mom. Her taste was significantly different from ours, clearly. My mother liked men who looked slick and put together, with killer smiles and sparkling veneers. Something about people who flaunted their money seemed to attract her. Katie and I saw through that. Guys like Danny didn't have anything else going for them. Of course, he had to show off his money to make up for his awful personality.

Meanwhile, I preferred a man much like Wesley Taves…if not exactly like him. Even though he had much more money than Danny, being the owner of a Fortune 500 company, he didn't have to throw his wealth in my face to make me pay attention to him. Everything in my body pulled me toward Wesley. He was magnetic. Effortless. From the moment his arms were around me, I was under his spell and I couldn't look away.

I hadn't been able to shake the depth of his dark brown eyes and the smell of his musk, his protective touch, and the sound of his deep voice. The only sense I had not used was taste.

And God, how I would have liked to taste him.

I cleared my throat. *Get over it, Cara. A man as sexy as that could have any woman in the world. Why would he want you? Besides, he's probably twice your age.* "Right…well. Danny was Danny. Cocky and oblivious. So much so that he nearly ran me over with his car."

My parents had the gall to laugh. Katie gaped. "What the hell, guys?"

"I'm serious! He nearly —" I huffed. "If Wesley Taves hadn't been there to pull me out of the way, I'd be in traction!"

Dad got his act together faster. "I'm sorry, Cara. It seemed like you were being dramatic at first."

Any time I tried to express myself, I was being dramatic. I couldn't even tell my parents I was nearly hit with a car without them thinking I was making things too big a deal.

"Did he apologize?" Mom asked.

"He wanted to make it up to me — the whole debacle with another potential buyer being there, so he asked if I wanted to grab dinner tonight, but —"

Mom gasped, clutching her chest. "Why didn't you go?!"

"Yes, pumpkin, you should have gone!"

My parents were clearly interlopers. I had no doubt they talked daily with the Mordens about ways to set Danny and me up. "Dinner doesn't make up for nearly squashing me with the front of his car. Besides —" I went on with a glimmering, sweet smile "— I had dinner with you guys."

Mom waved her hand, as if it was nothing. "Well, you can always see us. You should have gone, sweetie."

I pursed my lips. I didn't have it in me to tell them I didn't *want* to go on a date with Danny. Lucky for me, Katie came to my rescue.

"Ugh. You guys, Danny is *not* Cara's type. He's too obsessed with looking cool and way too frat boy. Cara's never been into that." She was right. I was into the suave and stoic type. The Wesley Taves type. He could go right into the dictionary next to the definition of my type. "Besides, he's a total dick."

I snorted into my wine. I grinned and mouthed *thank you* to her. She had a straightforwardness I could only dream of. For some reason, it didn't seem like our parents were as controlling of her, although she still lived at home. Maybe having eyes on her helped.

Mom clutched her heart, scandalized. "Katie! Don't say such a thing. Danny is a nice boy."

"To you, maybe. But he's such a fuckboy."

"That's enough," Dad boomed. "Katie. Apologize."

"He nearly hit Cara with his car!"

"*Katie.*"

"*And* he lives in Midtown!"

I cackled at that. Living in Midtown *was* one of Danny Morden's biggest crimes.

Katie was such a pro at diverting attention that we didn't speak of Danny Morden or Wesley Taves the rest of the night. When it was time to go, I gave each of my parents a kiss on the cheek and Katie a big hug. "You're the best."

"I know."

I went out to my car to drive to my apartment, but Katie followed me outside, barefoot and wrapped in a quilt. "You're going to catch a cold like that!"

"I'm not leaving you alone until you call Wesley Taves."

I stared at her. "I don't know, Katie. I need to sleep on it."

"Bullshit."

"You heard Mom and Dad. Maybe they're right. I've worked with really privileged people before, they can be —"

"Forget all that crap Mom and Dad were talking about. This is a huge deal, Cara." Katie reached into my coat pocket and pushed the phone into my face. "*Call him.*"

"Katie, it's like, 10 pm, he wouldn't —"

"Just leave a message. Come on. What do you have to lose?"

I took the phone and pulled the business card out again. My heart fluttered at the idea of seeing Wesley Taves. Just the two of us this time. This could be the beginning of the rest of my life.

Or it could be my fucking downfall.

## Chapter 4

### Wesley

"Lucy! Where's your other shoe?!" I had one of her snow boots in my hand but the other one had disappeared into the mess of shoes in the front hall.

"Daddy, did you know that if a lion fought a tiger, the tiger would win?"

I huffed. *I don't fucking care who would win.* "No, I didn't know that." I got up from the floor, abandoning my search. "Lucy, would you please stop reading and come put your coat on? We have to get to school!"

I walked into the living room where Lucy was fully dressed but curled up reading a book she had checked out from the school library. On one of her feet, she wore the missing snow boot. *Bingo.* "Luce. What are you doing with one boot on and one boot off?"

She grinned at me from behind her book. "I got distracted."

"Looks that way. Come on, I don't want you to be late. It's the first day back after winter break!"

"But I'm almost done with my —"

I snatched the book out of her hand. "You can read it in the car. Look alive, kiddo."

Mornings were always like this. Lucy was a curious chatterbox. She was a very talented reader for her age, and consequently, was always eager to share things with me that she'd read in books. However, it was easy for her to get engrossed in a book to the point of tuning out the entire rest of the world.

Being late to school meant that I would be late to the office. And being late to the office was one of my least favorite things. From the time the clock struck nine, I would be inundated with an avalanche of emails. I had to be ready at my desk to put out fires as quickly as possible.

I got Lucy's coat and held it out for her. She slipped her arms in and smiled up at me. "How's the loose tooth?"

She pushed her front tooth with her tongue.

"Oof. Really loose."

"Pull it out! Pull it out!"

"*Noooo*, definitely not for me. Come on, get that boot on and let's head to school."

I shepherded Lucy out of the house and into the car. While the morning routine could be stressful, I adored drop-off for the most part. Getting to watch Lucy walk down the hall of her school and greet her friends and teachers was extremely gratifying. She was becoming her own person. A little person, but still. A person, nonetheless.

"'Kay, Luce. We're here."

We got out of the car and made our way into Lucy's ivy-covered, college-tuition-expensive private school on the Upper East Side.

"Wesley!"

My entire body cringed at the sound of that overly

sweet voice. I pasted on a smile as Greta Powers, the mother of one of Lucy's classmates, hustled over to us.

Greta was about my age with two children of her own and a recently finalized divorce. Her bleached blonde hair and makeup was always pristine for this early in the morning. I don't know how she did it when I felt like I barely had time to run a brush through my hair.

"Hello, Greta."

"Let's walk in together, shall we?" She hooked her arm in mine and pulled me close. "Lucy, you and Gerald can walk ahead of us."

Lucy eyed Gerald, her snotty-nosed classmate, and sighed. "Come on, Gerald."

Greta and I ambled behind our two children. I could feel eyes on us from every direction. Ever since Lucy was born, I had felt eyes on me when I was with her, especially when she started school. Mothers and teachers alike seemed to watch me with greedy interest.

I'd only been hit on a few times at Lucy's school. After all, most of the mothers were married and the teachers had a duty to be professional. However, on occasion, there were ladies like Greta who made no attempt at hiding their…interest in me.

"Tell me all about your Christmas."

"It was great. Lovely."

"Did you travel? Stay home?"

"We were here for the holiday and then took a quick trip to Tahiti."

Greta clutched my arm harder. "Oh! That's why you two have such good color."

Gerald and Lucy had walked a good distance ahead of us. I watched her shrug off her coat and hang it in her cubby, starting to chat with friends she hadn't seen since before winter break.

"How about you? Nice holiday?"

She sighed. "Well, first one since Tim and I divorced. But I had the kids, thank God. I don't know what I would have done without them. I would have probably lost it." Greta laughed wildly, as if it wasn't the saddest thing in the world.

"That's lucky."

"Bye, Daddy!" Lucy waved from the doorway of her classroom.

"Wait!" I broke away from Greta and swept Lucy into a great big hug. "Have an amazing day."

She squirmed. "Daddy! You're squeezing too tight!"

"Sorry, sorry." I pulled back and looked into her face. I was glad she looked so much like me — in all ways except one. Her smile. It was exactly like her mother's. It hurt that some days her smile, her sign of happiness, could break me. "Maybe you'll lose that tooth today, huh?"

Lucy gasped. "Then I could put it on the tooth chart!"

I gave her one more hug and a kiss before she skipped into her classroom.

"You two are just so cute together. So close. My boys barely let me hold their hand anymore."

I smiled at Greta and began to back away down the hallway. Out of her grasp, I could make a break for it. "Yes, they do get to be that way, don't they. Anyway, I have a meeting to get to, so I'll see you soon, take care."

I bolted toward the exit, unable to make out what Greta called after me. Frankly, I didn't care. Sure, she was pretty. And it was abundantly clear she was interested in me. But I didn't have space for any women in my life. I was entirely focused on Lucy. Sure, I had a fling here and there. Never with someone I'd have to run into in everyday life. That would make things complicated.

I carried this rushing energy with me all the way to the

MediaDeck building in Midtown. First Monday after the holidays would inevitably be a doozy.

I rode the elevator up to my office, said my *hellos* here and there, grabbed a coffee from the coffee bar, and settled heavily into my desk chair.

Having to get Lucy ready for school made every day feel as if I needed a nap before the start of my workday. I needed to figure something else out.

Out of the corner of my eye, I saw the red voicemail light on my office phone blinking. That was unusual. People knew to call my assistant to take any messages. I put the receiver to my ear, pressed the button, and listened.

"H-hi, Wesley. I mean, Mr. Taves. It's Cara. Cara Smith. I was the woman looking at the building with you? Anyway, I'm sorry I'm calling so late, but if you get this, I just wanted to confirm that I'm available for a — um — a meeting on Monday."

The sound of her voice brought back memories of Saturday. I could picture her full pink lips as she chastised that cretin realtor. My cock stirred as I remembered how her warm brown eyes held a bit of heat when she became riled up. *Down boy.*

"So give me a call back. I'm flexible. You know I lost my job, so I'm free as a bird, ha! Um, anyway. Looking forward to hearing from you."

When the message ended, I noted the huge smile on my face. Relief pumped through my veins. This was going to work out. It had to.

I dialed Cara back. It rang once. Then her voice sounded on the other end. "Mr. Taves?"

"You have my number saved in your phone?"

She sputtered, "W-well, yeah. In case you called back I wanted to be…to be prepared."

"That's a good way to be. Listen, can you meet me at

eleven? The Starbucks on the first floor of the MediaDeck building. You know where that is?"

"Yes, obviously. I can see it from Brooklyn."

I chuckled. "Great. I'll see you then."

I hung up. There was much to do before my meeting with her. I couldn't be troubled with idle chatter. I dialed the line to my secretary. "Janene, hi. Cancel my eleven o'clock if I have one. And contact my bank to cut me a check for a hundred grand. Actually, make it a quarter million." I smiled to myself. "I've got a deal to make."

# Chapter 5

## Cara

The MediaDeck building was the latest addition to the New York City skyline. It was a sleek building that looked like a teardrop and glistened like one, too. My parents thought it was an eyesore, but I always thought it rather beautiful, especially compared to older, blockier buildings.

Inside, though, sitting at a table at the MediaDeck branded Starbucks, I didn't give a goddamn about how beautiful or important the building was. All I could think about was what the hell Wesley Taves wanted from me.

I had barely taken a sip of my iced latte when the lid, which must not have been secure, slipped off. Coffee slid down the front of my white dress top. Shit! Just my luck. Now I was wearing a wet coffee-stained shirt for my meeting with billionaire Wesley Taves. And I didn't have time to do anything about it. Oh well, I managed to catch it before too much spilled. I dabbed at the spot with a napkin.

I checked my phone. He was already twenty minutes

late. *How hard can it be for him to just come downstairs on time?* I decided I'd give him a piece of my mind. No one, not even media mogul Wesley Taves, had the right to be rude and leave someone waiting indefinitely.

"Ms. Smith. Good to see you."

I stopped dabbing at my shirt and looked up to find Wesley Taves standing in front of my table as if he'd just stepped off a magazine cover. Reflexively, I stood up to greet him with a handshake. "Mr. Taves. Thanks for meeting with me on such short notice."

Wesley looked down at my hand. A tiny smirk appeared on his lips that made my insides melt, but also brought back the memory of my parents' warning. This man was all business, all the time. There was no telling what kind of schemes were brewing behind those chocolate-brown eyes. "The pleasure is all mine." He took my hand in his and gave it a firm shake.

His touch sent electricity through my arm and made me dizzy. *What the hell was that?* I had the urge to hold fast to his hand, but he broke the handshake and sat down in the seat across from mine. "I wish you would have waited." He gestured to my coffee. "Your coffee would have been on me."

I flushed and forced a laugh. "Well, actually, it ended up on me — literally."

Wesley raised an eyebrow. His gaze slipped to my wet top and lingered where the coffee had spilled on my chest. Unbidden, my nipples hardened from the cool air. Or was it from his attention? Finally, he looked up, clearing his throat and shifting in his seat.

"Bad joke. Anyway." This wasn't a great start.

"Mmm. Well. Let me cut right to the chase, Ms. Smith. I'd —"

"Cara. I've never been called Ms. Smith in my life."

I could tell he wasn't used to being interrupted. "*Cara*. I'll remember that."

He said my name carefully, sounding like a caress. I wanted to hear him say it over and over, preferably in more…*intimate* circumstances. *Where the hell did that thought come from?*

"I'll keep it simple. You're a nanny without a job and I'm a father without a nanny. I need someone for at least two months while I get my new project off the ground. Twelve-hour days, seven to seven, five days a week. Is that something you'd be willing to take on?"

I sat up taller in my seat. Hell yeah, I'd be willing to do that. And this man had *money*. I could make up what I'd lost from the Nolan family firing me. "Very willing."

"I like your spirit, Cara. Your positivity."

*I like that you like that about me.*

"So, what's your price?"

Shit. I'd never been good at this part. The negotiations. I never knew how to price myself in a way that felt fair to both me and a potential client. "Um…well…"

Wesley chuckled.

*Screw you, buddy.* I narrowed my eyes. "What's so funny?"

His brown eyes widened. Like warm caramel with flecks of gold. "Not funny. I promise. You're just very inexperienced, aren't you? You have big dreams and you're passionate about your cause, but you aren't *quite* there yet where business acumen is concerned. I understand. That was me twenty years ago."

Twenty years? How old was this guy? I had pegged him to be in his midthirties.

"Tell you what. I'll start negotiations. I'll make an offer and you can counter. I promise, I'll be fair." Wesley leaned forward; my eyes caught on the muscular forearms where his white dress shirt sleeves were rolled up. *Jesus, Cara. Focus!* "You're going to need about 25 percent of the building cost for a commercial loan to start your day care. That's at least two hundred fifty thousand."

I blinked.

"I know you want it. I know you can be good at it if given the chance. I can read people like that. So. I'll give you that amount up front." He pulled an envelope out of his suit jacket and held it across the table to me.

I took the envelope carefully, as if it might bite me, and opened it. Inside was an unsigned check for the exact sum he'd specified. "Holy…" *Don't say shit, Cara.*

"After two months, I'll match that amount. I can be a silent partner as long as you're for-profit."

It was believable he had this level of money to throw around. After all, he was one of the most high-powered businessmen in the country. What I *couldn't* believe was that he was giving it to *me*.

"This is, of course, all contingent on how you and my daughter get along."

I looked up at him. I couldn't believe he was offering me this kind of money. "This is way too much."

"Not to me."

"But…why?"

"'Why?'"

"Yeah, why? You can get a nanny, hourly, for a fraction of this amount. You're offering me five hundred thousand for two months of work. Half a million —" I stopped short. Holy shit. This guy was offering me *half a million dollars*. I felt lightheaded.

Wesley paused, sucking his lower lip into his mouth. He crossed his arms and leaned back in his chair, sizing me up. "I'm not giving it to you. I'm giving it to your business.

Your *purpose*. That's a very different thing. Call it intuition, but I think you've got a lot of potential."

I gulped, remembering all the things my parents said about Wesley Taves the night before. He could use his money to control me. The last thing I needed was another person who thought they could control me.

"And I liked the way you interacted with my daughter. That's the most important thing. She took a shine to you. I'm not sure why. But if she had a good feeling about you, I trust her instincts."

My racing thoughts slowed. Though Wesley Taves was a clean-cut businessman who looked like he had everything together, I could tell behind his eyes there was something… troubled. I let my eyes fall to his left hand. No wedding ring. I had to ask. "You've discussed this with your daughter's mother?"

Wesley's expression hardened, his jaw tensing. *Okay.* I might have just walked into a minefield. "Lucy's mother is out of the picture."

*Single dad.* A zing of excitement ran through my body. Almost as quickly as that emotion, I considered what that might mean. "I'm sorry."

He shook his head. "It's alright. She's not deceased. It's not that kind of tragedy."

Not *that* kind. But a different one. That explained the look in his eyes.

"So. What do you say? Do we have a deal?"

This would be the biggest decision I'd make so far in my life. I should have slept on it or called someone to talk it through. But I couldn't contain my eagerness. I wanted it. I wanted it so badly. And maybe the opportunity to spend time around such an attractive man sweetened the deal even more.

I slid the check across the table. "Sign it."

Wesley grinned. My stomach flipped, seeing that smile directed at me. "Fantastic." He pulled a pen out of his pocket and started to scribble his signature onto the check. "Can you start tomorrow?"

"Yes."

"Good." Wesley capped the pen and slid the check back to me. A quarter of a million dollars was now mine. "Lucy has the day off from school. Something to do with some seminars for the teachers. It'll be a good opportunity for you two to get to know each other."

"Terrific. I'm looking forward to it. She made a great impression on me."

Wesley's expression filled with warmth. "That makes me happy to hear. She's a very special little girl."

"I can tell."

Our eyes met for only a moment, but it felt longer. The air seemed to crackle around us as I stared into those warm brown eyes.

Wesley cleared his throat and stood up. "I look forward to working with you, Cara."

I couldn't bring myself to stand for fear my legs would give out from under me. "You too."

"We'll discuss some sort of stipend for your living expenses once we get the first week under our belt." He reached into his pocket and pulled out a hundred-dollar bill, setting it in front of me. "For the coffee and a new shirt." The corner of his mouth ticked up in a smirk.

I rolled my eyes. "Thank you."

Wesley nodded and walked out of the coffee shop.

If I had been at home alone, I would have jumped up and done a happy dance. I was on top of the world and nothing could stop me. Nothing would.

Without taking the time to think twice about it, I pulled out my phone and immediately called Danny Morden.

"Cara, sweetheart, I was going to call you later —"

"I want to make an offer."

"An offer?"

"On the building we saw Saturday." I stared at the check, like it was my lifeline. "I'm ready to make an offer."

# Chapter 6

## Wesley

I was at the door mere seconds after she rang the bell. I had been anxiously pacing, waiting for her well before 7 am.

Cara greeted me with a smile. "Good morning."

Her appearance was fresh and casually professional in leggings, a loose sweater, and flats. Even though it was early in the morning, she looked put together and ready for the liveliness of an active six-year-old. From her bright amber eyes to the way her loose waves hung to her shoulders, I was endeared to her from the start. *Stay professional, Wesley.* I cleared my throat. "Morning. Come on in."

Cara stepped into the front hall, eyes wide as she scanned her surroundings. "Wow. This is a beautiful home."

"You haven't even seen all of it yet."

She flushed. "Well, I can tell already."

Before I could say anything else, Lucy scrambled in, sliding on the hardwood floor in her socks. "Lucy! What did I tell you about sliding across the floor?" Last time she had done that, she'd fallen backward and nearly given herself a concussion.

Lucy smiled sheepishly. "Sorry, Daddy."

Cara giggled. "Hi, Lucy. Do you remember me?"

Lucy nodded. "Daddy said you're my new nanny."

"Yes! Is that okay with you?"

Lucy smiled wide, the loose tooth still proudly front and center. "Depends on what games you know how to play."

"*Games*? Oh boy, do I know games."

*I could think of a few games I'd like to play with Lucy's new nanny.*

My daughter laughed. She was ready to get busy playing. My heart swelled. "Before you start on any games, let me give you a rundown on everything."

"Perfect."

I led Cara into the kitchen. "Lucy's school starts at eight most days. I pack a lunch for her the night before and I'll leave that in the fridge for you. Important to note, Lucy is allergic to peanuts."

"Does she have an EpiPen?"

I nodded. "There are several throughout the house. Easiest access is this drawer here."

"Got it."

"On days off, you two can go on any outings you like. We have memberships at most of the museums and the park is right nearby." I rattled off the rules and systems without pausing. Cara wasn't even taking notes, but I could tell she was cataloging everything in her brain. "Is that all clear?"

Cara nodded. "Yes. What's your screen time policy?"

Ah, yes. Forgot that. "Limited through the day, but while you're making dinner, she can have as much as she likes. Which reminds me, if you can start dinner before I get home, I can finish it up and you can take off."

Cara smiled. "Okay. That's the only question I have for now."

"Great." I looked from Cara over to Lucy in the doorway of the kitchen. "Well. That's it, then."

"Great."

"Great!" Lucy twirled in a circle. "Game time!"

My chest tightened. "Well, come say goodbye to me first."

"Oh! Right!"

We went back into the front hall. Cara hung back while Lucy and I hugged goodbye. I squeezed her tighter than I had in a long, long time. "Daddy, you're squishing me!"

"Yes, I am." I kissed her on the cheek, relishing her giggle, and then put her back down on the ground. "You remember the rules, yes?"

Lucy stood at attention with her hands behind her back. "Be the goodest girl ever."

I chuckled. *Not quite, but that'll do.* "Yes. And Cara, if you have any trouble, you can call my office number whenever. Don't worry about me, I'll —"

"Thank you, Wesley, but I think we'll be okay. I have a good feeling." Cara and Lucy exchanged a smile as if they had known each other forever. *Huh.*

I snapped my mouth shut. There was that confidence I saw in Cara Smith shining through. I had to admit, I liked the look of it on her. "Well, alright. Have a good day, girls." Saying that sent a pang through my heart. I had always said that before leaving Lisbeth and Lucy when Lucy was only a baby. I hadn't said it in…well, years.

I'd missed it.

Throughout my drive to work, I couldn't stop my thoughts from racing. At least Lucy and Cara seemed confident with the situation. I, on the other hand, had been questioning my intuition all night long, tossing and turning. I hadn't even asked Cara for a background check. What if she was some sort of criminal? Or a corporate spy? I had let my mind run away with improbable scenarios.

*Calm down, Wes. It'll be fine. Your sixth sense hasn't been wrong in a long time.*

I'd count on that as long as I could.

---

DAYS AT MEDIADECK were typically fast-paced and I had little time to think about anything but the business. I often attended back-to-back meetings or I was on calls and answering emails.

However, on that particular day, I was preoccupied with thoughts of Lucy and Cara. I wondered what they were doing, if Cara had made Lucy a nutritious lunch, if Lucy was having fun, or if Cara was truly as wonderful as she seemed. I was zoning out at meetings and on work calls. Even during lunch I was distracted and barely ate my salad.

I glanced at the clock. A little past four. I started daydreaming about arriving home after my day at work. I hoped when I opened the door I would be greeted with Lucy's huge grin and stories of her fun-filled day. And if I was being honest, I wondered if Cara would be happy to see me…

*Knock, knock.*

I looked up and smiled. "Jenson! What's up?"

Jenson Styles was my closest friend. He also happened to be the CFO of MediaDeck. Though we worked closely together, we had less time to shoot the shit than we used to. I always appreciated when he dropped by.

"You busy?"

I leaned back in my chair. "Nope. Come on in."

Jenson closed the door behind him and came over to perch on the corner of my desk. "I wanted to hear how this morning went."

"Oh. Good, I think."

"Good, you think. Wow, that's fascinating."

I chuckled. "Well, I don't know. I only was with her about fifteen minutes before I left for work."

"But how do you feel? This is your first nanny in forever."

I appreciated Jenson's ability to keep tabs on me. "I'm nervous."

Jenson rolled his eyes. "I knew it."

"What? Wouldn't you be?"

"Sure, but my kids have had the same nanny since they were babies." I couldn't help but be a little envious of what Jenson had. Jenson had twins, a boy and girl, just a bit older than Lucy, and had been with his wife, Kerry, since they were freshmen in college. That was the kind of life I always saw for myself. "If Eliana left, I think we'd all have a mental breakdown."

"Well, Cara is on a two-month contract. I know that Lucy is aware it's short-term. So we'll be ready when she leaves."

"What if you want her to stay longer?"

I shrugged. "Another contract."

Jenson scratched his stubbly chin. "This is a nanny we're talking about, Wesley. Not a lease on a parking spot."

"Well, I don't know. That's a bridge we'll have to cross when we come to it."

Jenson looked away for a second. "What's she look like?"

I raised an eyebrow. "Pardon me?"

"You know what I mean. Is she cute? Easy on the eyes?"

I shook my head. "That's a dangerous game, Jenson, and you know it."

"Oh, come on, Wesley. You must have noticed."

I felt hot under the collar. I would not let myself consider the attractiveness of Cara Smith. At least not actively. "And you know I don't believe in conflict of interest."

"Just because you think she's cute doesn't mean you're going to do anything about it. Yeesh. Who do you take me for?"

I smiled. "You know I don't like this kind of water-cooler talk."

Jenson pulled his phone out of his pocket. "What's her name?"

"Jenson —"

"*Name.*"

I narrowed my eyes at him, but it was clear he wasn't backing down. "Cara Smith."

"Smith? You're just trying to make it difficult."

"Swear to God, her last name is Smith."

Jenson began typing. "Fine. Cara…Smith…nanny." Jenson held up his phone. "This her?"

Sure enough, the very first result was a picture of Cara. Possibly from her daycare days. She had two kids on her lap and another leaning over her shoulder. They were all in the midst of laughter. Cara's hair was shorter in the picture. But she still had that vivacious energy about her. It shone through the screen.

"Um. Yeah. That's her, you creep."

Jenson snorted. "Please, you love me." He considered the photo for a moment. "She's young. Cute. But young."

"Exactly why I didn't want to have this conversation."

*Cute* wouldn't even be the tip of the iceberg of ways I would describe Cara.

"You wouldn't date a younger woman?"

I sighed. "I don't know, Jenson. The opportunity has never presented itself."

"I find that hard to believe."

I rolled my eyes. "Okay, sure, there have been opportunities. But women her age are usually immature and I don't have time for that."

"Well, let me present an opportunity to you. Kerry just finished up working with a client and we think you'd be a great match. She's twenty-nine, so a bit of a gap, but —"

Alarm bells went off in my head. "Sorry, Jenson, but no."

"I haven't even told you about her yet."

"You don't need to. The last time you set me up was —"

"Rough. I know. How was I to know she was an ex-con? But this one is different. She's a chair designer. Like, she only designs chairs. How cool is that?"

I eyed him. He knew my answer was no.

Jenson huffed and then got to his feet. "Fine, if you want to hold out for your nanny, be my guest."

"I'm *not* holding out for my nanny!"

"Then go on this date and prove it!" Jenson shot back just before leaving my office.

I hated being fixed up. But I didn't want him to continue hounding me about Cara. I knew she was off-limits, even if I did find her completely appealing. But I was already determined to resist any inklings of attraction. Even if I did find myself thinking of her sweet curves and bright amber eyes way too much today. But I couldn't deal with him exacerbating that. *"Fine."*

"You'll do it?"

"*Yes.* Now get out of my office."

"You won't regret it. Friday, eight o'clock. Somewhere nice. You choose. And Wesley?"

"What?"

"Do me a favor and smile more. You don't want to drive her away by looking like you're at a colonoscopy appointment."

The second he was gone, I felt my stomach turn sour. On top of the stress of work and everything to do with Cara, I had a fucking date to worry about.

I forced myself to smile just as Jensen had instructed and felt my cheeks burn.

This was going to be worse than I thought, I could just feel it.

# Chapter 7

## Cara

"Okay, the water is boiling, so carefully…that's it." I guided Lucy's hands that held the box of spaghetti over the pot of boiling water. "Now, go ahead."

Lucy poured the dried spaghetti into the pot carefully. "There you go, spaghetti!"

"Good job! You're a pro at this!"

Lucy bowed her head and bent at the waist. "Thank you, thank you."

Lucy was helping me make spaghetti for dinner, as was her request. She was eager to help me in the kitchen rather than watch television, as her father had suggested that morning. I was happy to have her company, especially since it indicated to me that she liked me.

We had a fabulous first day together. It helped immensely that Lucy was one of the best behaved children I'd ever worked with. But I could also tell we had a good rapport. In the morning, after playing some introductory Go Fish, Lucy suggested we play with her stuffed animals. I thought she would have us make a zoo, but instead, she wanted us to be scientists studying the animals in the wild.

"This penguin is sick!"

"Oh no, should we take care of her?"

Lucy's face drooped. "No, we can't interfere with the circle of life. Scientists should only ever observe."

I had to stifle a huge laugh. Clearly, animals were her thing and it was totally adorable.

For lunch, we made sandwiches and granola which we ate on our "animal expedition." Every moment flowed easily into the next. It didn't even feel like work at all.

After we got tired of that game, Lucy read for a bit while I familiarized myself with the house.

It was a massive townhome in Park Slope. I didn't even want to know how much it likely cost. There were three floors of rooms to explore. I looked forward to an opportunity to play hide and seek so we could get lost together.

I crept around the house, taking stock of where the rooms were located. Lucy had the whole top floor to herself while Wesley had the second, plus a guest room.

Now, I'm not a snoop. Just curious. And the Taves house was going to be my place of work for the next two months, at least. I thought I should at least get a lay of the land. So I peeked into all the rooms, including Wesley's bedroom.

Though it wasn't anything out of the ordinary, the furnishings looked luxurious. From the art on the wall to the fluffy duvet, everything was as if it'd been picked out of *Architectural Digest*.

I couldn't help but wonder what it felt like to lie in the luxuriousness of Wesley Taves' bed, snuggled within his embrace. My mind wandered to the feel of his muscular build and his delectable scent the day he saved me from Danny's careless driving. *He's your boss, Cara. Don't go there.*

Shaking off thoughts of my sexy employer, I spent most of my time looking at the photographs that lined the stairwell. All of them were of just Lucy and Wesley. No pictures of her mother, indicating that whatever had happened was *definitely* not amicable.

One picture in particular caught my eye. Lucy must have been only a couple of years old. She was bundled up in Wesley's arms outside this very house. He looked different. His hair was a bit shaggier, stubble was decorating his chin and cheeks, and his eyes were shaded with sleeplessness.

But his smile was big and full. Pure joy.

My heart melted for him and I secretly hoped that maybe someday I could make him smile like that, too.

⊂⊃

"CAN I TASTE THE SAUCE?" Lucy asked.

"Sure you can. But you have to be careful. It's hot." I dipped a wooden spoon into the pot of simmering sauce, brought it up to my lips, and blew away the steam. "Okay, give it another blow and then you can try it."

Lucy did so and then stuck out her tongue as far as it would go to carefully taste the sauce. "Mmm. It's so good. Usually Daddy just uses sauce from a jar."

"Well, that's just as good. Doesn't take as long as making it from scratch."

"Yeah, but it's not as tasty."

We smiled at each other. I already felt like we'd known each other a lot longer than just one day. I hoped she felt the same.

The front door opened. I could hear Wesley take a few heavy steps inside. "Hello?"

Lucy jumped in excitement and skittered into the front hall, crying out, "Daddy!"

I threw a glance at the clock on the stove. *Just past seven.* Pretty good for a billionaire mogul. I followed slowly as to give them a moment to greet one another. When I peeked into the hallway, Wesley and Lucy were entangled in a big hug. It was clear she adored him.

*Screw what my parents say. This guy is a good man.*

"How'd it go today?" he asked, eyes flicking up to me.

Thank goodness Lucy spoke first because I was rendered speechless by his gaze. The tired look I had seen in the picture was there…something about that made me want to take care of him. Make him dinner, put him to bed, and maybe *take care of him* in some other more *unmentionable* ways, too.

"It was great. We played Go Fish, and with my animals, and Cara let me eat lunch in my room, and —" she slapped her hand over her mouth "— I wasn't supposed to say that."

I gulped. There was a gap of silence and I felt he was surely going to reprimand me, but then Wesley spoke. "I guess it was a special day." He eyed me. "But not something to make a habit."

"Of course, it was just a…" I finally found my voice. "We were on an expedition. It couldn't be interrupted. The penguins have a virus going around and it was very intense."

Wesley laughed as he got to his feet. "Oh, she's got you roped into one of her expeditions, huh? Well, I guess you're right, not even a scientist can stop for lunch."

I bit my lip. Phew. That could have been bad. "We had a really great day."

Wesley smiled. "That's wonderful to hear." He sniffed the air. "Wow, something smells delicious."

I'd completely forgotten about the savory aroma of dinner. All I could smell was Wesley's cologne — warm leather and earthy.

Lucy grabbed his hand and dragged him into the kitchen. "We're having spaghetti and Cara made sauce from scratch!"

"Wow. It smells amazing."

I grabbed my coat off the hall tree and slid it on as I followed. "There's garlic bread in the oven. And I steamed some broccolini earlier. Just pop it in the microwave to warm up when everything's ready."

Lucy's eyes went big. They were the exact same color as her father's. "You're leaving?"

"I…" I looked to Wesley. "Well, that was the plan, I thought."

"Yes, absolutely. Cara's got her own life and plans, Lucy. We can't keep her here forever."

Her face fell. She tugged on Wesley's arm.

Wesley sighed. "Sorry, Cara." He bent down so Lucy could whisper in his ear. Though I couldn't make out the words, her whispering was loud and scratchy. "I suppose you could."

Lucy giddily clapped and started toward me.

"But you can't be upset if she says no, Luce," Wesley added.

She nodded and then looked up at me. "Cara…would you please stay for dinner?"

I felt a rush of excitement. Although, I wasn't sure whether that had to do with spending more time with Lucy or with her father. Maybe it was both. "Of course, I'll stay." I turned to Wesley. "As long as it's truly alright with you."

Wesley glanced between Lucy and me. A smile spread across his lips. "It's more than alright."

"WHAT ARE YOU LEARNING IN SCHOOL?"

Lucy tried to reply with a mouthful of spaghetti, the noodles escaping from her mouth.

Wesley held up his hand. "Lucy, chew and swallow first, please."

She went silent and tried to chew faster.

"Sorry, that was my fault." I sheepishly looked across the table at Wesley.

He smiled and shook his head. "I appreciate that you care enough to ask." His plate looked as if nothing had been on it in the first place. He'd devoured my cooking, remarking frequently how delicious it was. If there's one thing better than being told you're a good cook, it's being told you're a good cook by a devastatingly handsome man.

Lucy gulped down her spaghetti. Sauce stained her mouth. "We do math and reading and writing and science and —"

"But what's your favorite class?"

"Well, in social studies, we're learning about traditions."

I raised my eyebrows. "What kind of traditions?"

"Like holidays and family traditions. So we've been talking about what we did during the Christmas break. Some kids didn't even celebrate Christmas!" She gestured wildly with her hands as she spoke.

"Mmm. Yes. A lot of people don't."

"So tomorrow, we're going to start a report on our favorite family tradition."

Wesley chuckled. "A report? In first grade?"

Lucy raised her chin proudly. "Yes."

I leaned toward her with an eager smile. "What tradition have you decided on, then?"

Lucy's excitement dissipated. She started to stab a piece of broccolini with her fork repeatedly. "Well, I don't know. We don't really have any family traditions."

I immediately noticed Wesley's posture change. "What do you mean? Of course, we do."

Lucy leaned her chin on her hand. "Like what?"

"Well, we…you know, we…" Wesley's eyes darted around the room, desperate to come up with something. "We read books before bed."

"Everyone reads books before bed, Daddy."

"Okay, well, we always do something fun on Saturday. We have adventures on the weekends."

"*Everyone* has fun on Saturdays. That's the point." Lucy drooped more and more, staring at her food.

I could sense Wesley's embarrassment growing. "We can start a tradition right now."

Lucy and Wesley looked at me. She smiled curiously. "What kind of tradition?"

"Maybe the tradition is that once a week I eat dinner with you and your daddy." I looked over to Wesley for permission. "How does that sound?"

Wesley answered with his eyes; they softened at the corners in relief. *Yes.*

"Seriously? That'd be awesome! I could definitely write a report on that!"

The conversation was interrupted by my phone buzzing in my pocket. I checked to see who was calling. It was Danny Morden. "I'm sorry, I have to take this. It's my realtor."

Wesley's eyebrows jumped, his interest piqued. "It's no trouble."

I got up and stole into the hallway to answer the call. "Hello?"

"Cara! How's my favorite client?"

"You know, it's quite late to be calling me."

"I'm sorry, but I thought since we're old friends —"

"What's going on? I'm sort of in the middle of something, so if you could be quick."

Danny cleared his throat. "Alright, alright. Sorry to interrupt. I just have some good news."

I took a deep breath of anticipation. Since I was able to get the loan started for the building, I knew things would start moving faster.

"The owners will accept your offer."

"Really? That's great!"

"If you drop the contingency."

My joy turned to disappointment. "Oh…"

"Trust me, Cara, this would be a *steal*. It'd be totally worth it."

"So if we drop the contingency, that means no inspections?"

"Exactly. You can get those done once the building is yours."

I pursed my lips, thinking for a moment. "So they'd take my offer right now."

"We'd be in and out of escrow before you know it."

Suddenly, I heard a voice right behind me. "Don't do it."

I turned to find Wesley towering over me.

"You need the inspections."

I pulled the phone away from my ear. "Have you been listening to me?"

"That place is going to eat up all your capital if you don't take proper precautions. Tell him the contingency stands."

There was no room for argument when it came to Wesley Taves. I wanted so badly to accept the deal, but then I remembered — it was his money. And if I wanted his investment later on down the road, I had better make him happy in this process.

Mom was right. *They do whatever they need to get what they want.* Even if that was listening in on private phone calls.

Danny's voice came through the phone. "Cara?"

"I'm not taking the deal."

Wesley nodded appreciatively. As much as I hated to admit it, I liked the feeling of his approval.

"What?"

"You heard me. The contingency stands."

"Cara, you —"

"Bye, Danny." I hung up the phone. Wesley and I stood in silence in the front hall. "I wish you hadn't done that."

Wesley sighed. "It was for your protection."

"I don't need to be protected." The air crackled with electricity. In spite of myself, I felt my body sway toward him.

Wesley sucked in a sharp breath and clenched his hands into fists, as if to prevent himself from reaching for me. If Lucy hadn't been in the next room, maybe he wouldn't have been so measured in his responses. "You're still learning, Cara. Don't get cocky."

"Would you be saying that to me if I wasn't a woman?"

"I'd say that to anybody. It would be reckless to buy that building for such an exorbitant amount without an inspection." He wrapped his hands around my shoulders. My mouth went dry and my heart started to race. His touch made me dizzy. "You have to trust me."

Wesley had trusted me with his daughter today. Maybe I owed him some trust in return. But between my frustration with his antics and the confusing feelings I felt from his touch, I couldn't offer him my trust.

"I have to go. It's getting late."

Wesley let go of me. "Of course, we don't mean to keep you."

I hurriedly grabbed my coat and bag, pulling on my boots as fast as I could. "I'll see you both tomorrow. 7 am."

I didn't wait for Wesley's reply before rushing out the front door to my car. Not until I was safely inside my sedan with my hands around the wheel could I catch my breath.

Wesley Taves was in control of me. That was a fact.

And if I was being honest with myself, I wasn't sure I minded it one bit.

## Chapter 8

### Wesley

I adjusted my tie in the mirror. Jensen told me wearing one on a date would make me look old, but I felt naked and vulnerable without it.

I'd been dreading the date from the moment I told Jensen I'd go. Now that it was the day of, my stomach had been churning and queasy. I hadn't been able to eat anything, anxious to meet this woman — the chair designer.

I didn't have a lot of optimism for dating. In fact, I didn't have a lot of hopefulness about relationships in general. Lisbeth's desertion of our marriage — and of Lucy — had damaged my heart to the point that it felt like a much smarter idea not to even open myself up to the possibility of getting hurt again.

Additionally, my experience with women since the demise of my marriage hadn't been positive. It seemed they were only interested in my money or social standing. Subsequently, I tended to make it clear I wasn't interested in anything long-term. I stuck to seeing those who under-stood it was physical only, to satisfy our mutual desires.

Moreover, if by some miracle I met someone I liked and brought her into my life, I always ran the risk of hurting Lucy, too. I wouldn't be able to forgive myself for that.

A burst of laughter echoed from downstairs. I smoothed out my tie and took a deep breath.

*Just get it over with. It'll be over soon.*

I ran my hand through my hair one last time and then went downstairs.

Lucy and Cara's voices echoed through the house, full of joy and laughter.

"Oh no! Not Plumpy!"

Lucy squealed in amusement. "You have to go all the way back to the beginning, Cara!"

I looked into the living room. Cara and Lucy were lying on the ground, playing a game of Candy Land. I smiled to myself. Lucy had taken to Cara like a fish to water. Every morning, she waited for Cara at the front door and every evening, she wished her goodbye with a long hug.

Cara noticed me in the doorway and her full lips perked into a smile. She cocked her head to the side. "Well, you look nice."

My heart squeezed. "Um. Thank you."

"You're welcome."

Things between Cara and me had been strange since the very first day. Admittedly, it was wrong of me to listen in on her conversation with the realtor. But I couldn't just let her flounder in the negotiations with that slimeball Morden. I wanted to help any way I could.

Unfortunately, my version of helping clearly crossed a boundary.

Since her first day, which was only a few days earlier, we were tiptoeing around each other, barely looking each other in the eye when we spoke.

"I'm about to head out. I won't be too late."

Cara waved her hand. "Take your time. Have fun."

I grimaced. "We'll see about that."

She touched Lucy's back to draw her attention away from the game. "Say bye to your father."

My daughter grinned. "Bye, Daddy! Good luck on your date!"

I went over to her and kissed the top of her head. "Thanks, kiddo. I'll need it." My eyes drifted to Cara. She was smiling tenderly at Lucy. The way she looked at her made my insides turn to mush. I needed to find someone who looked at Lucy like that. Someone who would be willing to take on the role of mother, right from day one.

Cara would have been perfect…if I wasn't so much older than her.

I'd be lying if the thought didn't cross my mind, though. More frequently than I cared to admit.

"Cara, could I speak with you for a moment?"

Cara got to her feet. "Sure."

We walked in silence to the front door. "Well, bedtime is nine on weekends."

"Got it."

"She'll probably try and squeeze as much time as she can out of you before she actually goes to sleep."

Cara giggled. "Don't they all?"

Yes, Lucy was just one of many to Cara. I had to remind myself of that. "And she has a night-light on her bedside table. You'll have to turn it on. But she'll remind you."

"I got it."

"If you need anything, you have my number."

Cara touched my arm. "We'll be fine, Wesley. Seriously. Have fun. Let loose."

I bristled at her touch, despite wanting to lean further into it. "Do you think this tie makes me look old?"

She laughed. "Old?"

"Yeah, my friend told me not to wear a tie." I ran my hand down the emerald tie hanging from my neck. "Said it would make me look too mature."

She raised an eyebrow. "Is that a bad thing?"

I gulped. "Well, I don't know. My date's quite a bit younger than me. I don't want to come off too..."

Cara took the tie from me and observed it. "If she's going out with an older man, then she wants someone who's mature." Her amber eyes flicked up to mine. "I like it."

I snaked the tie out of her hand, hoping I hadn't turned beet red. "Really, well, fantastic. I'll tell him that's what you said."

She smiled and then drifted back toward the living room door. "Bye, Wesley."

"Bye, Cara."

With a deep breath, I strode out to the car with all the composure I had left in me. The entire drive, I clutched the steering wheel tightly, attempting to think unsexy thoughts to stifle the half erection I'd gotten from Cara Smith being so close to me.

---

"I HOPE you don't mind, but I have some questions."

I took a sip of my second glass of wine and smiled at the woman across from me. "Go right ahead."

This was going better than I expected. Not great, but not horrible. Cheyenne Brumley was a very attractive young woman with olive green eyes and tan skin who wore her dark hair in a smart pixie cut. From the moment we sat down, I wanted to lean into the chemistry I hoped we might have, but my mind kept returning to Cara.

Women don't believe it, but while they are beautiful with makeup, they're even more so without it. Cheyenne was made up to the nines with fake lashes to boot. Beautiful, but when I remembered Cara's soft skin and her long wavy hair held back by a headband, I felt distracted.

That's the kind of woman I could imagine waking up to every morning.

*Focus, Wesley. Cheyenne's a beautiful girl.*

I opted to focus on her low-cut dress and her perky breasts. Maybe that would get Cara out of my mind.

Cheyenne reached into her purse and pulled out several index cards.

"Oh, wow, you came prepared."

She smiled. "I don't want to waste time beating around the bush on a date. You understand, right?"

I nodded and took another, longer sip of wine. "Yes. I can appreciate that." Index cards were definitely *out there*, but I wasn't ready to write her off just yet.

"So, Kerry told me you have a daughter."

I nodded. "Yes."

"How old is she?"

I smiled proudly. "She's six. First grade."

"Aw. Cute. Do you want more kids?"

I did everything in my power not to let my face portray my shock. That was an awfully forward first question for a first date. Though, I couldn't blame her for wanting to be careful. Dating was a hellscape for me. Must have been ten times worse as a woman. "Um…"

"Because I really don't want to have kids. Unless it was surrogacy."

"Sure. I understand. It can be hard on your body."

Cheyenne rolled her eyes. "I don't understand why a woman would opt into that. Feels maniacal."

This felt like a red flag, but I let it slide for now. "If I met someone who wanted more kids, then I'd be more than happy to oblige. But also, Lucy is a great kid all on her own, so I'm not necessarily compelled."

"Is she actually a good kid or are you just obligated to say that as her father?"

"Excuse me?"

Cheyenne shrugged and tilted her wine glass back and forth. "Parents aren't the most objective measures of their children's goodness. Don't you think?"

"I…uh…wow…" I half laughed. This woman was something else. "I can forward you her report card, how about that?"

"That'd be great."

She clearly didn't understand sarcasm when she heard it.

"Now, let's see…" Cheyenne flipped through her cards. "Ah. This is a good segue. What's your relationship with your parents like?"

Jesus Christ, this woman was really trying to get to the point. "Nonexistent."

Her eyes bugged out. "Whatever for?"

I rubbed my chin. *Stay calm. Don't be an ass.* "They're dead."

"Oh my God, Wesley." Cheyenne reached across the table and squeezed my fingers. "I'm *so sorry*."

I shook my head. "It's alright."

"When did they die?"

This had to be a prank. I couldn't believe this woman was actually going on dates and acting like this was a normal way to behave. "My father passed from a heart attack when I was still a kid. My mother never got over it and died just shy of her eighty-first birthday a couple years ago."

"Heart issues run in your family, then?"

"Is that what you got from that story?"

Cheyenne laughed as if I was joking. I wasn't. "You're a single dad and an orphan. Yeesh. What's that like?"

*What's it like to be an emotionally devoid bitch?* "Just fine."

"Now, on to your ex. Why'd that end?"

That was a bridge too far. The other questions annoyed me, but I could answer them without feeling like my guts were spilling out onto the table. But this one…

This was more than personal.

"Creative differences." I downed the rest of my wine.

"Oh, you business guys are always talking the lingo." Cheyenne rolled her eyes. "Tell me the truth. What'd she do that was so bad you ended up with custody of your kid?"

"Lucy. My daughter's name is Lucy."

"Aw. So cute."

I'd met toddlers with more emotional maturity than Cheyenne Brumley.

"So. What's your answer?"

I blinked at her and then knocked her glass of wine over. It spilled across her index cards and right into her lap. She pushed herself back from the table with a loud gasp. "What the hell was that?"

"Sorry. I'm such a klutz sometimes."

"You did that on purpose!"

I reached into my pocket and pulled out my wallet. I dropped a few bills on the table. "This is for the wine." A few more. "And this is for the dry cleaning. Have a nice life."

I walked away from the table without turning back,

knowing Cheyenne's tantrum would most certainly not be quiet.

Once outside in the cold night air, I found my anger at her turn to self-loathing.

Maybe if I wasn't so damaged, this would be easier.

*Maybe I'm too damaged to be with anyone at all.*

# Chapter 9

## Cara

*Ten o'clock. Must be going well.*

I was curled up in front of the television downstairs watching some rerun of a reality TV show, something nondescript and trashy. Lucy was sound asleep upstairs. We'd had quite an eventful night. After playing some games, we had a movie night complete with popcorn. A rogue kernel caused her loose front tooth to pop right out. She insisted on going to bed early so the Tooth Fairy would come sooner.

After some stories and a bit of cuddling, Lucy was off to dreamland. I found it hard to leave her there and spent a few minutes stroking her blonde hair as she slept.

In four short days, Lucy had I had become close. Very close. We needed each other. She needed a mother figure and I need to fill that hole left from being fired by the last family I was working for. It was practically a life require-ment for me to nurture children, or in this case, a child. I found myself hoping that Wesley would see this and realize he should keep me on longer than two months.

Wesley, though, was an issue in and of himself. I didn't quite know how to act around him. He was intimidating and commanding with his presence and yet could be so gentle and soft. Those two sides of him combined made him so intriguing.

I wanted to know more.

The front door opened and I heard Wesley take a few steps into the front hall. Then he sighed heavily.

I turned off the TV and got to my feet. "Hello?"

"Oh, hey Cara. It's just me. Hope I didn't scare you."

I went into the front hall to find Wesley slouching on the bench Lucy used to put on her shoes. I knew without asking how it had gone.

Wesley looked up at me. "How were things here?"

I leaned on the doorframe and smiled. "Lucy will be getting a visit from the Tooth Fairy tonight. You may want to give her a call."

All the exhaustion on his face immediately dissipated. He smiled. "She lost that front tooth? Finally?"

"While eating popcorn and watching *Encanto*. It was the highlight of her night. She was hoping you'd be home before bed to see it."

Wesley sighed. "Damn. Me too. Was she okay with the blood?"

"Oh yeah. She was staring at her gums in the bathroom mirror. That kid isn't squeamish, let me tell you."

"Brave girl." He ran his hands back through his hair. It looked like he had done that many times already with how his blonde locks mingled together messily. "Well, thanks, Cara. You get home safe, alright?"

I didn't move from my spot. "You okay, Wesley?"

"Hmm? Oh, I'm fine."

"You sure?"

Wesley chuckled. "Are you trying to get information out of me?"

I frowned. "No, not at all. You just seem…crestfallen."

He leaned his head back against the wall. "Crestfallen. Yeah. That's a good word for it." He folded his hands between his legs. I couldn't help but stare at his long fingers and wonder what they were capable of. "It was just disappointing, that's all. I didn't even have my hopes up and —"

"It lived down to your expectations."

"Precisely."

I couldn't very well leave him here all dejected like that. But clearly, he wasn't just going to come out and tell me what had happened. I had to find another way. "You know, the last first date I went on was a complete nightmare."

Wesley raised an eyebrow, as if to say, *I'm interested*.

"He was working on a political campaign; mind you, it was a really low-level one. Like city council or something. I was like, 'That's sweet, he cares about local government.'"

"Is that what gets you going, Cara? Local government?"

I blushed and my body heated. If Wesley Taves knew he was the newest addition to the list of things that got me going, I was in big trouble. "I thought it was honorable. Anyhow, I get to dinner, and he's dressed in a nice suit and wearing campaign buttons on his lapel. Really into it. A little too into it. He spent the whole date trying to convince me to vote for the guy, Redmond Sax."

Wesley laughs. "Oh no."

"The kicker is, I remember Redmond Sax's name, but I don't remember the name of the guy I went on the date with."

"I guess he did his job."

I rolled my eyes. "I guess. Anyway."

Wesley considered me with a lopsided smile. "Tell you what, I'll pay you back with my bad date story over a glass of wine. How does that sound?"

*Fucking amazing.* "I could do that."

"Perfect."

───

"SHE DID *NOT* HAVE INDEX CARDS."

"She did. Swear to God."

It took a full glass of wine to get Wesley to actually start talking about his date. I had sucked mine down quickly due to my nerves from sitting alone with him at the kitchen island, sharing a drink. *How is this happening?*

"And the questions were…intense."

"What do you mean by *intense?*"

Wesley let out a big sigh and reached for the bottle of wine. "That's going to require another drink."

"That bad?"

"Yes Cara, that bad."

I loved the way my name sounded coming out of his mouth. Every time he said it felt very intentional. I couldn't help but look at him when he said it. This handsome, successful, sexy man saying *my* name so intimately? *Impossible.*

Wesley started to pour me a glass but stopped short. "Will you be okay to drive?"

"I can have one more." *Careful, Cara.* "Maybe just half a glass. So I'm good to drive."

The wine sloshed into my glass. True to my instructions, it was just half a glass. "I'd be happy to call you a car if not. Or you can even stay over here if you need. That's always an option."

"I think Lucy would be bummed if there was a sleepover going on that she didn't know about." *Sleepover* made it seem like we'd be sleeping together, in my mind. I tried my best not to blush at the thought.

Wesley chuckled. "We'd have to make it up to her." He took a long sip of wine.

"So. Index cards."

"Oh, yes. Just stuff you probably don't even learn about a person until…I don't know, the fifth date, if I can help it. Although it's been so long, I'm not sure I even know how it works anymore."

"You don't date a lot?"

Wesley's eyebrows jumped. "No. No way. No time for it." He looked into his glass, swirling the wine. "And if I'm honest with myself, no energy, either."

"Mmm. I get it."

He smirked. "You're way too young to get it."

I winced internally. That certainly reminded me of the place I had in his mind.

"What I mean is…you should have the energy to date and find what you like. What you're looking for. Have fun. You know what I mean. Am I sounding really old?"

I laughed and shook my head. "It's nothing I haven't heard before. I'm just not too interested in 'exploring.' I feel like I know what I want and I'll know when it comes along. You know?"

Wesley observed me for a moment. I held my breath. It looked like he wanted to eat me up — in the best way possible. The thought of his mouth on me made me shiver. His voice came out huskier than usual. "Well, what is it you want?"

"Something easy."

He cracked up, throwing his head back, showing off his prominent Adam's apple. "Don't we all."

"Don't laugh!" I smacked his knee. "You know what I mean!"

"Well, relationships aren't easy, Cara."

"I know that. I just meant it should be easy compared to any bullshit I've had to put up with." I pressed my lips together. "Sorry. I promise I don't swear in front of Lucy."

Wesley leaned back in his chair. "I work in corporate America. My ears aren't that sensitive."

I smiled sheepishly.

"I'm sorry you've had to put up with guys being idiots. I know I definitely doled out some of that bullshit in my twenties. You deserve better."

Our eyes met, but I looked away quickly. I couldn't get lost in the deep brown depths of his eyes. "I think by *easy*, I just mean someone who's willing to show up and give their whole self as imperfectly as they are, just how I would. I just want to find someone who sees me. Do you know what I mean?"

He nodded. "I do."

This was the sorriest "sleepover" I had ever been to. It was me who was bringing down the mood, so I decided to lighten it back up. "I can't imagine you have too much trouble out there."

"How do you mean?"

"I don't know. Maybe I'm making an assumption about people with money —" *Shit, this wine. It's like truth serum.* "Sorry, that's so impolite of me to —"

"No, you're not wrong. You definitely get a lot of attention when your net worth is updated on the internet daily." Wesley shrugged. "It can be the wrong kind of attention, though."

"Well, it's not just the money." I was digging myself a deep grave. "I mean, you're a good-looking guy. I'm sure you get attention when you're out and about, too."

Wesley smiled and tilted his head to the side. "I could say the same for you. Not the guy part, but…"

I let out a loud, awkward-sounding snort to cover up how nervous he was making me. I was good-looking to Wesley Taves? Not possible. "It was just an objective observation."

"Oh, of course. Mine was, too. Purely objective."

Just two people very innocently pointing out each other's attractiveness. Nothing suspicious going on at all…

"But see, let's say I separate out the gold diggers and find maybe a handful of women that are actually well-intentioned, not just in it for the money and the looks, as you objectively pointed out."

"You're not going to let me live that down, are you?"

"Absolutely not. It's too fun to see you squirm."

*This man will be the death of me.*

He continued, "I'm still dating kryptonite because…" He gestured for me to fill in the blank.

I had no idea what he wanted me to say. "Because…?"

Wesley frowned. "I've got a kid."

My jaw fell slightly. I never understood why that drove some women away from men. It was an obvious sign of compassion and care. Who wouldn't want a man who had opened his heart like that?

"Don't get me wrong. She's everything to me. I wouldn't trade her for the world. And I would love to give her a positive female role model. A…a mother who's actually around. But it's hard to find someone willing to step into a ready-made family."

"That's crazy. I don't get why someone wouldn't want that. Like, as long as a guy wanted more kids, I wouldn't care. You know?"

My smile faded as I realized how his gaze had heated. And he was looking at me so intently.

I downed the rest of my wine. *When will you learn to shut up, Cara?* "I should go." I hurried out of the kitchen, into the front hall, and pulled on my coat.

Wesley followed, much to my chagrin. "Let me walk you out."

He wouldn't take no for an answer, I was sure of that. Wesley followed me out to my car and stepped in front of me to open the door. *Aw hell, he's a gentleman, too.*

"Hope I didn't keep you too late."

"No, it's okay. It's…" I trailed off. "I know I haven't known Lucy very long, but I think we're really getting along well."

Wesley nodded. "I think so, too."

"She's a great kid."

"Thank you."

A cold January wind danced around us. Wesley wasn't even wearing a coat. Goose bumps broke out on his skin, but he didn't flinch.

"I know you have so many responsibilities. But I know she'd love to see more of you. I don't mean to overstep or anything, but —"

Wesley interrupted quickly. "I'm working on it, Cara. That's why I've brought you on. I'm working really hard to have everything automated for the summer so I can take some time off and be with her. It's hard when I'm on my own."

"I know, I didn't mean to —"

"I know you didn't."

I grabbed his hand. "Thank you for trusting me with her." I hadn't meant to do it, but once I had, the warmth of his hand in mine shot through me.

Wesley glanced at our hands and then back at me, tucking a loose strand of hair behind my ear. I fought not to close my eyes, lean into him. "Let me know when you get home, alright?"

"I will."

After I got into the car, Wesley waited on the curb until it started, and I drove off. I watched him in my rearview mirror until the very last moment, when I turned off his street.

And I didn't stop thinking about him the rest of the night.

# Chapter 10

## Wesley

I awoke to my phone buzzing on my night stand, its vibrating even louder and more ominous than usual.

I cracked my eyes open and groaned. I'm no light-weight when it comes to drinking, but four glasses of wine had left me with a horrible headache. I'd need coffee as soon as possible to avert a hangover. I couldn't afford hang-overs with Lucy around, especially on the weekends.

I grabbed my phone and looked at the screen to see who was calling.

*No. No fucking way.*

Lisbeth. My ex-wife. Lucy's mother. The only time she called was holidays and Lucy's birthday. She and I hardly ever spoke if we could help it. There was never anything to say. We'd made it through the divorce by the skin of our teeth. That meant we were done. That's how I'd always seen it.

So why was she calling on a random Saturday in January?

I let it ring and buried my head under my pillow. Maybe I could eke out just a bit more sleep before —

"Good morning!"

Wishful thinking.

Lucy ran into the room and leaped onto the bed, slamming right onto my stomach. I groaned. "Luce! What did I tell you?"

"I know, I'm getting too big, but look, look, look!" She grinned big, showing off her missing front tooth.

I smiled and wrapped her face in my hands. "Look at you. Did the Tooth Fairy come?"

"Yep! She left me a fifty-dollar bill!"

I swore it had been a twenty when I snuck it under her pillow the night before. The tooth was in a plastic bag in my nightstand table with the rest of the ones she'd lost. I didn't have the heart to get rid of them. Was I just supposed to throw my only child's teeth in the garbage? That felt so wrong.

"Wow. My big girl. What am I going to do with you?" I pulled her into my arms and snuggled up to her.

Lucy squirmed. "Daddy! Too tight!"

"Sorry, sorry." She was getting too big for all my affection. She wanted to have her own space and control over her boundaries. I had to respect that. My biggest fear in raising a girl as a single dad was not instilling in her the ability to say "no" and to not take shit from anyone.

Luckily for me, after I loosened my hold on her, she snuggled right into my chest. I kissed the top of her head. Hangover miraculously cured. "What do you want to do today, Lucy Goosey?"

"Hmm…breakfast in bed."

I laughed. "We can do that. And we can watch a movie."

"Yeah! And then we should go have an adventure."

"What kind?"

"Central Park Zoo!"

"Isn't it a little cold for the zoo?"

Lucy frowned. "We'll bundle up."

I sighed. "Whatever the queen says."

———

NOT ONLY WAS the zoo frigid, but Lucy insisted on getting ice cream. I was completely flabbergasted at her ability to keep her core temperature regulated when I was shivering in my wool coat. But there we were, standing in front of the sea lion exhibit, watching their feeding time.

"Want some?" Lucy held up her ice cream cone to me.

"No. Thank you, though. I'll stick to my coffee." I sipped the dark liquid that was already tepid due to the frosty winter air.

Surprisingly, the zoo was pretty busy, despite the chilly weather. And the sea lions didn't seem to care at all. They were eagerly flopping around as the keepers challenged them to do tricks in exchange for silvery fish.

"Can you see okay?"

Lucy was standing up on her tiptoes, peeking over the railing of the enclosure. "Yes."

I laughed. Trying so hard to be independent already. "Come here."

I carefully scooped her up onto my hip with a grunt, careful of our coffee and ice cream. Soon, I would not be able to do this. I wanted to relish every moment I could.

We'd had a lovely morning together with breakfast in bed and a viewing of *Charlotte's Web*, one of Lucy's favorites. But in the back of my mind was Lisbeth. Her phone call. What did she want? I kept checking my phone to see if she'd left a message, but no message ever came through. For her to call out of the blue and not leave a message made no sense. Either she was regretful for having called in the first place and happy I didn't pick up or…

She wanted to make sure she caught me off guard.

"Look, Daddy, look!"

Lucy pointed across the sea lion enclosure to a keeper who was entertaining a little sea lion cub. It was furry with big eyes and didn't have the same coordination as all the adult sea lions. But it was way too cute for its own good.

"It's a baby." Lucy grinned at me, showing off the gap in her teeth, which I still hadn't gotten used to. There was chocolate on her chin.

"I know it's a baby. He's pretty cute, huh?"

"I think it's a she, Daddy."

"How can you tell?"

She shrugged. "How can you tell it's a boy?"

I laughed. "Fair point. Well, he or she is very cute."

We watched the sea lions a little longer. The sea lion cub sidled up to a bigger sea lion and started nudging and nuzzling at them. "That's like us, huh?"

Lucy shook her head. "That's a mommy, not a daddy."

I twisted my lips to the side. She never meant to hit me with daggers, but she could do it pretty easily with an offhanded comment like that. "You're probably right, though." In nature, most fathers weren't really around like the mothers were. I hated that everywhere we turned, the world showed us examples that a daughter and a father alone together wasn't the norm. "Do you think sea lions have nannies?"

Lucy laughed. "No."

"Really? Don't you think a mommy sea lion needs a little help every once in a while?"

She finished up the last bits of her ice cream cone,

licking her fingers clean of chocolate ice cream. "Sea lions don't need to have jobs, so they don't need nannies."

*Ouch. Again.* "Good point. You're so smart."

The sea lion feeding finished up and all the lions basked in their full bellies. We watched a little while longer before Lucy wanted to move on to the penguins. We walked hand in hand through the zoo. From time to time, I felt eyes on me. This was a normal occurrence. I was a recognizable person. I tried my best when I was out with Lucy to be discreet. I would wear a hat, sunglasses, just a little something that would make someone unsure it was actually me.

I tried to ignore it and focus everything on Lucy. However, it was a constant reminder that my life was not ordinary. I couldn't walk around and just blend in with the crowd, couldn't have a typical marriage and family for my child, couldn't have a normal conversation with my nanny that didn't end up going somewhere…unusual.

I'd gone to bed with thoughts of Cara in my head. All her comments about my attractiveness and eligibility — not in spite of being a father but *because* of it. Well, that was a lot to think about.

I squeezed Lucy's hand as we ambled through the zoo. "So. A week with Cara. What do you think?"

"I like Cara."

"Yeah? Why do you like her, honey?"

Lucy's expression was so bright I thought it could chase away the clouds of this gray winter day. "Well, she's nice. And she's fun. And she's very good at playing pretend. And she lets me help with dinner. And…"

The list seemed endless. I soaked up every positive thing Lucy said, happy that my instinct about Cara had been right.

Her list halted. "Do *you* like Cara?"

I half laughed. "Um. Yes. I like her. For all the reasons you like her."

"But what about the reasons *you* like her?"

God, I *had* made a list. I didn't want to admit it, but I did, at least mentally. Unfortunately, mine started with beautiful eyes, followed by a luscious body, and hair that I wanted to gather in my fist while…*don't go there, old man*. But the more I'd come to know Cara, the more those superficial traits fell to lower places on the list. They were replaced with things like her sense of humor and her kindness and her commitment to what she wanted. How much she knew herself.

"I think she's one of the nicest people I've ever met, Lucy. And that's pretty special, don't you think?"

Lucy pulled my gloved hand to her cheek and leaned on it. "Oh, Daddy…"

"What, baby?"

"Do you think Cara could be like my mommy someday?"

*I think I'd like that. Fuck.* "I…uh…well…you know, Lucy, Cara's got her own life, her own family, and —"

"I know, but isn't that how everyone starts? Two people with two different families make their own family. That's what you and Mommy did. Kind of. Right?"

Damn, she was wise beyond her years. I patted her hand gingerly. "Cara's your nanny, sweetheart. Is that okay with you?"

Lucy's face fell. "Yeah. That's okay. Let's go see the penguins."

I wished I could have told her what she wanted to hear. Made her smile for the rest of the day. For the rest of her life. But I would have been lying to her if I'd said there was a likelihood that Cara would ever be anything more than her nanny.

But even though it was improbable…didn't mean it was impossible.

And there, in front of the penguins in Central Park Zoo, I realized something that terrified me. I not only liked Cara. I wanted her. And that feeling was not going away any time soon.

## Chapter 11

### Cara

I was sitting at a coffee shop near Lucy's school, waiting for Danny Morden. I had to wonder how lately, I seemed cursed to have to wait for men in coffee shops when they were running late.

After I told him I wasn't accepting the deal without the contingencies — or should I say, after *Wesley* told him that — Danny was eager to meet up with me to talk about the deal.

Despite being furious with Wesley for interceding the way that he did, I had to admit, he was right. It would have been reckless to accept that deal when I didn't know what could be wrong with the building. And if I had to shell out a little more money for the property, that was the price for my peace of mind.

Yesterday, I'd decided to give Wesley a call to ask for help. It had taken about an hour out of my day just working up the nerve to call, but I knew I needed his expertise.

"Cara, what a surprise. Is everything alright?"

"Yes. I was hoping you could give me some pointers. I have a meeting with my realtor tomorrow and I want to make sure I'm going in with all the tools I need to…to not back down."

I could hear his smile over the phone. Picturing it my mind's eye, I felt the impact to my core. "I'd be happy to help. You have something to take notes with?"

Wesley and I spoke on the phone for a while as he explained to me everything I needed to know to stand my ground when it came to Danny Morden. His skills were clear. I had a lot to learn. At the end of the call, Lucy hopped on to say hello and how excited she was to see me the next morning. She'd already found a home in my heart.

And Wesley was sneaking in there, too.

So anyway, back to the coffee shop. Danny finally showed up, nearly half an hour late. Aviators plastered on his face and hair greased back as usual. "Cara, baby! How are you?"

"Hi, Danny." I stood up to greet him, letting him kiss my cheek, even though it made me cringe.

"Sorry to keep you waiting. Busy, busy, busy. You know how it goes."

I tried to smile. "I do."

We sat down. Danny whipped off his glasses like he was some sort of Hollywood star. "So tell me, how're your parents?"

*You've got to be kidding.* "Good."

"And Katie? How's Katie? I haven't seen her in years. She's gotta be a grown woman now."

I didn't like the way he was talking about her. A grown woman? What the hell did that mean? That she had breasts or something? "She's good. Business school."

"Mmm. She was always a smart girl."

"Can we get started? I have to pick up the girl I'm caring for in about half an hour and —"

"Oh, shit. My parents mentioned you'd moved families. How's it going?"

No doubt my parents had gossiped with his after church. "It's just been a week but we're getting on really well."

"Who's the family? Maybe I know them."

I let myself relax. *This will be fun.* "I'm nannying for Wesley Taves."

Danny's beady eyes bugged out of his head. "What?"

"Yeah, we talked a bit after you left the showing. He was looking for a nanny and it just sort of made sense."

"No wonder you came up with this capital all of a sudden. Ha! You've got Taves on your side."

I glared at him. "I don't think it matters where the capital came from."

He leaned back in his chair and crossed his leg over his knee, drawing attention to his crotch. *Eww.* "Okay, yeah. Let's get down to it. Don't want to keep you too long. Just long enough." He winked.

My mouth moved into a tight smile, but it didn't reach my eyes.

Danny cleared his throat. Down to business. Finally. "I know you told me you didn't want to accept the offer without the contingency. I get it. It's a risky move."

"Right. Exactly. I don't want to have to deal with cleaning up somebody else's mess."

"I get that…but…I want to warn you there's another potential buyer."

I observed him for a moment. Wesley had warned me about this. His words echoed in my head. *"People trying to make a deal their way will lie to get what they want from you. Be careful."*

I'd be careful. I'd make him proud. "Really."

"Yes, and they're considering buying without a contingency." Danny lifted his chin. So smug, the bastard.

"Why didn't you tell me about this the last time we talked?"

"Well, I can't help a new buyer being interested. That's not something within my control."

I zeroed in on Danny. Wesley had reminded me, *"Stay firm. Up the offer if you have to. I don't doubt that place is in rough shape. You'll be able to counter with less."* I'd do just that. "I can't sign the deal without the contingency."

Danny's face fell.

"I'll throw in another, say, thirty thousand to the offer."

"Jeez, are you made of money, Cara?"

I laughed. "No, just got Wesley Taves on my side, remember?"

Danny grimaced. "Right. Well. That'll get you pretty far, then."

"That's my final offer. I'm not accepting any deal without inspections. That'd be…" What was the word Wesley had used? "Ludicrous."

Danny nodded reluctantly. "Okay. I'll see what they say. But don't be disappointed if it falls through."

Wesley's voice popped up again in my head. *Don't show your emotional hand. Be indifferent.*

I shrugged. "Then you'll find me some place else."

He tried to smile but it came out more as a sneer.

"It's your job, right?"

"Yes, of course. I've got plenty of spaces that would be perfect for you, Cara." He ran his hands up his thighs and I couldn't help but feel the suggestion of that sentence had to do with what was between his legs.

I smiled. "I'm sure you do, Danny. Well, this was great, but I should be off. School pickup can be a *bitch*. You understand, right?"

"Well, wait a second, why don't we sit and catch up and —"

I got up out of my seat. "Another time. Places to be, people to see, yada, yada, yada. Talk soon. Call me as soon as you know."

I threw my bag over my shoulder and waltzed out of the coffee shop without looking back. I could feel Danny's eyes like daggers in my back and I knew I'd done a good job.

*"Always leave them wanting more from you and knowing they'll never get it."*

———

WESLEY HAD BARELY WALKED in the door when I pounced on him. Before either of us could really react, I threw my arms around his neck, hugging him tightly. Our bodies were so close, even closer than the first day we met when he rescued me — chest to chest, hip to hip, my feet barely touching the floor. I didn't want to admit how it made me feel. *Tingly. Hot. Aroused.* "Thank you, Wesley. Thank you so much!"

"Woah! Okay." He acted as though he was off-balance, but his arms were strong and steady around me.

When I drew back, my arms still resting on his shoulders, Wesley looked at me with confusion. "What was that for?"

Now that I was in his arms, I never wanted to leave. If I had the confidence of a more experienced woman, I could have even kissed him. But that would have been awkward, more awkward than this already was. I let go of him and stepped back. My body already missed the feel of him. "My meeting with Danny. Your advice was so helpful."

Recognition passed over Wesley's face. "Right, that was today. Forgive me, I —"

"Have a lot on your mind. I know. I don't hold it against you."

Wesley smiled at me. "No, I was thinking about it this morning, actually, and I forgot to wish you good luck. So good luck. Retroactively. Sounds like you didn't need it, though."

God, he was thinking about me? I could have melted into a puddle right there in the front hall.

"Tell me all about it."

"Well, I did everything you said, and it worked. Apparently, there's another buyer, but I remembered what you said and —"

"Oh, he's totally lying."

"Exactly! So I acted like I didn't care. Stayed firm with the contingency. Upped the offer a little bit and then told him to let me know and —"

"You're shaking, Cara."

I looked down at my hands. They were trembling. "I can't help it; it was just so exhilarating! I didn't think I could do it, but I did."

Wesley took my hands, squeezing them tight. My body released all the tension at his touch. He rubbed his thumb back and forth against my skin. I had to stifle a groan. "I knew you could do it."

"I owe it all to you."

"No, don't do that. You did it all on your own. I'm really proud of you."

I looked up at him. It would have felt more romantic if he hadn't just said he was proud of me, like I was a kid coming home with straight A's on their grade report. Still, I wouldn't let that ruin the moment. "Well, thank you. Your advice was…invaluable."

A soft smile crossed his lips. "Any time, Cara. Seriously."

"Daddy!"

The sound of Lucy's voice had me shying away from Wesley, folding my arms in front of me. I didn't want her getting the wrong idea. I already could feel her getting more attached to me than she should since I was only meant to be there a short time.

Lucy and Wesley greeted each other with clear affection. Kissing and hugging as if it'd been days, not hours. My body burned with the memory of his touch.

"Well, dinner is in the oven. It's a shepherd's pie."

"Cara, can we have our traditional weekly dinner?"

I smiled at Lucy. "It's up to your dad. But I'm game." Of course, I was. I craved even a second longer with Wesley Taves.

"Oh, of course. I'd never get in the way of tradition." Wesley's eyes glinted with humor as they looked between Lucy and me.

I didn't come down from my high the rest of the night. Sitting at the dinner table with Lucy and Wesley, I felt so comfortable and safe. It had only been about a week, and I was already feeling like a part of the family.

From time to time, I caught myself looking at Wesley, admiring him. The way he looked at Lucy, or his prominent cheekbones, or the way his shirt was unbuttoned, revealing the smattering of chest hair. When I realized I was staring, I'd look away quickly.

But all it took was one time for him to notice me ogling him. And when he did, his eyes found mine, locking me in his gaze. A prolonged, nerve-racking moment. What was in his intense stare? Was it desire?

Our eye contact was only interrupted by Lucy announcing she was done with dinner. When he looked away, I decided to keep watching. I wanted him to feel my stare so viscerally it felt like I was touching him.

Wesley might have been teaching me the ways of the business world, but I had found an even better use for them right here.

If I could make Wesley aware of me as a woman, maybe I could even make him want me.

# Chapter 12

## Wesley

"Wesley…"

"Mmm."

Lips against my neck. I sighed. The heavenly feeling of a tongue teasing my skin.

"You've been so bad." A woman's voice. Familiar.

"Have I?"

I squirmed, but a slender hand pressed down on my chest. *I can't move.*

I laughed. "That bad, huh?"

The figure above me was obscured by darkness, her image fuzzy. "Thinking about me the way you do."

I could now make out the contours of her face.

"Wanting me…"

*Oh God.*

"When you know you can't have me."

Cara's amber eyes cut through the dimness like a smoldering fire. I suddenly felt her hips weighing heavy on mine. Her pelvis moving back and forth over me. *I'm hard.*

It felt so wrong and yet…*so good*. I could have lived the rest of my life underneath her, between her thighs. "Fuck, Cara."

"You're foolish if you think you can resist, Wesley."

I loved the sound of my name coming off her tongue. "Kiss me."

Now her smile. Those perfect pink lips. She leaned down and pressed them to mine. My senses exploded. I could feel her, taste her, touch her, hear how she sounded when her body was against my own, yearning for pleasure.

*This can't be real.*

Her tongue dipped between my lips. *She could devour me if she wanted and I'd let her.*

"Touch me."

I swallowed the words into my mouth, lifting my hands to her breasts. They fit perfectly in my palms. Her nipples were hard. "Let me see you."

Cara retreated again, tearing off her shirt in one fell swoop. *I knew she didn't wear a bra under there.* She tossed her head to the side and her hair came into focus. Perfectly tousled from my hands, her bangs framing her beautiful face.

"Do you like what you see?"

"God, yes."

She bent down, arching her back, and pushing her exposed chest toward me. I caught one of her breasts in my mouth, sucking and licking at her nipple. My hand teased the other, pinching and pulling the peak gently. A simple distraction that allowed her to snake a hand into my pants and wrap her hand around my cock.

I jerked underneath her and moaned. Just her hand on me…*fuck*. If I wasn't careful, I would come too fast. "Cara." Her name, so sweet to me. "Cara, be careful."

"Why should I be careful?" She lowered her mouth to my ear. "We've already risked everything."

How did I get here? I was having trouble cataloging the steps that we must have taken to get into…were we even in my bed? Where were we? I blinked my eyes open, trying to focus on the ceiling, the wall, anything to tell me where I was.

Nothing.

*Shit. This truly isn't real.*

A dream. A really fucked-up and fantastic dream. Pinned to the bed by Cara, my daughter's nanny. I'd had this fantasy when I was awake and shoved it away guiltily until it went away. But in sleep, things were harder to control.

Now that I was here…what was the harm in indulging?

A lucid dream now and again could do wonders for the soul. Maybe if I worked out some of that frustration here, I wouldn't be so focused on trying *not* to be attracted to her once I woke.

Her hand continued to stroke me. Dream Cara had a look on her face that I'd never seen on Cara in real life. Her eyelids were lowered in lust as her hand pumped me. "You're so big, Wesley."

God, even in my dreams I fantasized about the thing all men wanted to hear.

"Can't wait for you to be inside me."

"Let me taste you first."

"Uh-uh."

"Cara, please." Would I be able to taste her in my dream? "It's my dream, dammit. I'm in control."

Cara laughed, a giggle that was innocent until it very suddenly wasn't. "No, you're not, Wesley." And without another word, she ducked her head down and wrapped her lips around my cock.

Subconsciously, I knew when I woke that I would be a mess. I hadn't had a wet dream in years. Sure, sometimes I'd wake up hard, especially when there was a woman in my bed. But a dream that pushed me all the way to coming?

*Something must be wrong with me.*

Cara worked me over, sucking and licking while humming her pleasure. Feelings of ecstasy built through my body until I was just at the brink. I pulled her off me. "Stop, let me feel you. Let me come inside you."

"Oh, Wesley. I thought you'd never ask."

Just as she reached for the button on her jeans —

I woke up, gasping for air and sweating. I reached down and grabbed my dick. I shuddered at the touch, my nerves sensitive and raw. "Holy shit." I was leaking pre-cum.

I turned my brain back into the fantasy. Cara about to take me inside herself. I'd already gotten this far, I wasn't going to give myself blue balls when I was alone in my own bed. I pumped my cock the fastest I ever had until I crested into an orgasm. I groaned loudly into my pillow and gripped the bed sheets.

*How did she do that?*

Even though I'd taken care of the problem between my legs, my blood was coursing harder than it ever had. You wouldn't know it was winter from how much I was sweating and the heat I felt all over my body.

I closed my eyes tight and immediately opened them back up when I realized the image emblazoned on my eyelids was Cara's face, alight with ecstasy.

An ecstasy I had never and *would never* see.

Cold shower. That was the only answer.

I threw the sheets aside and scrambled into the shower

as fast as I could. When the water hit my skin, my entire body flinched. "That's fucking cold!"

*That's the point, dumbass.*

A few moments later, I'd gotten used to the freezing water. I braced myself on the tiled shower wall, trying to gain my composure.

It was just a dream. A really fucking awesome dream, but a dream, nonetheless. It had no bearing on my reality.

But it had happened. The thoughts I had banished from my waking mind had attacked me all at once, scrambling together into the most visceral and erotic dream I'd ever had.

How the hell was I going to face her in two hours?

———

"DADDY, WHAT'S WRONG?"

I was hurriedly scrambling eggs for Lucy's breakfast. "Nothing, sweetheart." I turned around to throw some carrot sticks into her packed lunch. "Why?"

"Your face."

"What about my face?"

"It's like this."

I looked over my shoulder at Lucy. She was frowning and her mouth was tight. "Is that what I look like?"

"Yes. When you're thinking very hard."

I laughed dryly. She wasn't wrong. I was thinking very hard, concentrating on *not* thinking about Cara's upcoming arrival, which actually made me think about Cara *more*.

I turned back to the eggs, my hand slipping with distraction, nicking the edge of the searing hot pan. "Ah, fuuu —" I held in my curse for Lucy's sake.

"Oh no! You burned yourself!"

"Yep. Yeah, Luce. I did." I rushed over to the sink and

ran my hand under cold water as a blister formed, taking measured breaths.

"Are you okay?"

"Probably. Hopefully." *Damn shit motherfucker.*

Then, to my horror, I heard the front door open. I was suddenly regretting giving Cara a key.

Lucy squealed and ran out into the hall. "Cara, Cara, Cara! Daddy hurt himself!"

"I'm fine!" The way my voice broke, however, did not make my words very convincing.

Cara rushed into the kitchen. "Oh my God, what happened?"

"Eggs are burning!" Lucy announced.

I was thankful to have something to occupy my attention and keep me from looking at Cara, even if it was burning eggs and a burn on my hand.

Cara turned off the burner and threw the pan into the other side of the sink. Without asking, she grabbed the wrist of my injured hand. "You burned yourself?"

The burn seemed much less important than the current state of my dick, which was growing hard, just from her innocent touch. "Um…"

"Oh God, it's pretty bad."

"It's fine. The water helped a lot."

Cara didn't let go of my wrist, closely examining the burn. I got a whiff of her perfume, vanilla and lavender. I turned away, clenching my good hand into a fist, and pressing it up to my nose.

"I'm so sorry, did I hurt you?"

"Mmm. No, no. It's okay." I yanked my hand away from her and stepped back. "It's fine. I'm going to be fine."

Her brow folded with worry. "Are you sure? It looks pretty —"

"It's already blistering. Just some aloe and I'll be good.

I've got a big meeting today and — shit, would you look at the time! I gotta —"

"Daddy, you said a bad word."

I took a deep breath. This was going poorly, to say the least.

Cara had already disappeared upstairs before I had a minute to respond again. She returned in a flash with a green bottle of aloe and a bundle of gauze. "Give me your hand."

I stared at the way her hand gripped the bottle of aloe and immediately thought about my dick. No. I could not let her touch me. "I'm running late already." I held out my hand for the materials. "I'll do it in the car."

Cara's lips cracked into a smile. *Is she daring me to kiss her? Because I will if she looks at me like that one more time.* "It'll only take a second."

"Fine." I held out my hand doubtfully.

Cara went to work. I closed my eyes, not noticing any pain, completely fixated on keeping my erection down.

But her hands…her touch was so tender as she patched me back up. I would have fumbled with one good hand, trying to wrap gauze around the other. "Does that feel better?"

I wriggled my fingers and looked at my now gauze-wrapped hand. "Much. Thank you."

"Maybe you should call a car. Might be hard to drive with this on."

She was right. But I wasn't willing to look any more vulnerable than I already was. "I'll be fine." I stuffed my hand in my pocket and went through my usual goodbye activities. Throw on my coat, grab my briefcase, give Lucy a hug and now…

One last longing look to Cara. I didn't realize it was a

habit until it already was. Today, she noticed. And she smiled. "Be careful with that hand."

I smiled. "Don't worry, I had a good doctor."

Cara's face turned pink, highlighting her cute freckles.

*Dude. You're totally screwed.*

# Chapter 13

## Cara

Arriving late to family dinner was the last thing I needed. Since taking the job with Wesley Taves, my parents had been on the edge, the most I'd seen since I missed curfew junior year of high school.

The day had started weird and ended weird. Walking in on Wesley trying to nurse a burn on his hand at 7 am was probably the last thing I would have expected. He always seemed to have it together in his perfectly pressed suits. Seeing him frantic and in pain caught me totally off guard.

Not to mention, he seemed like I was hurting him more than helping him. Men can be so prideful sometimes.

Although right before he left, I had sworn there was something in his hypnotic brown eyes. A look I'd never seen before. As if he was trying to see right into my soul. For a split second, I wanted to ask him to stay home the rest of the day and let me take care of that hand. Then from there it wouldn't be so hard to ask him to stay the rest of my life. *Hopeless romantic, Cara. As always.*

The rest of the day was nothing out of the ordinary. I took Lucy to school, I did work on the daycare business plans back at the Taves house, took a call with Danny (*ick*), picked Lucy back up and spent the evening with her.

In the middle of cooking dinner, Wesley had texted me.

**Going to be late.**

No context, no nothing. Just four words that annoyed me. I had a life, too. Did he think he could just change his schedule willy-nilly, with no explanation, and not act the least bit remorseful? In fact, he knew I was seeing my family that night because I had mentioned it the day before over dinner.

"It must be so nice to be so close to your family," Wesley had said.

"A blessing and a curse."

He chuckled. "As all family is."

His lateness was a reminder that I was putty in his hands. To be shaped and used to his will. And I had to let it happen…no ifs, ands, or buts. A quarter of a million dollars will do that to a person.

When he arrived home, he muttered an apology, barely looking in my direction. I had to admit, it broke my heart the slightest bit. Between sharing wine and talking about dating to the celebration we had the previous night over my successes with Danny, all the way to that tiny look I caught this morning before he walked out the door, it felt like we had moved the meter of our relationship a bit more toward friends. And if I was honest with myself, I'd hoped maybe even more.

Of course, though, Wesley Taves had a habit of subverting my expectations. Before I made it to my car, he rushed out from inside with a bottle of wine and handed it to me. "I'm sorry to keep you late, Cara. Give my regards to your family."

"Oh, this is…really nice. You don't have to do that. It's no big deal." *You're a big liar, Cara.*

"Please. I insist. It's the least I can do."

I clutched the wine to my chest and smiled at him. "Thank you."

Now, Wesley's bottle of wine sat in the passenger seat as I pulled up to my parents' house in Oceanside. As soon as I was parked, I snatched the bottle and bolted for the front door. It was unlocked. Everyone was already seated for dinner and their plates were mostly finished.

"Sorry I'm late!"

Katie was the only one who looked happy to see me. "Hey, Car!"

I went to her and kissed the top of her head. "Hi, honey." I went then to both my parents and gave them kisses as well. "Sorry, I got held up with work."

"It's okay. Glad you made it." Mom patted my arm, but I could tell by the thinness of her lips that she was only saying it was okay to make things nice.

Dad, on the other hand, was not willing to make those concessions. "Dinner's cold."

"Oh, I don't mind. I can throw it in the microwave or…" I glanced down at my full plate that had already been made for me. "Or I can just have it cold. Totally fine." I remembered the bottle of wine in my hand. "This is from Wesley."

"Ooh! That looks expensive." Katie immediately pulled out her phone to Google the wine.

I sat down and began to eat quickly so as to catch up to where they were at in their dinner schedule.

"Did Wesley get held up at work?" Mom asked carefully.

Katie interjected before I could speak. "A hundred fifty dollars! He just gave this to you, Cara?"

I swallowed a big bite of pork chop and potato. "Mmm. Yeah. An apology for being a little late tonight. You know, he's got a new project underway that's taking up a lot of his time. He usually keeps a pretty good schedule." Unwilling to answer any follow-up questions, I turned the conversation to Katie. "How's school, Katie?"

"Oh, it's great. I ditched my last business plan. I'm starting on a new one and I'm having so much more fun with it."

"I liked the last one! What was it again? It had to do with sustainable wool and —"

Katie waved her hand toward me to cut me off. "The market just isn't interested in sustainable wool at this point. Too expensive."

I laughed. Katie was still in college but always trying to create her magnum opus of business plans. She was interested in fashion and trends, as evidenced by her ever-changing wardrobe. Lately, she had been focused on neutrals. Everything was tan, khaki, or gray. Very effortless and elegant. I wished some of my baby sister could rub off on me. Maybe dressing more maturely would pique Wesley's interest a bit more. "So, what is it now?"

As I scarfed down food, Katie raddled off some business jargon regarding fast fashion and making slow fashion more accessible to consumers.

"That's so cool, Katie. You're so smart."

"Oh, shut up."

"I mean it!"

She blushed hard but was grinning. I couldn't believe how much she had grown up and was stepping into her own. Just yesterday, we were playing dress up.

"I'm so proud of you."

"Thanks, sis."

"So, Cara, sweetheart…" Mom shifted the conversation without much of a segue. She glanced at Dad and then back to me. "How's work?"

"Mmm. It's good."

Dad raised an eyebrow. "Must be since your boss is giving you small investments in the form of wine…"

"What's that supposed to mean, Daddy?"

He cleared his throat. "Just saying, most people would just apologize. Not buy you off with —"

"Oh, please, he wasn't buying me off. He's a nice guy. He's generous. We have a rapport. Alright?"

I could hear the alarm bells going off in my dad's head. "What kind of 'rapport'?"

"Like a normal rapport! What is with you guys?"

Mom tried to be more delicate. "A hundred-fifty-dollar wine is not a normal rapport, pumpkin."

I dropped my fork and sighed. "Look, I know you guys are just looking out for me, but Wesley's a really nice guy. He knew I had plans, he was sorry, he gave me this wine as a peace offering. That's not some psycho businessman machination."

"He's got money and he's a man, Cara. And you're a beautiful young woman. I don't think it's unreasonable for us to be worried about this man's character."

Katie stepped in to stand up for me. "This is ridiculous. If Wesley was a woman, you wouldn't be worried about this. Besides, Cara's a grown woman. If she wants to —"

"Katie! That is *not helping*!" I ran my hands over my face. "Nothing's going on. Nothing *will* go on. I promise you, we're just friends. The only thing we care about is Lucy's well-being. And if he wants to give me a bottle of wine, he can give me a bottle of wine." The room went quiet. I was being awfully defensive…trying to cover up any cracks in my story. "I don't even think you said thank you."

Mom and Dad both went silent and looked at the unopen bottle of wine. Mom touched Dad's wrist and smiled pleasantly at me. "You're right. That was very generous of him."

Dad huffed and grumbled something under his breath. Then he looked up at me. He was going to set aside this argument for now, for the sake of the family dinner. But I could tell he wasn't done thinking about it. Not by a long shot. "Yes, very generous."

"It seems like he's a very respectful man. And if so, maybe you should focus some of your energy off all your work and put it onto…" Mom trailed off and shrugged plainly. "Dating."

Both Katie and I groaned. *Solidarity, sister.* "These conversations are getting old and boring." Katie started collecting finished plates from the table.

"Oh, Katie. I'm just saying. It's been a while since you've brought a young man home, Cara. Maybe it'd be nice to find someone to be able to lean on…in that way. You know. And then none of us have to worry about anyone being inappropriate."

I rubbed my eyes. "First of all, finding someone to date isn't like going to the store, Mother."

She laughed. "I know that."

"Second, I've got too much on my plate."

"Then let us do some of the work for you!" Dad now was excitedly taking the reins of the conversation. "We've been putting a good word in with the Mordens, you've been spending more time with Danny, and —"

"Okay, you know what, I'm done. Thanks for dinner. Keep the wine." I pushed myself out from the table and started for the front door.

Both my parents jumped to their feet and followed me. "Honey, he's a good boy!"

"It sounds like you're talking about a dog, not a man, Mom."

"He's got a good job. He's your age. He could support you. Why are you so averse to that?" Dad got to the front door before me so I couldn't leave.

I looked between my parents. "How is that any different from dating my employer? Which I'm not doing, but since you two are so worried about it —"

Mom rubbed my arm. "Danny's a friend, Cara."

"And I'm *working with him*. I'm trying to do business with him. That's a conflict of interest, too, so I'll thank you both to stay out of my personal life until I explicitly ask you to get involved. This is absolutely ridicu—" My phone buzzing in my pocket cut me off. I pulled it out.

Speak of the devil. Danny was calling me.

"I have to take this." I pushed past them back into the house and answered the phone. "Hi, Danny."

Mom whispered loudly to Dad, "Oh it's Danny! It's him!"

I glared back at her.

"Hey, Cara. You got a minute? I've got good news."

All the frustration with my parents melted away. Good news — I needed some of that. "Of course. What's up?"

"You got it."

I couldn't breathe. "What?"

"The owners have agreed to your offer. We can sign the contract and go into escrow and run inspections as soon as you sign on the dotted line."

I couldn't help letting out a humongous scream of excitement. "Are you serious?!"

"You bet I am. Now, it took some finagling on my end,

a little bit of groveling, which I am *not* a fan of, but I got it done."

"Oh, thank you, thank you, thank you."

"Let's find a time for coffee. Or even better, a drink. And we can get you to sign and —"

*Nice try.* "I'll come into your office tomorrow. What are your hours?"

Danny sighed and gave me the information I requested. I'd see him first opportunity I had. We said our goodbyes and I turned around to my parents and Katie who'd joined, trying to listen in on my conversation. "They accepted the offer. The building is mine."

For the first time all night, everyone seemed happy. My family crowded around me with hugs and congratulations. I slipped into their embrace. My dreams were finally coming true.

Good thing they didn't know that the man responsible for sponsoring my dream was their adversary, Wesley Taves. I'd keep that information to myself as long as I could.

# Chapter 14

## Wesley

"Hello?" Her voice was a soothing balm coming through the car speakers.

"Cara? I'm headed home."

"Oh! It's a little early, isn't it?"

I felt bad for keeping her late the day before. I had disguised my reasoning with work, but the truth was, I couldn't build up the courage to go home and face her. I paced my office back and forth, terrified of what I might feel — or do — if I was in the same room with her again. Then I was late. "I owe you for yesterday."

"Please, Wesley, really, it's not —"

"I do. I'm stopping at the supermarket on the way home. I'll make dinner. Don't lift a finger."

Cara hesitated. "Are you sure?"

"Unless you wanted to stop whatever fun you two were having."

Cara laughed. "No, no. We're actually just put the finishing touches on our blanket fort."

I imagined Lucy and Cara curled up under the blankets of the fort, pretending they were on a secret expedition.

"But I don't want you to injure yourself again." Was there a teasing tone in her voice?

I looked at my left hand, wrapped in fresh gauze. "I promise I'll be careful. You two relax. I've got dinner taken care of."

I was quiet a moment, tightening my hands around the steering wheel. *Just say it, Wesley.* "And if you'd like to stay…for dinner that is, well, I'm sure Lucy would love that." *And I would love it, too.*

Cara hesitated.

"There's no pressure. I already took time from your night yesterday and —"

"No, I'd love to."

*Love.* Not just like, but love. My heart jumped at the implication. *Jesus, get a grip, you pussy.* But at least I was doing something right. Or maybe Cara's motivation really did have everything to do with Lucy. Either way, at least I could look forward to another few hours spent with Cara Smith. I'd take it.

"Perfect. Anything you girls are in the mood for?"

"Let me ask."

I heard Cara's voice grow distant as she asked Lucy, "What do you want for dinner, Luce?"

Lucy's voice came through clear as a bell. "Pizza!"

"Okay, besides pizza."

Lucy groaned in frustration. That kid would eat pizza every day of the week if I let her.

"Tacos!"

"Mmm…tacos. That sounds good." Cara moved back to the receiver. "The lady wants tacos."

I smiled. "You're in for a treat, then. I make the best

tacos on our block. Which isn't saying much, but it's saying something."

Cara giggled. I tried to memorize the sound so I could savor it later. "Well, I look forward to your block famous tacos."

"Now, I never said they were famous, but —"

"They'll certainly be famous to me."

A car honked behind me. I realized I had been idling at a green light. Cara was doing things to my brain that were making it nearly impossible for me to function normally.

"Be home in a bit."

"Looking forward to it."

§

When I arrived home, I was greeted by peals of laughter from the living room. I poked my head in, arms full of groceries and smiled at the sight. Cara and Lucy had somehow gotten tangled in the blankets. Their fort had unraveled to just a pile on the living room floor. And while I could imagine Lucy getting upset over her creation falling apart, there was no sign of disappointment.

"Oh gosh, hi —" Cara had to break for laughter. "Hi, Wesley!"

"What happened to you two?"

"Cara got tangled in a blanket and it all came tumbling down!" Lucy squealed, hiccups of laughter under each word.

"I'm sorry I missed out on all the fun."

Cara patted Lucy on the back. "I'm sorry, kiddo. We can rebuild it."

Lucy continued to laugh and snuggled into the crook of Cara's arm. It did something to me, seeing my daughter feel so comfortable with and close to another adult, particularly a woman. In that moment, I realized it wasn't just Lucy who was developing feelings for Cara.

I should have known then things were going to get complicated.

"Well, I'll leave you two to rebuild while I work on dinner." I held up the bags. "I've got all the fixings for a fiesta right here."

Lucy pushed the blankets off her. "Ooh! Can I help?"

"Are you abandoning the fort, then?"

Cara waved her hand. "Lucy, go ahead and help your dad. I'll fold up the blankets and put them away."

"No, Cara, she should help clean up."

Cara gave me a look. "It's not every day she gets to help her dad make dinner."

She was right about that. "Okay. Follow me, Lucy. But I'm doing all the cutting!"

"Got it!"

We left Cara in the living room and started on the tacos. Lucy was always an amazing sous-chef, especially for her age, and tonight was no different. I left her to do all the stirring and mixing while I did the cutting. But she was done with all of that quickly, leaving her at my elbow, begging to use the knife.

"I'll let you help, but we have to do it together, okay?"

Lucy nodded and dragged her kitchen stool beside me. She stood up on the stool triumphantly, now at an appropriate level to cook at the counter. "Alright. What do I do?"

Just then, Cara walked in, wrapping her sweater around her. Her eyes were more tired than usual, but she wore a serene smile. Even tired, she still looked beautiful. "Ooh…getting in on the chopping action, I see. You're a big girl, huh, Lucy?"

I half laughed. "Don't remind me."

"Is there anything I can do?"

"No, Cara, you sit. Relax."

Cara rolled her eyes. "Please, there must be something I can do."

I smiled and shook my head. "No. Nothing. I'm in charge tonight. Open a bottle of wine for us, yeah?"

Cara moved to the wine fridge. "What kind?"

"Your pick."

"If it's up to me, I'm going to end up picking something super expensive."

I shrugged. "That's just fine with me."

Cara shook her head. "I'm not used to that."

I didn't grow up with a ton of money, but I was often reminded of how fast it had become the norm. I was used to not worrying about the prices of things nowadays. It was quite a blessing that I didn't often reflect on.

As Cara picked out a bottle of wine, I guided Lucy through the mechanics of chopping vegetables. "Never stick your fingers out. You want your knuckles to be up like this." I let her hands rest on mine as we chopped a tomato. "Cut away from you. See?"

"Yeah."

"You feel how the knife is moving?"

"Mm-hmm."

We were so concentrated on the cutting that I didn't realize Cara had been watching until the tomato was all finished up. I raised my gaze to her. She slid a glass of wine in front of me across the kitchen island with a sneaky smile.

I picked up the glass and narrowed my eyes. "What's that face?"

"I just wanted to make sure I was on hand in case you cut yourself."

I laughed and sipped my wine. I felt so at ease. The three of us here in the kitchen, laughing and cooking together, felt so utterly domestic in a way that Lucy and I had never had. The last time that feeling was present, Lucy was a baby. And even then, Lisbeth always had one foot out the door. That sense of a family unit was always floating out of my grasp. "Up until yesterday, I'd never hurt myself in all my years of cooking." I handed Lucy the cutting board. "Pour the tomatoes into the bowl and then we'll start on the cilantro."

"That's a pretty good track record, I have to say."

"Exactly. Don't worry about me, Cara."

"Oh, Wesley. I'm built to worry. It's my job."

"Okay, now." I put the cilantro out on the cutting board. "You need to go over there." I pointed to a stool at the opposite end of the island.

Cara shrugged, then sat down with a glass of wine in front of her.

I was about to get started on chopping the cilantro, but my heart was beating terribly fast. "And turn around."

She looked puzzled. "Why?"

"Because you're…you're making me nervous."

Cara's eyes widened, as if something clicked into place. *Oh shit, too late now.* Yes, she was making me nervous in every way possible. I wasn't just attracted to her. I wanted to look good in front of her. And that was making this whole arrangement very complicated.

"Cara! Turn around! You're making Daddy nervous!"

"Sorry! I'll turn around." Cara turned around as I had requested, and I tried not to linger on the way her hair tumbled past her shoulders. I struggled not to think about what it would feel like in my hands. I stifled a moan, took a breath, and turned back to the task at hand.

Lucy and I chopped up the rest of the vegetables. In the meantime, Cara left briefly and returned with a sheet of paper, scissors, and tape, working quickly on something I couldn't see. "Lucy, come here."

Lucy leaped off her stool and rushed over to Cara.

"If you're going to be a chef, you need a hat."

My little girl gasped as Cara revealed her creation. From just paper and some tape, she'd created a chef's hat. "Put it on, put it on!"

Cara placed it delicately on Lucy's blonde hair.

"How do I look, Daddy?"

I grinned. "Amazing. Exactly like a chef."

Lucy threw her arms around Cara, thanking her profusely. It was clear that she loved Cara. And for that, I was grateful. But also…terrified.

I let my eyes linger on her. Yes, she was young. Very young. Early twenties…that seemed a world away from me. But she acted so mature. I could picture her as a mother herself one day. And I'd be remiss not to admit that I could conjure up a whole fantasy where I was the man who made her one.

What kind of man thinks about his nanny like that?

# Chapter 15

## Cara

I washed the dishes in the sink while Wesley and Lucy played a game of Battleship at the kitchen table. I wouldn't let Wesley lift a finger when it came to cleaning up after he had done everything but kick me out of the kitchen to keep me from making dinner.

"D5."

"Miss. G9."

"Miss. D7."

"Hit."

I looked over my shoulder and watched as Wesley reluctantly stuck a peg into one of his battleships. I couldn't tell if he was losing on purpose, because Lucy was absolutely creaming him. He only had one ship left for her to sink, and she'd just hit it right on the bow.

Wesley hadn't been exaggerating. His taco skills were incredible. My eyes were way bigger than my stomach, but thankfully, it balanced out all the wine I was drinking.

It was my nerves. I was guzzling down the wine like it

was water. But between the smoldering looks and his kind gestures, the situation with Wesley had made me jittery. It felt like something was happening between us, something I couldn't quite control or understand. Luckily, the wine soothed my anxiousness. However, it did make me silly in the process.

"E7."

"Hit."

"F7!"

"Hit! You got me!"

"I did it! I won!" Lucy jumped up and down, still wearing her chef's hat. "Look, Cara, look!"

I went over to look at the boards. Indeed, all of Wesley's boats were full of red pegs. "Wow. You're a champ!"

Wesley moped playfully. I couldn't resist touching his shoulder. "Sorry for your loss."

He smiled at me and shook his head. "It's okay. I'll get her next time."

Lucy laughed. "No, you won't."

"You better believe I will! Now come here!"

Wesley swiped her out of her chair and pulled her onto his lap, tickling her until she begged him to stop through a loud, breathless laugh. The two of them together were picture-perfect. She was his doppelgänger, with beautiful blonde hair and deep brown eyes. I would have loved to see a photo of her mother to confirm she was a complete photocopy of her dad.

Wesley kissed Lucy on her cheek. "Okay, how about we get your pajamas on and then turn on a movie?"

"Can Cara watch the movie with us?"

"Oh, Luce, Cara's already stayed much longer than usual."

Lucy pouted. "But if I ask and she says yes, can Cara

stay?"

Wesley sighed and closed his eyes. "Yes, but —"

"I have to be okay with her saying 'no.' I know!" Lucy then looked up at me with a big smile. "Cara?"

I played the fool as if I hadn't just heard their entire conversation. "Yes? Do you have a question for me?"

"Will you stay and watch a movie with me and Daddy?"

I looked from her to Wesley. "Only if it's really, really okay with your daddy."

Wesley smiled up at me, a lock of his blonde hair falling over his forehead in a smooth curl. "It's really, really okay with me, Cara."

*Does that mean* he *wants me to stay?* I tried to shake off the thought. I was already acting much more friendly with him than I should have been. I welcomed the lines being crossed, the small touches and the utterances of our names, as if we weren't employer and employee.

"Okay, you get ready in your pajamas, I'll make some popcorn, and then we'll meet in the living room."

Lucy jumped off Wesley's lap and ran upstairs to get her pajamas on as fast as possible. Wesley got to his feet more slowly to follow, but when he stood to his full height, he stopped and looked down at me. "Cara, you really don't have to."

He was too close, lingering over me. One more inch and I would have thought he was going to kiss me. "It's fine. I want to."

Wesley licked his lips and conceded, "Alright. As long as you're not doing it just to be nice."

"No, never. I have too much fun with you two. It's getting to be a problem."

"It is, isn't it?"

Wesley then went off to follow Lucy. I gulped. Yes, it

was getting to be a problem. I was starting to enjoy my life with the Taves — more than my actual life. Their family was just a part of my day. Taking care of Lucy was my job. That couldn't be my whole life. It had an expiration date.

I focused on popping the popcorn. *One thing at a time, Cara.* Once that was all ready, I met Lucy and Wesley in the living room. Lucy was dressed in a cute little nightgown, resting in the crook of Wesley's arm. I took the spot on her other side and without thinking, she extended her feet onto my lap. "So, what's on tonight?"

"*Raya and the Last Dragon!*"

"Ah, a favorite. Okay, start it up, Lucy Goose."

The movie started playing and Wesley dimmed the lights with just a voice command to his Alexa. We watched for a while, the only sounds being the movie and the three of us munching on popcorn.

We were very cozy on the couch, Lucy connecting the space between Wesley and me like a bridge. The longer I was there, the more I leaned toward the two of them. Before I knew it, my head was only a few inches from his. And even though I noticed it…I didn't draw away. I indulged in this closeness. I could smell him, his cologne tinged with the scents from our dinner. My pheromones were going wild.

"She's sleeping."

I looked down to find Lucy's head tilted back on Wesley's stomach, mouth hung open, and her eyes shut. She was snoring softly.

"Man, she's sleeping *really* good."

Wesley chuckled softly. "I could use a sleep like that."

The movie played on in the background, but neither of us watched. We were totally engrossed by watching Lucy sleep. Wesley stroked her hair and caressed her cheek. "I think we're stuck here, Cara."

I looked down at my lap where Lucy's legs were resting and giggled. "There are worse places to be stuck."

Our eyes met, heads resting on the back of the couch. *I could be stuck here with him forever.*

Neither of us looked away. Not distracted by the movie or the little girl entangling us together in our laps. The world around us ceased to exist.

It was just me and Wesley here on the couch. He was close enough I could feel his warm breath on my face.

His eyes fell to my lips. He licked his own.

I wanted nothing more than for him to kiss me. And at the same time, I knew I'd have to refuse him.

Not for lack of want or desire. There were too many voices in my head that weren't my own, overwhelming my decision-making. Suddenly, my mom and dad were in the room with me, reminding me of Wesley's money. Of his ability to use me up. If I already felt under his thumb due to how much capital he was promising me, I knew I'd feel completely under his spell with just one kiss.

What was to say that after my two months were up as Lucy's nanny he would want to continue an affair? Maybe he would easily discard me as his employee and as a lover in one fell swoop. I didn't know if my heart could handle that kind of rejection.

Wesley leaned in, his eyes hovering shut. And just when his lips were about to press against mine, I shoved my hand up against his chest and drew my head back. "We can't."

His eyes shot open. But he did not pull away, our faces only inches apart now. "What?"

"We…" I glanced down at Lucy. "I think we're confused."

Wesley frowned. I couldn't tell if he was angry or hurt. He then drew away from me. I yearned to wrap my arms around him, hold him tight to my chest. Apologize. Take it back. Rewind the clock and try again. "You're right. I'm sorry. I don't know what got into me."

"Please, don't apologize."

"No, I shouldn't have —" He ran a hand through his hair and leaned back on the couch, focusing again on the movie. "I hope I didn't make you uncomfortable."

I couldn't say no, but I also couldn't say yes. His lips hovering toward mine made me the best kind of uncomfortable.

"*Mmgh.*"

Lucy stirred in our laps, stretching her body out long.

Wesley welcomed the distraction. "Sleeping beauty awakens."

Lucy didn't open her eyes, burying her face into Wesley's abdomen. "Did I fall asleep?"

"Yes, and I think that means it's time for bed."

"No…I'm not tired…"

I giggled. "Says the girl who's snuggling up to her dad and hasn't even bothered to open her eyes."

I felt Wesley look at me and smile. I couldn't bring myself to meet his gaze again. "Okay, kiddo. It's bedtime."

Wesley hauled himself and Lucy up off the couch, holding her at his shoulder as if she weighed nothing.

"Why don't you say goodnight to Cara?"

"Goodnight Cara…" Lucy limply waved her hand at me as Wesley carried her out of the room.

"Goodnight, Lucy."

Wesley took her up the stairs without another word. I sat awkwardly for a minute, debating whether I should go. The thought of being alone with Wesley terrified me. If we were alone, if he made another move, I wasn't sure I'd be able to refuse.

I rushed to the front hall to get my boots and coat on,

fumbling wildly. I was shaking, my nervous system on high alert.

"You're leaving."

I froze and turned to the stairs. Wesley stood on the bottom stair, hand on the railing. "It's getting late."

He nodded. "I'm sorry I kept you."

"No, please don't be sorry. It was…" I tried to stand up straighter. "It was a really nice night."

Wesley smiled sadly. "I'm glad you thought so."

Even at this far distance, my body called to him. *Go to him, Cara. Kiss him.*

"I'll see you tomorrow."

"You're good to drive?"

The wine was no longer making my head spin. But my nerves were. I grabbed the doorknob and with one foot out the door, I called over my shoulder, "Y-yes. I'll be fine. Goodnight."

As I drove home, I thought about the kiss that almost was. Wesley's full lips looked soft and luscious. I imagined his strong arms wrapping around me as he kissed me deeper. How would it feel to have those lips on my neck or nipping at that sensitive spot behind my ear? I probably never would have left. Who knows what would have happened then?

Maybe I would have had another peek at that beautiful bedroom of his.

For half the drive, I regretted not kissing him. The second half, I tried to convince myself I was glad I had resisted.

Then I came to a precarious realization.

No matter what I did, Wesley and his money would always have control over me. Damned if I do and damned if I don't.

*I might as well do exactly what I please.*

## Chapter 16

### Wesley

Again, at work the next day, I was unable to focus.

From the moment Cara refused me, I spiraled into a state of self-loathing.

*You're an idiot. A creep. A predator.*

She had been so gentle and polite, and yet it had cut me so damn deep. Had I been reading the signals wrong? Had it really been that long since a woman had paid attention to me that I didn't know when she was into me and when she was just being nice?

I wouldn't have even been surprised if Cara hadn't shown up the next morning for work. It would have been completely reasonable for her to not want her employer to be making moves on her.

Thankfully, though, she did show up. And as awkward as things were between the two of us, it didn't seem to rub off on the way she treated Lucy. She was a professional. A mature young woman.

And she was driving me *mad*.

My dreams, both sleeping and waking, were plagued with Cara. Thoughts of kissing her, of fucking her, of just feeling her in bed next to me were never far from my mind.

And it was starting to impact my work.

"Hey, you got a minute?"

I looked up from my computer, abandoning an open document in which I didn't have a single word written, to find Jenson in the doorway of my office. His expression was grim. *Shit. What have I forgotten this time?* "Yeah, come on in."

Jenson stepped inside, closing the door behind him. He had been very patient with me the past week or so as my brain started turning to mush. I hadn't confided in him my feelings about my nanny, not wanting to prove him right in the first place. But I knew he could tell something was up. It would have been fully within his right to be annoyed at having to pick up my slack.

"What's going on?"

Jenson didn't take a seat in the chair across from my desk. He stood awkwardly opposite me, holding his laptop close to his chest.

"Shit. Did I miss a meeting?"

"No, Wesley."

"Well, from the look on your face, it looks like I fucked something up. So tell me what it is and I'll get right to it."

"Wesley."

I stopped my monologue and looked Jenson dead in the eye.

"Lisbeth's engaged."

I didn't process his words at first, unable to connect the name and the adjective. "What?"

Jenson put his laptop in front of me and opened it. I was assaulted with an image of my ex-wife and an overly tan man that looked at least fifty years old. The caption on the photo read, "Miami's most eligible bachelor puts a ring on it."

"What kind of website is this?"

"Some website called 'Ocean's Edge.' It covers Miami high society or whatever bullcrap."

I stared harder at the photo. Lisbeth was ensconced in the man's arms, looking like an enigmatic siren. Her dark hair was flowing in long waves, a catlike smile perked at the corners, her hand on his chest, showing off a huge, gaudy ring.

"Who the hell is this guy?"

"Yves St. Pierre. He's in yachting. Apparently been breaking hearts since the moment he hit puberty."

I shook my head. "That's not Lisbeth's type at all." And it wasn't. I wasn't some playboy that she tamed. Lisbeth and I had both been ambitious and young. We barely found enough time to see each other between our work hours, until we finally realized how much we wanted to be together. How much we thought we wanted to be together…

I scrolled down to read the article, but only phrases jumped out at me as my eyes blurred. "…romantic proposal on the beach…" and "…been courting her for two years…" Until I landed on the last sentence of the article. "When asked if she would take his last name, Lisbeth Anderson smiled. 'Lisbeth St. Pierre' has a nice ring to it, don't you think?'"

I felt sick. Lisbeth had been adamant about holding onto her last name when we got married. I didn't mind and didn't push her, even though I'd doodled the name "Lisbeth Taves" once or twice.

Now she was going to be Lisbeth St. Pierre, just like that?

I slammed the laptop closed and pushed myself out of my chair. "Fuck."

"Hey, Wesley. Calm down."

I started to pace, remembering the phone call from the weekend I had ignored. She tried to warn me. But if she cared enough, she could have left a fucking message. "What the hell am I going to tell Lucy?"

"You don't have to tell her anything. She's six. She's got other things on her mind."

I ran my hands over my face. "This is the last thing I need, Jenson."

"It's okay, man, relax." Jenson came over to me and touched my shoulder. "I wanted you to hear it from me before you went out and started hearing it through the rumor mill."

"People are already talking about it?"

Jenson nodded solemnly.

I looked toward the door of my office. I hated to imagine everyone whispering about me. Getting into my private life. "I think I'm going to take off early today."

"I think that's wise. Take as much time as you need. I know it's…" He trailed off. He didn't know. How could he, when his life was so picture-perfect with his wife and children and mine was so…convoluted?

"Thanks for telling me." I shrugged off his hand. "I'll be in tomorrow."

"Or not, you know. Take the time you need. Be with your daughter and —"

"I'll be in tomorrow." It came out harsher than I meant it to. "We've got work to do on Readly and I can't afford to be…elsewhere."

I collected my things, threw on my coat, and walked out, mumbling a goodbye and not waiting for his answer.

§

I walked into my house, midday on a Thursday. I rarely saw the light this way, streaming in through the blinds, creating an ethereal feeling to the space. "Hello? Cara?"

Silence.

I sloughed off my coat. "Anyone home?"

Still, nothing. That was for the best. I was sure Cara was working on something for her daycare center or out running errands. I had the slimmest amount of hope she might be there, though. I could have used her smiling face to calm me. Even if I'd made things complicated.

My heart had not stopped racing since I'd heard the news about Lisbeth. I was unsure why. I'd worked very hard over the years to get over her. Therapy and time were the most beneficial. And yet, as soon as I heard she moved on, I was spiraling.

I didn't want to be with Lisbeth. I was long past that stage.

But knowing she had moved on while her little girl grew up with little more than a phone call on her birthday? What kind of life was she looking to start with this Yves St. Pierre character?

I needed to get the anxious energy out. I could get past this, but I needed to focus. I decided to go for a run and lift some weights down in the basement workout room, which I rarely used because of how much time I spent at the office.

I went up the stairs two at a time, stripping my clothes along the way. Totally alone, I could have walked naked around the house if I wanted. It'd been years since I'd done something like that. In my bedroom, I rummaged around for some running shorts, but couldn't find any. *What the fuck?* I couldn't remember the last time I'd worn them. *Must be lost in the laundry room.*

I started back down the hall, naked except for my boxer briefs, on a mission to find my running shorts.

But suddenly, the bathroom door swung open and Cara emerged, balancing cleaning products in her arms.

As soon as she saw me, she screamed. All the bottles and rags fell from her arms except for the Windex, which she clutched in her left hand like a weapon.

"It's just me! I'm sorry, I didn't mean to scare you."

"I didn't know you were home!"

"I called out, but no one responded."

Cara removed earbuds from her ears. "I had my head-phones in, I —" Her eyes dropped down from my face to my naked chest. "Oh my God."

I ran my hand across my sternum, as if I could somehow cover up my nakedness. But it was too late. She'd seen me.

And her expression as her eyes drifted over my mostly nude body…did something to me.

Cara's terror morphed into curiosity, her jaw falling open at the sight of me. From my bare pecs, to my abs, to the growing erection in my briefs, Cara practically devoured me. Her pupils dilated.

I couldn't help but smile.

"I'm so sorry…" Her voice was barely audible. She made no effort to turn away or move, feet firmly planted in the spot where I had surprised her.

*Now*, I was tempting her.

And she was tempting me, too. Without any makeup on, Cara was a natural beauty. She wore a wide-necked T-shirt that revealed one of her shoulders and a pair of tiny biker shorts. And she was barefoot.

I craved her in her most natural state.

I was fully hard now just staring at her. "You see what you do to me?"

Cara blinked and then nodded.

"What am I supposed to do when just looking at you makes me feel like this?"

A slight smile appeared on her lips. Her chest was heaving with breaths of anticipation.

"I don't know."

That smile was it. My permission.

I closed the space between us, snatching the Windex from her hand and throwing it to the ground. Then I took her in my arms and kissed her.

It was better than in my wildest dreams. *How is that possible?* Her lips were softer than they looked; her tongue snaked into my mouth, winding with mine, and she drew me in as close as possible.

I broke the kiss, Cara clinging to me, arms around my neck. "Tell me to stop."

"No."

I pushed her up against the wall, returning my lips to hers. "Cara, tell me to stop before it's too late."

"I don't want you to stop."

*Fuck. She's so hot.* I ran my hands down the curves of her body. "We can't go back if I — if we —"

Cara pushed her hips up against mine and grabbed my backside. "Wesley. *I want you to fuck me.*"

Well. I didn't need to be told twice.

# Chapter 17

## Cara

I couldn't believe this was happening. Wesley Taves was kissing me, pressed up against a wall, totally hard for me. And I'd barely done a thing.

This was beyond my most enthusiastic wishes.

As soon as I told him I wanted him to fuck me, a flip switched. He no longer held anything back.

Wesley kissed me ferociously, pressing me tight to the wall. His mouth devoured mine and then moved down to my neck. I whimpered as he sucked on the sensitive skin, his hands sliding down my body to my ass.

He growled. "Fuck, your body, Cara…" His wide-palmed hands seemed to envelope me completely. I felt so secure in his embrace.

Wesley slid one hand from my ass into the waistband of my shorts, gliding his fingers through my folds. I gasped.

"You're so wet for me."

"Yes."

Wesley slipped two fingers inside me, curling them until

he found my G-spot. His thumb pressed against my clit. I threw my head back against the wall, crying out and gasping for breath. "Fuck, Wesley."

"Mmm. Say my name again."

"Wesley…"

He groaned into my ear. "Where do you want me to fuck you?"

"Anywhere."

"Right here?"

"Wherever you want."

Suddenly, his hand left my center and he hoisted my legs up around his hips. "I want you in my bed."

I locked my arms around his neck. "Take me there."

Wesley's arms were strong and safe. I didn't think for one second he would drop me as he carried me down the hall to his bedroom, kissing me hungrily the whole way there.

Once inside his bedroom, he deposited me on the bed and stood over me.

*God, he's gorgeous.* Standing tall above me, he looked like some kind of Viking warrior. Broad chest, covered in hair, his jaw hard, and his eyes traveling up and down my body with wicked intent.

Not to mention his cock bulging in his briefs. I couldn't wait to have him in my mouth, between my legs…wherever he wanted.

Wesley pulled my shirt up over my head, revealing my breasts. He sucked in a tight breath. "Damn, you're not wearing a bra."

"I never do."

"I didn't think so."

I laughed. "You've been looking."

Wesley cupped my breasts in his hands, thumbing my nipples. My back raised off the bed in pleasure. "Obviously, I've been looking." His dark eyes found mine. "You're so fucking sexy, Cara."

I had never been called sexy, at least not by a man I desperately wanted inside me. It made me weak.

Wesley's hands slid down from my breasts to the waistband of my shorts. He yanked them down, off my legs. Now, fully naked in front of him, I was exposed, nervous for him to see every imperfection.

But from the look in his eyes, I could tell he felt the exact same way as he had a moment before.

*Sexy.*

"God, the things I want to do to you —"

"I want to see you, too."

Wesley raised his chin, eyelids lowering. "I'm big."

"I can tell."

"I don't want to hurt you."

"You won't."

Wesley pulled on the band of his underwear, revealing a patch of pubic hair first, then low enough that his cock sprung out.

Big was an understatement.

Wesley looked down at himself and then at me to gauge my reaction, self-consciousness bubbling in his eyes. "Told you."

I stifled a laugh. I'd never met a man so embarrassed to have a nice cock. I sat up and ran my hands down his chest to his thighs and pushed his briefs the rest of the way down. "I love it."

He smirked. "Yeah?"

"Yeah. I'd love it even more if it were inside me." I stroked his length, then kissed the tip, swirling my tongue around the head.

Wesley hissed, pulling me back up. "Jesus Christ, Cara. What am I going to do with you?"

"You want me to say it?"

Wesley chuckled and leaned down to kiss me. "I wouldn't mind hearing it again."

I ran my hands through the locks of his blonde hair. It was softer than I had imagined. "Fuck me," I whispered against his mouth.

Wesley growled and wrapped one of his hands around my jaw, drawing back to look into my eyes. "Tell me if you want me to stop."

"I won't want —"

"I'm serious, Cara, tell me if you want to stop. I don't want to hurt you." He lowered our bodies to the mattress.

I smiled. He meant in the broader sense. Ever my protector. In this instance, I appreciated that. But also, the need I felt for this man was so great, I wasn't thinking about the possible consequences. I only wanted to live in this moment, here with him. I wriggled my hips up against his, feeling his cock nestle into me.

Wesley shut his eyes tight and grit his teeth. "Christ…I need a condom."

I slid my hips back and forth, coating his length with my wetness. "I'm on the pill. We can go without one. It'll be okay."

"You sure?"

I nodded.

Wesley positioned his dick so the head nestled right into my opening. His eyes met mine one last time. And without words, we agreed.

This was happening.

Wesley shifted his hips forward, pushing himself into me. I jerked under him, throwing my head back and gasping. It felt so good to be stretched by him after imagining what he'd feel like.

Slowly, he started to move his hips, pulling almost completely out before gliding back in, deeper each time.

"Oh my God. You feel so good. I'm so full…"

Wesley smiled, but said nothing, focusing entirely on creating a steady rhythm. His lips caught mine in a kiss and he began to speed up. "Good girl…"

I wanted to be his good girl. Wanted him to praise me and adore me every moment of every day. And here, in his bed, I wanted to make him feel amazing.

I wrapped my legs around his hips and drove up toward him, taking him deeper.

Wesley cursed. He gripped the comforter in his hand until his knuckles turned white. "Taking me…so well…"

"Fuck me harder."

He pumped into me with more force, our pleasure building by the moment. Warmth was pooling in my belly. I'd never felt this good with anyone else.

Wesley moved back onto his knees and wrapped his hands around my hips to control my rhythm. I moaned. "Faster…"

"Jesus, you're so fucking beautiful."

I loved the way his eyes devoured me, from where our bodies were joined, to my swaying breasts, all the way up to my eyes. When our gazes locked, the fire burned hotter inside me.

Suddenly, Wesley slid out of me. I whined, "What are you doing?"

He moved onto the bed beside me, so our centers were lined up. "I want to make you come."

"But I was so close."

He shook his head. "Better than that. I want to be in you as deep as I possibly can."

With more control than I thought possible, Wesley

lifted my top knee and plunged his cock back inside me. We both moaned, lost in the sensation.

I mewled in ecstasy, burying my head in the pillow. "Oh, fuuuck."

Wesley was in complete command. He shook his hair out of his eyes, his head tipping back. He shut his eyes and parted his lips, almost as if he was praying for the strength to hold on as he fucked me.

I reached toward his navel and pressed my hand against his taut muscles. My fingers dug into his hip, as if I could somehow pull him closer to me. Wesley pulled my hand up and pushed his mouth into my palm, kissing it sweetly. "Oh God, Cara…"

I raked my hand back through his hair and pulled him closer. "You're gonna make me come."

"Yeah?"

"Yeah."

He moved his hips faster. "Come on my cock, Cara."

The tingling in my core grew stronger.

Wesley grabbed me by the chin, pulling my face toward him so our gazes locked. "Eyes on me, beautiful. I want to watch when you come."

There was no going back. While he plowed into me mercilessly, his brown eyes stared at me so intensely, letting me know I was safe.

I came with a scream, reaching for something, anything to make me still feel like I was on earth while my body burst into stardust.

"Good girl…that's right…come for me…"

His tender voice drew out my pleasure for longer than I thought possible. I fell limply onto the pillows, breathing heavily.

Wesley bestowed kisses from my clavicle up to my neck.

"You're so gorgeous. The most exquisite woman I've ever seen."

When he reached my mouth, he stopped. I tenderly cupped his cheeks in my hands. "We're not done," I whispered.

"I don't care about me."

"I care. I want to feel you, Wesley."

His Adam's apple bobbed.

I kissed his chin, the short bristles of budding facial hair scraping my lips. "Please. I want you to come inside me."

Wesley pulled back and looked at me with a serious expression. "Are you sure?"

I played with a lock of his hair. "I'm on birth control. It's okay."

Wesley's eyes dropped to the place where we were still connected. He sighed, his breath full of want. "If you're sure…"

"Wesley —" I readjusted myself on top of him, bringing my knees around his hips and working my body up and down his shaft. I brought my mouth to his ear. "Fuck me."

He moaned, a slave to his own pleasure, and began to thrust his hips up.

"That's it…you make me feel so good." I leaned back, reaching a hand out to cup his balls. "Let me make you feel good."

"Fuck! Cara…that feels amazing."

"I want to make you feel *even better*."

"Jesus Christ, Cara."

As though he couldn't resist, Wesley angled himself up and caught one of my breasts in his mouth. He teased and gently bit my nipple, soothing the sting with his tongue.

Suddenly, I could feel another orgasm building. *Fuck, this man is incredible.*

Our mouths came together, and we kissed just as recklessly as our bodies coming together. Biting lips and knocking teeth.

"Cara, I'm —"

"Yes! I'm all yours."

Every muscle in Wesley's body went rigid and he grabbed my hips, fucking me mercilessly.

I cried out as my second orgasm ripped through me, my pussy clenching around him. "Come with me, Wesley."

With that, he released inside me with a grunt, his cock surging several times.

"That was amazing." I said softly as my orgasm faded.

"Yes, it was."

Wesley pushed up, rolling me off him. The emptiness he left behind ricocheted through my bones. I wanted to stay joined with him as long as possible.

We lay side by side, catching our breath. Nervously, I looked over at him and him at me. We exchanged a smile and then looked away from each other. Shy laughter bubbled from our lips.

"I'm sorry."

I frowned. "Why?"

"Well, I…I don't know."

"Do you regret this?"

Wesley shook his head. "No, not at all. I just…"

We looked at one another again, this time unable to look away.

"You're my daughter's nanny."

I smiled. "That's true."

"And I don't ever want to make you feel uncomfortable."

"Do you think I felt uncomfortable while begging you to fuck me?"

Wesley smiled. "No. I certainly hope not."

I put my hand on his chest. "Can I be honest?"

Wesley rested his hand on top of mine. "Please."

"I've wanted to do this for a long time. I never thought you'd feel the same or that it'd ever happen, but —"

"Me too."

I resisted a huge grin, but it came out anyway.

"Cara…" Wesley touched my cheek and ghosted a finger over my lower lip. "I think about you all the time."

I wondered if his thoughts of me were just sexual or if there was more there. But at the root of all of this were a few simple facts. One: he was my boss. Two: he was much older than me. And three: everything about this was wrong.

So why did it feel so right?

"Then we should do it again. If you'd like."

Wesley smiled, a satisfied look in his eyes. "I'd like that very much."

"Good. Me too."

Without another word, Wesley gently pulled me into his chest and kissed the top of my head. "I hope you don't mind, but I like this part, too."

I held my tongue from saying what really was on my mind. *I don't mind at all. In fact, you could keep me right here forever, if you want.*

## Chapter 18

Wesley

I pulled up to the house midday on a Friday to pick up Cara for her appointment with Danny.

Cara came out of the house in a wool winter coat and waved to me as she flew down the stairs. In a flash, she'd thrown herself into the front seat of my car and planted her lips on mine.

"Mmm." Her lips on mine still filled my entire body with warmth. "Hello."

She giggled. "Hello." She kissed me again quickly. "Thank you for coming with me today."

"It's my pleasure."

"You know it means a lot to me." Her hand slid down to my bicep and she squeezed.

I had insisted on going with her so I could assist her. But really, my motives were selfish. I'd noticed in our short encounter all those weeks ago that Danny Morden was less than professional with her. Coupled with Cara's passing mention of his advances, I was on high alert.

Protecting Cara had been a priority since the moment I saved her from being hit by Danny's car. I felt a possessiveness that I didn't want to examine too closely. I just hadn't really acknowledged it until we'd made love.

From that moment on, we'd barely been able to keep our hands off one another. Two weeks of blissful rendezvous, hidden from the light of day and of course, from Lucy. But with each other, nothing was off-limits.

Even though Cara was not explicitly mine, I wasn't going to let some other man try and pull her away from me.

"You better to be careful with those hands, or we might not even make it to the appointment."

"Is that a threat?"

"It's a promise."

Cara laughed and let go of me. "Alright, I'll be good."

"Good."

We drove off to the building in Brooklyn, catching each other up on our days, sharing laughs, and of course, flirting. My new favorite pastime was finding ways to make Cara blush. And boy, was I good at it.

When we pulled up to the building, two cars were already out front: Danny's and the inspector's. Cara's mouth formed into a thin line. "We'll have to be good in front of Danny. I don't want word getting back to my parents about us."

She hadn't meant for that to sting, but it did. Our relationship wasn't one for public consumption, but I'd be lying if I said I didn't want that. To be able to walk down the street with Cara Smith on my arm was a daydream I had regularly. "That's fine. I'll be good. I can keep my hands to myself."

She raised an eyebrow. "Can you now?"

I scoffed. "You don't trust me?"

"I just know how hard it is for you to keep your hands off me. We've almost gotten in trouble before."

There had been a few instances over the two weeks when I had pushed a bit too far and Lucy had almost walked in to see. From stolen kisses to a groping of the ass, I was always trying to see what I could get away with. "I'll be good."

"Good. You'll be rewarded handsomely later." Cara got out of the car.

I leaned my head back with a sigh. *She can't just say those things and not expect it to affect me.*

I got out of the car and followed her across the street to the front door of the property. Danny Morden was there to welcome us in all his smarmy glory. "Cara, it's good to see you." He grabbed her hand and pulled her in close, kissing her cheek.

My blood boiled.

"Hi, Danny."

Danny turned to me with a wry smile. "Is Mr. Taves your new chauffeur?"

Cara lifted her chin. "Sorry, I thought I mentioned it. Mr. Taves is my business partner." I had told her to call me this. Not only was it mostly true, but I knew it would rile up Danny.

Danny removed his aviators, a look of shock and bewilderment on his face.

"Why do you look so surprised, Danny?" Cara asked with faux innocence.

He shook off the surprise quickly. "Well, I knew Mr. Taves was, um, *investing* in your business, but business *partner*, that's…" He looked me straight in the eye. I raised my chin and smiled subtly, daring him to say anything more that might piss me off. "Good to see you again, Mr. Taves."

"You too." I shook his hand and then greeted the inspector beside him.

The inspector was a man a little older than me wearing a hardhat and a reflective vest. "Let's get started, shall we?"

Cara and I exchanged a look. I would let her take the lead until she needed help. She smiled at the inspector. "Sounds good."

Once inside the building, the inspector set to work. That left a lot of down time for us. Or should I say *torture*. I couldn't touch Cara, couldn't flirt with her, and had to be party to watching Danny constantly hovering around her, making small talk, and so obviously checking her out.

"I tried this amazing Korean place in the village. We should go some time."

"I always like when you wear makeup. You'd look amazing with some red lipstick."

"I still can't believe you're single. What's wrong with those guys? You know, if you were with me…"

I kept my hands in my pockets so no one could see they were balled into fists.

From time to time, the inspector grunted out something that none of us really understood, but I could tell things weren't going well. Even though I felt bad for Cara that the building was probably in shambles, I still felt smug that I'd been right and Danny had been wrong about the need for an inspection.

The last thing that needed to be looked at was the roof. We all followed Danny through the access door and into the breezy February day.

Cara reflexively moved closer to me as a chill ran down her body.

"It's a lovely view from up here, isn't it?" Danny spread his arms wide to the expanse of Brooklyn before us.

"V-very l-lovely." Cara's teeth were chattering.

If only I could have reached out and warmed her up. I had plenty of ideas on how to do that.

"Over here, Cara, look at this —" Danny walked to her and grabbed Cara by the hand, pulling her away from me.

I quietly fumed as he pointed something out to her in the distance, whispering in her ear. Cara laughed politely, but I knew she was just trying to humor him.

I tried to keep my attention on the inspector, engaging in small talk as he knocked his boot against different parts of the structure and muttered complaints under his breath about the cold. All the while, my whole body screamed at me to follow its instincts and protect what was mine.

Cara was mine. She just didn't know it yet.

Abruptly, the inspector stood up straight. "Okay. Whew. Done." He started scribbling something on his clipboard and then scanned the three of us. "This place is in need of some serious TLC."

I spoke first. "What are we looking at here?"

"Well. Plumbing needs a complete overhaul. Electrical is a mess. And I'm surprised this roof doesn't have more damage than it already does. There's no drainage system. And that's just the tip of the iceberg."

I smiled politely, though I could feel Danny's smoldering glare on me. "Let's talk about it inside, hmm?"

The inspector continued to list issue after issue that he had found in the inspection. I was glad I'd steered Cara in the correct direction and pissed off Danny Morden. At least, I could tell he was melting with embarrassment.

"Well, thank you so much for taking the time to come out here." Cara shook the inspector's hand. "You've really done me a big favor."

The man shrugged. "Just the job. Have a great day."

As soon as he left, the three of us were plunged into silence.

"Well." Danny laughed nervously. "That was…not as expected."

I crossed my arms. "Really? You didn't expect the bowels of this place to be a wreck just by looking at it?"

"Wesley…" Cara glanced my way.

Danny raised his hands. "Listen, you never know with old buildings like this. I was optimistic. Clearly, that was the wrong way to go about it." He then turned to Cara, cutting me out of the conversation. "How about we go grab some coffee and talk over the offer? With all this information, I'm sure we can come to something that suits both sides better."

I stepped between them. "Sorry, she's not going with you."

"All due respect, Mr. Taves, I'm trying to talk to Cara, so —"

"I think you're abusing your preexisting relationship with Ms. Smith and I'm not afraid to point that out. I think the next best course of action is for us to take a step away and discuss how we're going to proceed." I narrowed my eyes. "But you can be sure the deal as it stands now is off."

Danny stepped back from me. Intimidation was a necessary hazard of my job. I didn't always love doing it. But intimidating a piece of work like Danny Morden filled me with satisfaction.

"What he means is…" Cara moved toward Danny, putting her arm out casually between the two of us, knowing there was tension brewing. "I still want the place. But I think we'll have to lower our offer unless some changes are made."

*That's exactly right.* She'd known just what to say when my hotheadedness had almost interfered with the sale.

"I can appreciate that. Let's talk Monday. Take the weekend to mull it over with your *business partner*. Alright?"

The three of us walked out of the building. I kept my distance from Danny and started for the car, else I would put my foot in my mouth again and let my jealousy ruin the negotiation.

*This is why mixing business and pleasure is a bad idea, Taves.*

Cara and Danny said their goodbyes and she hurried over to join me. As soon as the car door was shut, she tore into me. "Okay, what was that?"

"I knew this place was a mess."

"That's not — that doesn't excuse the way you were behaving, Wesley. You almost lost me the building."

"Oh, come on. He wouldn't have canceled the contract with you. He needed to be put in his place."

Cara huffed. "I can handle him. I've known him practically my whole life. You don't need to save me, Wesley."

"You wouldn't have had the inspection if it weren't for me."

"And I'm grateful for all your guidance. Seriously. But that…"

She didn't finish her sentence. "What?"

Cara chewed on her lower lip, staring out the windshield. "If I didn't know better, I'd say you were jealous."

I glanced out the window. Danny had already driven off. We were alone, in the privacy of my car. "You're right. I was jealous."

"Why? It's just Danny."

"I had to stand there and watch him flirt with you. It pissed me off."

"Are you mad at me?"

I shook my head. "Of course not, Cara. You didn't do anything wrong. He just —" I smacked my hand against the steering wheel in frustration "— made me so fucking mad. And I couldn't even do anything."

Cara was quiet. She reached over and cupped my cheeks in her hands, turning my face toward me. Her touch was soft against my skin, and her honey eyes entrapped me. "Wesley, you know there's no one else, right?"

She didn't owe me loyalty. We'd never discussed it explicitly. But to hear her say it…

I knew I wanted Cara to be mine and mine alone.

One of her hands moved down my chest, lower and lower, leaving a trail of fire behind. "No one makes me feel like you." Her hand cupped my groin. "No one ever has."

I pulled in a tight breath as she massaged my dick through my pants. "Christ, Cara…"

Cara leaned in to kiss me, smiling. "You're cute when you're jealous."

I closed the space between us, kissing her hungrily as she continued to stroke my length.

"Get on my lap," I growled into her mouth. "*Now*."

In a frenzy, I pulled Cara over onto my lap, tilting the seat back as I did. Though such close quarters made it difficult, we managed to remove all the necessary items of clothing so that I could slide inside her. Cara had shown herself over the past two weeks to be quite brazen in the bedroom and her willingness to fool around in the car only made my desire for her grow.

"Ooh, you feel so good," she murmured in my ear as I guided her hips up and down over me.

"*You* feel good…so tight…" I nipped and kissed her neck as she rode me.

Faster and faster, our hips worked in a frenzy. We were both breathing so heavily, the windows were fogging up.

Cara clutched the headrest of my seat. "Oh God, Wes, *fuck* me."

I merely grunted, the hot pleasure creeping through my veins. But if I could have formed words, only two came to mind.

*You're mine, you're mine, you're mine.*

But I never would have dared say it.

# Chapter 19

## Cara

By Valentine's Day, Wesley and I had been having our affair for twenty days. I was embarrassed to admit I was counting. But every day that passed and Wesley was still mine felt like a dream come true.

Of course, I didn't expect anything from him on Valentine's Day. That holiday is saved for romance the world can see, for those in a committed relationship. And though my feelings for him were growing, I knew we were keeping our relationship — if that's what it was — a secret.

But it didn't stop us from having a celebration with Lucy that night. Wesley brought her a bouquet of roses and I set the table with a white tablecloth and candles. Our meal was personal pizzas, which we all topped ourselves, and sparkling apple cider in champagne glasses. Dessert was chocolate covered strawberries.

While it was all for Lucy, I couldn't help but get swept away in the evening myself, stealing as many glances at Wesley as I could.

It had become a habit for me to stick around through dinner and past Lucy's bedtime so that Wesley and I could steal some private moments together. And this night was no different, although I wanted to give him a special treat.

As he read Lucy her bedtime story, I snuck off to his bedroom and slipped into something a little more sexy — a flowy black nighty that came down just past my hips and closed at the center with a thin little ribbon. I had felt lost in Victoria's Secret until I laid eyes on it. I knew Wesley would love it.

He knocked before entering the room.

"Come in."

"She's out, so I'm all…" Wesley lost the ability to speak once he saw me. He blinked, as if he was dreaming. "Holy shit."

I twisted my hips from side to side, showing off the flowing fabric. "Do you like it?"

"I love it." Wesley approached me and wrapped his hands around my waist, gazing at my chest hungrily. "You won't be offended if I take it off you, though?"

I giggled and stepped closer to him. "Not at all."

He leaned down, kissing me softly as one of his hands slid down to the closure of the negligee.

"Happy Valentine's Day."

"A very happy Valentine's Day." Wesley pulled the fabric away from my chest and fondled my tits, his thumbs caressing my nipples. Despite having him more times than I could count, his touch still made me shiver. "You know, Cara, you're full of surprises."

I wrapped my arms around his neck, getting up on my tiptoes to bring our faces closer. "What kind of surprises?"

Wesley's hands slid down my waist and around the curve of my ass. "When I met you, I thought you were such a good girl. But it turns out you're really —"

I cut him off with a languid kiss. "What am I?"

His breath was warm on my face. He was silent for a long, heated moment. "Get on the bed and spread your legs."

I followed his instructions. Without any more conversation, Wesley shouldered himself into the space between my legs and began to devour me, his tongue and lips caressing my pink center with skill and perfection. I mewled in ecstasy. He had learned very quickly all my pleasure points and it was clear he was on a mission to make me come hard and fast.

Our eyes locked as he flicked my clit with his tongue, then wrapped his lips around the bud, humming. It sent tremors through my body, and I cried out as my orgasm crashed over me.

Without pause, Wesley flipped me onto my belly and took me from behind, plunging his rock-hard dick deep inside. I had become so used to him, and I was so wet from his mouth on me, I was more than ready for him to take me. Though I was still shaking from my orgasm, my body was primed to lose itself in him again.

"You're a dirty girl, Cara."

I groaned into the bedsheets as he thrust into me.

"You love when I fuck you."

I nodded.

"You can't get enough of me, of my cock."

"Yes, Wesley."

"Say it."

"I can't get enough of your cock."

He let out a hum of pleasure and started to play with my tits, pulling and plucking the peaks as he fucked me. "You're so good at being bad, Cara."

I lost myself to him, to his possession of my body, so close to coming again. "I need you to fill me up." He paused and I felt myself become desperate. "Fuck me hard, Wes." I clenched my core around him. "Come for me."

Only a few thrusts later, he lost control. He folded himself over my back, holding my hips tightly to his as he pumped into my pussy. I came, too, with a quiet moan into the pillow. We always had to be careful with Lucy around, even though she was on a different floor.

As we came down from our high, Wesley pressed kisses to my shoulder and rubbed the curves of my hips with tenderness. "You're so good for me."

I felt a pang in my heart. I knew not to believe anything a man said in the heat of the moment. And Wesley probably had only meant it in the context of sex. But in my heart, I wanted to tell him I *was* good for him — in every way. After only a month of being in his life, I knew this was true.

I had never stayed overnight with Wesley. It was much too complicated with Lucy in the house. Impossible to explain away, even though she was not yet at an age where she could fully comprehend what we were doing.

Every time we made love, though, I hoped it would be the time he'd invite me to spend the night in his bed and I could wake up in his arms come morning.

That would be a step toward something more serious.

This moment was no different. In the quiet, I sent out a silent plea.

*Ask me to stay. Let me wake up next to you.*

"I have something for you."

I raised an eyebrow. Not quite my wish, but it was something. "Oh?"

"Yeah. Give me a minute." Wesley kissed me languidly, our eyes meeting. I swore I saw more there than just lust.

But how could that be possible? He was a billionaire.

Over forty. He had a child. Why would he want anything more than sex with me? I shivered as my mind wandered into troubling territory while he left the bed to retrieve whatever he had for me. "You didn't have to get me anything."

"It's just a small gift."

I watched him go over to the dresser, open the top drawer, and pull out a red rectangular box. "Well, you didn't have to get me anything at all."

He smirked. "I could say the same about your sexy outfit."

I sat up and arranged the straps of the negligee, which we hadn't ever fully removed but exposed my front completely. "This is just a silly little thing."

"So is this." Wesley sat on the side of the bed and slid the box toward me.

I paled. The box was branded from Cartier. This wasn't just some silly gift. This was jewelry.

*Expensive* jewelry.

"Open it."

"I'm afraid to."

Wesley laughed. "You're so adorable."

I took a deep breath, picked up the box, and opened it. Inside was a gold bracelet with a butterfly pendant at the center, inlaid with what I could only guess was pearl.

"Do you like it?"

I couldn't hide my shock. "It's beautiful, but…I can't accept this."

"Of course, you can." Wesley gestured for me to give him the box, which I did. He took the bracelet out delicately, the diminutive chain glittering in the low light. "I saw it and it reminded me of you, spreading your wings. Seeing beauty wherever you go."

I swallowed nervously as Wesley clasped the bracelet around my wrist.

His penetrating brown eyes met mine. "I knew you had to have it."

My brain wanted to continue to refuse. *This thing must be hundreds of dollars, at least! You can't accept this!*

My heart was beating so loud, I was afraid Wesley could hear it.

I threw my arms around him and kissed him passionately.

It wasn't an invitation to stay the night, but it felt like an invitation to stay in his heart.

*I'm doomed.*

§

"Holy shit."

"I know."

"Wow!" Katie twisted my wrist from side to side, examining the bracelet with wide eyes.

The day after February fourteenth, while Lucy was at school, I'd driven out to the Bronx to visit Katie between classes. I hadn't taken off the bracelet since I'd received it, and I'd barely slept that night. I couldn't get Wesley off my mind. And I knew I had to talk to someone about it.

"Wesley gave this to you?"

I nodded solemnly.

"Just out of the blue?"

I pursed my lips. I hadn't told anyone about our affair. Katie was the only person I knew I could confide in who wouldn't judge me. "I need to tell you something."

Her eyes bugged out. "I knew it. I knew something was up."

"We've been…sleeping together."

She covered her mouth to avoid gasping loudly.

"For a couple weeks now."

"Cara! This is so exciting! He's totally obsessed with you!"

I jerked my hands down into my lap so she couldn't stare at the bracelet any longer. "I don't know, Katie. He's rich. He probably gives gifts like this all the time."

"Oh, come on! You're being completely idiotic." She pulled out her phone and started tip-tapping away. "Where's it from?"

"Cartier."

After just a few more seconds, she held up the phone, showing off a listing for the very bracelet I was wearing. "Yeah, I'm sure he just drops over a grand on all his friends."

I touched the butterfly charm, remembering how he'd said it reminded him of me. "He's a billionaire, Katie. That's a drop in the bucket."

"Cara, if he'd spent any more on you, he would've been showing his whole entire ass that he's obsessed with you."

I laughed, going red in the face. "I don't know about that."

"And you're totally obsessed with him."

"Katie…"

"Just tell me, how's the sex?"

"Katie!"

"Let me fantasize!"

I sighed. "Really great."

Katie squealed, making all the campus cafeteria patrons look our way. She, though, was unfazed by the attention. "This is so exciting."

"No, it's not. He's…he's my boss."

"Okay. And?"

"*And* I shouldn't be sleeping with my boss. And I sure as hell shouldn't be romantic with him. It's not like we work in an office, you know. I'm a part of his life. His daughter's life."

"Even more reason why he's totally obsessed with you."

"Would you stop saying that?!"

"Why are you so defensive?!"

"Because I don't want to get my hopes up!"

We both went quiet. My eyes fell to the burger I'd barely touched on my plate. Admitting it out loud felt like being consumed by a cloud of melancholy. Now I was vulnerable to getting my heart broken and other people witnessing that sorrow.

"Cara, it's okay to like him." Katie reached her hand out toward me. "It's okay to like him a lot."

I took her hand. Her touch immediately settled my nerves.

"You should say something."

"I couldn't do that."

"Why not?"

I blinked away tears. "Because there's no going back from that. What if he pulls back entirely from me because I tell him I'm feeling something for him? What if he fires me? He's doing so much for me already; I can't ruin it by —"

"Cara, you don't know until you know. He's a grown man. And if he doesn't act like one, you don't want to be with him, anyway. But it's useless to sit on your feelings and stress like this when you could just ask."

I eyed my little sister. Her brown hair, the same shade as mine, was long and sleek; held back in a claw clip, it showed off her strong bone structure and amber eyes. Though she was only twenty-one, she looked so grown up. "How'd you get to be so mature?"

She squeezed my hand. "Well, I've had a pretty great mentor."

I flushed. "Please. I can't work up the courage to tell a guy my true feelings. I'm not a mentor."

"You're being vulnerable to your feelings. That's so powerful, Car. Give yourself a chance at happiness. If you bottle your feelings, you're just going to suffer." Her eyes hardened. "It's better to know than to guess."

I looked at the bracelet on my wrist. The little pearl butterfly was calling to me. Wesley had said it himself; I could see beauty all around me. I was freeing myself.

And if I was going to live up to that, I was going to have to take a risk.

# Chapter 20

## Wesley

The pressure of running multi-billion-dollar businesses hadn't felt so stressful since Cara had entered my life. She had a way of soothing my anxieties. And if I became bogged down by fatigue and endless strain, I could retreat into my mind and imagine everything I wanted to do to her when I arrived back home.

I could also play a game of office basketball with Jenson. Although, admittedly, that activity wasn't as pleasurable.

"Kobe!" Jenson took a shot from the back corner of my office. The tiny basketball flew through the air toward the door where the basket hung, bounced off the backboard, and missed the net.

"Ooh. So close."

Jenson sighed, retrieved the ball, and tossed it my way. "Your turn, Lebron."

I chuckled and then took a shot from behind my desk. It swished right through the net. "Nothin' but net!"

"How do you do that? It's like you don't even try."

I shrugged and kicked my feet up on the desk. "Maybe I'm just better than you."

Jenson grabbed the ball again and lobbed it straight at my head. I held my arms up in front of my face, the ball bouncing off my forearms, and laughed. "Damn, you're a sore loser!"

"We're not playing for points. I'm not a sore loser. I'm just sore." Jenson took another shot and missed again. "Goddammit."

I stretched my arms up and sighed. "You want to go grab some coffee?"

Jenson's disappointment in his abilities with the ball transformed into a crooked smile. "What's gotten into you?"

"What do you mean?"

"You're like a whole different person."

I held back a smile. I couldn't let Jenson know he'd been right about the whole nanny thing. That'd give him fodder to rib me into the next decade. Plus, things with Cara were under wraps. It was an unspoken thing that our relationship was a private matter.

Although, especially after the night before, I was hoping we would speak to it soon. Cara's shock at my gift, however, didn't give me a lot of confidence. I couldn't read if she was happy or terrified at the prospect of me giving her jewelry. And while I played it off as a simple gesture, I had toiled over what to buy her for days.

When I didn't respond, Jenson took a moment to clarify. "You're more relaxed."

"Well, that's good."

Jenson narrowed his eyes. "Are you getting laid?"

Alarm bells went off in my head. "Bro, what the hell?"

"I just have to ask. I know you'd probably tell me if you were, but on the off chance you're hiding that from me —"

"I'm not. Since when do I have to tell you that I'm getting laid?"

A lopsided smile crept onto Jenson's lips. "You are, aren't you?"

"No!"

"Too defensive. You are. Who is it? It's not Cheyenne, right? Unless this is some hate sex fetish —"

"God, no."

"But it's someone."

I sighed. "Can we drop it?"

"If you're fucking your nanny and you're not telling me —"

"I'm not fucking Cara!"

Jenson's eyes narrowed momentarily, like he saw right through me. I was ready to respond with an even more defensive comeback, which would have proven my guilt ten times over, when my desk phone rang.

*Saved by the bell.*

"Hello?"

"I have Lisbeth Anderson on the line for you, Mr. Taves," came the voice of my assistant.

I hadn't given Lisbeth much thought since finding out about her impending nuptials. Cara had done a great job of keeping me distracted. Which is why hearing her name made my heart plummet all the way to floor.

"You okay, man?"

"Put her through." I covered the receiver with my hand. "Lisbeth."

Jenson's eyes widened. "You want me to stay?"

I shook my head and waved him out. He might have said something in return, but my blood was pounding so loud in my ears I couldn't hear him.

"Wesley?"

I did not tend to think of Lisbeth fondly, ever. But whenever she said my name, I was reduced to putty in her hands. Had been that way ever since we first met. "Lisbeth. You sound well."

"You've been ignoring my calls."

"Oh. Sorry. Must have missed them."

"That's alright. I know you're very busy." I could hear her smile through the phone, sly and cunning.

I picked up a pen and started to draw a spiral on my desk blotter to calm my nerves. "I heard you're engaged. Congratulations."

"Oh, thank you. That's very kind of you."

I closed my eyes tightly. There's something so painful about being made a stranger by someone who used to be your whole world.

"That's why I've been trying to call. I wanted you to hear it from me rather than someone else."

"Well, that's impossible when you're rubbing elbows with Miami elite, isn't it?"

She scoffed. "Don't be bitter, Wesley."

Anger flared in me. "I'll be however I like."

We were both silent for a long moment.

"Is that all you wanted to tell me?"

Lisbeth sighed. "No. That was just the preamble."

"Then spit it out, I've got a meeting in five." That was a lie, but I always had to make it known to Lisbeth that my time was precious. Otherwise, I found myself going in circles with her.

"Why are you always so cold to me?"

*Don't snap again, Wesley. Don't be cruel.* "You always catch me at the wrong time." There would never be a right time for Lisbeth to catch me. Though I'd moved on and had no desire for her in my life, the mere thought of her could tear open the stitches of the wound she'd left five years before.

"I see."

"Lisbeth, get to the point and tell me what you want."

A long pause. "I want to come visit Lucy."

I cleared my throat. "What for?"

"Well, I'm getting married, Wesley. She's a part of my life. And I'd like to introduce her to Yves. That's my fiancé."

*I know his goddamn name.* "That's completely out of the question."

"I'm sorry?"

"Lucy won't be meeting your fiancé. That would be incredibly inappropriate."

"Inappropriate? I'm her mother, Wesley."

*Then why don't you act like it?* "Lucy doesn't even know yet that you're getting married."

"I could tell her. I'll explain everything to her. You wouldn't have to do anything."

"Oh, thank you, Lisbeth. Thank you for doing me this one big favor. Mother of the year award." I couldn't hold back my temper. I was incensed that she thought any little thing she did for our daughter required thanks.

"I didn't *say* that. I'm saying rather than you painting this evil picture of me, I'd like to be able to explain my side of it. And Yves is so excited to meet her. She'll love him."

"I'm sorry, but that's not happening."

Lisbeth was silent. A chill went through my body. She was good at keeping me on edge. "You know that would be a violation of the court order, Wesley."

Our custody agreement, while mostly in my favor, did, indeed, allow Lisbeth some privileges in visiting Lucy. However, it was rare she exercised it. I couldn't help but feel this was total posturing to her new fiancé. I wondered what she had told him about me. Maybe she'd painted me out to be a villain, the one who took her daughter away from her when the truth was the complete opposite.

I tried not to remember the details when I thought about those times, banishing them from my brain. What I can never forget, though, is coming home. Lucy's squalling cry echoing through the house. Finding Lisbeth sitting, nonplussed on the couch, reading a magazine. And the definitive smile on her lips when she said, "Good, you're home. I want a divorce. And before you say anything, you can have her."

*You can have her.*

Like she was property. A commodity.

Once again, Lucy was just a commodity. Something to show off to Lisbeth's new fiancé.

"I'd hate to have to sort this out with a judge, Wesley."

So would I. Getting legal teams involved always posed a threat that our custody agreement could change. I had been told many times that parental alienation could get me in trouble. I wasn't about to start now.

*One meeting. That won't hurt us. Then I'll pick up the pieces.*

"Fine. When?"

"I'll be in New York at the end of the week."

"Jesus, you really love throwing me off guard, don't you?"

Lisbeth laughed. "I thought you might be happy to see me."

I didn't reply. "Friday."

"Perfect."

"But I'm going to warn her ahead of time about what's going on. She doesn't deserve to be blindsided like I was."

"Were you really surprised I've moved on, Wesley?"

*Moved on.* Like I was somehow still hoping she was hung

up on me. "It's hard for me to imagine my life after our marriage being about anything but Lucy. I forget that you're free to do whatever you please."

Lisbeth cleared her throat. "Fine. See you Friday."

She hung up before I could reply. I slammed the phone down into the cradle and ran my hands over my face. *Fuck. What the hell am I going to do?*

I started to think of ways to tell Lucy. Right when I got home from work? After dinner? Before bed? There was not a single moment that seemed right.

*Maybe Cara could help.*

My blood went cold.

*Cara.*

My beautiful distraction. The subject of my every waking thought for weeks now.

I'd become too caught up in her too fast. Consumed by her touch and the idea that she could be mine. I'd neglected everything else.

And with Lisbeth's arrival imminent, I couldn't afford a distraction. I needed everything to be focused on preparing Lucy and making sure nothing was amiss that would give Lisbeth any sort of ideas about our custody agreement. Though it seemed far-fetched, I was always terrified that a visit from her would come with the line "I've made a huge mistake" and she'd want to renegotiate.

The thing I'd always had over her was that, despite my workload, I was entirely committed to Lucy. She had been the only girl in my life since…well, since she was born.

I had to keep it that way.

Cara and I could not continue on as we had been. Not when my custody of Lucy was vulnerable. I tried to tell myself it was for the best. That based on her reaction to the bracelet, I didn't even know how deep her feelings went.

Regardless, I knew when I got home that night, I had to break my own heart and tell Cara things between us had to end. At least for now.

I just hoped I would only be breaking one heart and not two.

# Chapter 21

## Cara

I had practiced what I was going to say to Wesley over and over the rest of the day, whispering the words to myself like an incantation.

"*Wesley, I've really enjoyed spending time with you, and I'd like to take our relationship further,*" I whispered for the seventy-fifth time as I stirred the pot of chicken soup I had whipped up for dinner.

"What'd you say?"

I whipped around to find Lucy right at my heels. "Uh, nothing. Just talking to myself."

Lucy eyed me. "So it *isn't* nothing."

*Damn, this girl is too smart for her own good.* "Well, I was just…trying to remember what spices I'd put into the soup. Salt, pepper, garlic powder. And I thought there was one more, so I was going through them out loud to see if it sparked my memory."

Lucy laughed and turned around, back to her spot at

the table where she'd been coloring in a safari-themed book. "Cara, you're so weird."

"Takes one to know one."

We exchanged a grin before I turned back to stirring the soup unnecessarily. *Be careful. Tender ears are always listening.*

Every time I thought about backing out of my plan to tell Wesley how I felt, I remembered the bracelet on my wrist. Just a touch to the pearlescent butterfly reminded me of what I was moving toward. A possibility of a future with Wesley.

I could crash and burn.

Or I could fly. Like the little butterfly.

Only a little while later, the front door opened. My heart started pounding like a drum. *Boom, boom, boom.* I could feel the pulsing in my throat as I followed Lucy into the front hall to greet Wesley.

"Daddy! You're home!"

Wesley didn't have time to shrug off his coat before she bounded into his arms. He didn't hesitate to wrap her tightly in an embrace. He cradled her head in his hand, closing his eyes as he held her. "Hey, Luce."

I'd never doubted the love he had for her, but this moment was different. It was as if letting her go might wreck him. Of course, Lucy didn't know that and squirmed out of his embrace after only a few moments. "Cara made chicken soup and bought me a new coloring book. Let me show you!" She started pulling on his hand.

"In a minute, let me take my coat off and get settled and…" He lifted his eyes to mine. Something was wrong. I could just tell. His usually sparkling brown eyes held pain in their depths. And his shoulder drooped, almost as if he was carrying a huge weight on his back. "Lucy, I want to talk to Cara for a minute. Why don't you run along and color and I'll be there in a minute?"

Lucy looked between us and then shrugged. "Okay. Don't take too long."

I forced myself to chuckle, but smiling felt wrong when something was lingering in the air that seemed to be causing Wesley distress.

Lucy scampered back into the kitchen. I'd learned all the angles and curves of this house. I knew where Wesley and I could be seen and where we could hide away. Lucky for me, the kitchen table had no clear view into the front hallway.

I closed the space between us and wrapped my arms around his waist, underneath his coat. My body craved his warmth, his comfort. To know he wouldn't draw away.

He didn't.

I pushed myself onto tiptoe, so my lips weren't far from his. "Hi."

Wesley accepted my kiss. "Hi."

"Something's on your mind."

He nodded and touched my hip. But instead of drawing me closer, he pushed me away. My brain scrambled, now on high alert. Wesley took off his jacket and scarf, hanging them up with slow, deliberate movements.

"What's going on?"

Wesley swallowed. "Cara, we need to stop —" he gestured with his hand between the two of us "— this."

I couldn't hide my shocked hurt. His words cut straight through me. I had to school my expression and make a real effort to keep from crying.

"At least for a bit. I think we've become caught up in the excitement. And it's been amazing, really, but —"

"What's changed, Wesley?" I couldn't hold back. I

could not believe for a second he just came to this conclusion after giving me a gift like the one around my wrist.

Wesley looked away and his lips tightened. "My ex-wife."

Just the mention of her made my thoughts spin out of control. Did she want him back? Were they giving their marriage a try again? Was he leaving me for *her*, this woman I knew had broken his heart, even if he didn't speak about it outright with me yet?

"She's getting married."

*Thank God.*

"And she wants to come see Lucy. Introduce her fiancé to her. And I don't want her getting wind of anything going on that might be untoward. Do you get what I'm saying?"

Suddenly, Wesley felt so distant. The look in his eyes was not of tenderness and affection, but one of business. His detached, no-nonsense demeanor oozed out of him. Serious. More sophisticated. More mature.

*My boss.*

This had been wrong from the beginning. But I let my romantic nature get the better of me. There was a reason I had resisted him as long as I had.

Because this was always a bad idea from the start.

And him wanting to hide it from his ex-wife was proof of that.

"I don't want her to feel like she can change our custody agreement or think that somehow you're endangering Lucy's welfare by being involved with me while caring for her."

I bit the inside of my cheek to restrain myself from screaming at him. Anger never solved anything. And though I wanted to let him know what I thought about my *endangerment* of Lucy, I had grown in our short time together. I was more levelheaded in business dealings.

And that's what this was. Business.

Wesley took a step toward me and touched my hand softly. "Please understand —"

I pulled my hand back like his touch had burned me. "I do understand." I forced myself to smile. "I understand completely."

He frowned. "Cara —"

"It's what's best for Lucy. That's all that matters to me. Let's not…we don't have to go around in circles about it." I started to collect my coat and things. I would not be staying for dinner. That wasn't a discussion we needed to have.

"But I need you to know that —"

"Wesley, it's fine. This was a mistake, anyway."

He flinched at my words, as though they struck him physically. "Alright."

"You know why. It wasn't…professional of us. So it's for the best we end things now." I stood facing him, knowing the next thing I'd have to do was leave. But my feet were unwilling to move. The bracelet suddenly felt very heavy on my wrist. "Here." I started to undo the chain.

"No, no. That's yours to keep regardless of anything. It was a gift."

"But it's much too generous."

"It wasn't."

"I can't keep it."

"You have to."

"I *have* to?"

It was a standoff. His brown eyes held my own that were burning with fire. I was scorching him with my gaze, not meaning to cause harm but trying to maintain control.

Unfortunately, things like that never really worked.

I dropped my wrist and pushed my hands into my pockets. "Fine."

"Good."

Lucy was the queen of inconvenient timing, but at this moment, I wanted to thank her for it. She rushed in, holding her coloring book high. "Look! I finished! Giraffes!"

Wesley forced an expression of wonder onto his face. "Wow! That's an incredible coloring book! Let's go sit down and you can show me all the details, alright?" He hustled her into the kitchen, leaving me alone in the front hall.

He didn't look back, and I slipped out the front door noiselessly.

§

Going home to my empty apartment did not sound appealing. Instead, I drove directly to my parents' house on Long Island. Dad answered the door, shocked I had come over unannounced.

"Cara! I didn't know you'd be by for dinner. Did you tell Mom or Katie —"

"No, my plans fell through. But if there's not enough, I don't have to eat."

Dad chuckled. "There's always enough for you, Cara. Come here."

He gave me a big hug in the doorway.

"Is there a window open? It's freezing in here!" Katie yelled as she rounded the corner. Over Dad's shoulder, our eyes locked. Her frustration turned into confusion and then to understanding.

It hadn't gone the way either of us had wanted. Otherwise, I wouldn't have been there.

"Come in, come in. I'm going to go let Mom know to

set another place for you." Dad ushered me inside and then hurried out of the hallway.

Katie and I stood opposite one another, not saying anything. Ever since she was born, we had an uncanny connection. And we could feel each other's pain, even without words. She was feeling mine at that moment, her eyes filling with tears.

"Don't cry, Katie." I felt tears in my eyes, too. I hadn't cried on the way over. I had been willing myself not to.

"I can't help it. I'm so sad."

She closed the space between us and grabbed me in a fierce hug.

"Me too."

"I can feel you trying to be strong. Stop that."

I buried my face in her shoulder. "I don't want to cry, Katie."

"Why? That's stupid."

I laughed. Tears spilled down my cheeks. "Because that means it was real."

"Oh, Cara. Even if he doesn't feel the same way, that doesn't mean it's not real for you."

But that was just the thing. I didn't know if he didn't feel the same way for me. All I knew is that he had decided he *couldn't*. That was almost worse. He had decided to will himself not to care for me.

"He's made a mistake, Katie. It has to be a mistake."

"Then you have to let him make it."

And there, in Katie's arms, I relinquished my control. I couldn't make Wesley want me or love me. All I could do was show up the way I had every day since I met him. With my full, open heart.

Maybe then he'd see just how much he'd lost.

# Chapter 22

## Wesley

"How much longer until ten, Daddy?"

"About fifteen minutes."

Lucy sighed and leaned over the back of the sofa, looking out at the street as she waited for Lisbeth's car to arrive.

Since I had told Lucy the news, she'd been full of nervous energy, and not in a good way. My usually carefree, spirited little girl was now withdrawn and silent. She would zone out and need to be drawn back into an activity or a conversation.

"How about we play a quick card game, Lucy?" Cara sat down on the couch next to her and touched Lucy's back.

Lucy shook her head. "No. I just want to wait."

Cara looked up at me, brow folded with concern. I sighed. There wasn't anything we could do to distract Lucy from her anxiousness.

I was more grateful than ever for Cara. Despite the

obvious hurt I'd caused her, she didn't shrink away from her duty to Lucy. Every day, she came prepared with fun activities and games. She became the sunlight in our home and Lucy gravitated toward her warmth every minute she could.

I wanted to as well, although I had to keep my distance. Now I wanted her more than ever.

Though Cara was acting as a consummate professional, there was a slight shift in her attire. It felt egotistical to think it had something to do with me, but I couldn't help it.

Her tops were more low-cut and she opted for formfitting jeans and pants that highlighted the curve of her ass. Every time I looked at her, all I could think about was how many times I'd had her in my arms and how I wanted so much more with her.

On top of that, my bed felt cold and empty without her presence. And the house felt too quiet without her laughter late into the night.

When Lucy requested Cara be there that day, I wasn't sure it was a good idea. Cara could distract me, and I didn't want to cause Cara more pain, either. But this was about Lucy and what was best for her. So I let her ask Cara to be here. And she said yes.

*I should give her a bonus.*

"She's here!"

I went to the window and caught sight of Lisbeth climbing out of the car, her fiancé helping her out by the hand. "Well, this is the first time she's been early for anything…" I mumbled.

The three of us went to the front hall. Lucy tentatively opened the door and then rushed to my side. Cara lingered just a few steps back. While she was there to comfort Lucy, her presence also calmed me.

Lisbeth appeared in the doorway with a flourish. Her taste had become more expensive since we had been married, no doubt due to her new lifestyle, and she looked younger. *The miracle of Botox.*

She smiled, teeth blindingly white, lips slathered in raspberry pigment. "Is that my not-so-little girl?"

Lucy giggled, hiding her face in my leg.

"Would you give your mommy a hug, sweet girl?"

I wanted to growl. The fact she called herself "mommy" was laughable. But this was for Lucy. I patted her back reassuringly. "Go ahead, honey."

Lucy closed the gap between herself and Lisbeth and threw her arms around her neck. Regardless of the time between visits or her absence, Lucy always melted into her arms. No amount of hurt could change that she was her mother.

"You must be Yves." I stepped toward the overly tanned guy who was dressed for anything but winter in New York. His wool peacoat could not have been doing anything to keep him warm with his shirt unbuttoned so low.

He smiled smugly. "I am. Nice to meet you, Wesley."

We shook hands.

"And this must be Lucy. I've heard so much about you!" Yves cooed to her as if she was much younger than six.

Lucy looked at me and then back at Yves. She held out her hand to him. "Pleasure to meet you."

I could hear Cara stifle a giggle behind me. I smiled over my shoulder at her. *A woman after my own heart.*

"Ah. Yes. Like father like daughter, I suppose." Yves awkwardly shook her hand.

"And this is Cara, Lucy's nanny. I hope you don't mind

that she'll be joining us today." I stepped aside and gestured to Cara.

Lisbeth raised an eyebrow. "I didn't know Lucy had a nanny. I remember you saying just a couple of years ago that you didn't need one."

That was true. And also, wishful thinking on my part. Running multi-billion-dollar businesses definitely didn't equate to an excess of free time.

Cara stepped into the awkward silence and shook both their hands. "Nice to meet you. Your daughter is a joy."

"I'm sure she takes after her mother in that way." Yves put his arm around Lisbeth's waist.

I wanted to vomit.

"Why don't we move into the living room and you and Lucy can talk?"

Yves removed Lisbeth's coat and she shook out her long dark hair. "Yes, let's get started." She took Lucy's hand. "I don't want to waste a minute."

As she walked past me, her coldness seemed palpable. We hadn't even managed to greet each other. What kind of message were we sending our daughter?

Yves followed them, and then Cara, who squeezed my arm as she passed me.

Our eyes met for just a split second, and instantly, I felt at peace. She was more than I deserved, especially after I broke her heart. As she reached out, the charm of her bracelet hit my arm. It had to mean something that she hadn't taken it off.

Once settled in the living room, Yves and Lisbeth made quite a show of giving Lucy a present — a pair of slippers with giraffe faces on them. Lucy was enchanted by them and immediately took off her shoes to wear them. I had to give Lisbeth credit; she remembered the little things. But knowing favorite animals and colors were barely scratching the surface of what it meant to be a parent.

Lucy led the conversation. She sat in her own chair instead of next to any of us on the sofas, making it very clear this was Lucy's world and we were all just living in it.

I have to say, I was proud of her.

Lucy held a glass of chocolate milk with two hands in front of her, sipping it in between questions. "So you're marrying my mommy."

Yves chuckled. "That's right."

"Are you and Mommy going to have babies?"

I nearly spat out my coffee. Right to the point, this kid.

"Um. Well." Lisbeth hesitated.

Long enough to let me know the answer was at the very least *maybe*. Maybe even yes. I stared at her hard. Would she really be so cruel? Abandon one child to have more with another man?

Was I so awful that Lucy wasn't worth her time?

Yves cleared his throat. "You know, that's sort of a personal question, Lucy."

Lucy kicked her feet. "Well, this is sort of a personal situation."

Cara hid her mouth in her hand to stop another laugh.

"You're right, honey. This is a personal situation. Come here, would you?" Lisbeth invited Lucy onto her lap and held her close. "I brought Yves here because you two are the most important people in my life. And I want you to get to know each other. Is that alright with you?"

Lucy nodded and smiled.

Lisbeth was good with words. It's why she was in law. And Lucy wasn't yet able to distinguish that words didn't matter if they weren't seen in action. Where did Lisbeth get off saying that Lucy was so important to her when she barely made the time to visit unless it suited her? "Wesley, do you mind if we have a few moments together alone? To get reacquainted? I think in no time we'll be the best of friends."

My jaw hardened. I very nearly answered with a vehement "no" before I looked over at Cara. Her warm eyes were calling to me. Not at liberty to speak and tell me what she wanted, I had to rely entirely on her gaze.

Cara softened me. I didn't know if it was a good thing at the time, but I decided to trust her, despite every nerve in my body adamantly wanting to pull Lucy out of Lisbeth's lap and never let her go.

"Alright."

Lisbeth's lips curled up into a triumphant smile. The sight of her made me sick. She was viperous and manipulative. But I knew that if I kept Lucy from her, I ran the risk of Lucy holding that against me later in her life. "Thank you, Wesley."

"Sure. No problem."

Cara made the move to go, and I followed her, though my heart was sinking further and further into my stomach.

We went into the kitchen across the hall, not speaking. I stood near to the door so I could listen in on the conversation.

"You shouldn't do that, Wesley."

I glanced over at Cara, who was leaning against the counter.

"You're not going to feel better if you eavesdrop."

"I won't feel good *not* listening in, either. So what am I supposed to do?"

"Maybe this is a situation that doesn't feel good either way."

We stared at each other. I couldn't help but get the feeling she was referring to what had been happening between us, too. On one hand, keeping her away was killing me and on the other, keeping her close tortured me.

Maybe life was all about choosing the lesser of two evils. Or wielding the double-edged sword. Regardless, I was losing.

Cara reached out her hand to me. "Come here."

I went to her and put my hand in her open palm. She squeezed. And there was nothing more. She held my hand, comforting me, helping my pulse steady and my breath even out.

If Lisbeth or Yves or Lucy had walked in suddenly, I had every excuse to say I was nervous. That she was helping me. That we'd become friends. Close. We leaned on each other.

But even that broke my heart. Why would I need to make excuses? I was a billionaire, for Christ's sake. I could do whatever the fuck I wanted. But for now, I knew it was best for Lucy to maintain my distance from Cara. *Right?*

We sat in our own silence, overhearing bits of conversation and peals of laughter. It must have been nearly an hour just sitting there. And Cara never let go. Never moved away from my side.

Why had I failed her so miserably?

"Alrighty!" Lisbeth's shrill voice cut through the silence. "Wesley!"

I let go of Cara and leaped to my feet, eager to get back to Lucy. As I walked into the front hall, I found Lisbeth walking out of the living room with Lucy close at her heels. "We have to get going now, dear," she said, running her hand through Lucy's light blonde hair.

"Will you be back tomorrow?"

"Oh…no, honey. We're flying right back to Miami. I thought your father told you." Lisbeth glared at me.

"I don't seem to recall you mentioning that, Lisbeth."

"Well, I'm sure I did."

"I'm sure you didn't."

"Ahem. Well." Yves cut in and stepped forward, holding his hand out to me. "Thanks for having us."

I was both surprised and yet, unsurprised that Yves was managing to be much more cordial with me than Lisbeth. I shook his hand. "Nice to meet you."

Lisbeth gave Lucy a showy hug and a kiss on the cheek. "Goodbye, my love. I will see you soon."

Lucy hugged her back limply. Her eyes were tearing up.

I was afraid this would happen.

"Nice to meet you, sweetheart." Yves patted her head.

"Well, we'll be in touch." Lisbeth said with a flip of her hair. She didn't even notice Lucy's mental state.

Lucy followed them all the way to the door, waiting for something, anything else. But it was too late. Lisbeth was gone, shutting the door right in her daughter's face.

Silence fell over us. Cara and I looked at Lucy, waiting for her to burst into tears.

I stepped toward her. "Honey, I'm so sor—"

Lucy let out a scream and kicked off both of her giraffe slippers so they hit the door with loud thuds. Then, she descended into tears.

Cara and I both flanked her without hesitation, dropping to our knees to see if we could patch her up.

Hot tears dripped down Lucy's face, her lower lip trembling. "Why doesn't she like me?"

Cara rubbed Lucy's back. "Oh, honey, of course she does. She's just not so good at showing it."

Thank God Cara was there. Otherwise, I would have told Lucy the truth. Because her mother was heartless, cruel, and didn't deserve Lucy's love. I bit my tongue, rubbing my little girl's back, hoping that somehow, I could make her understand that I was enough.

Lucy sniffled. "It's not hard to show that you love someone."

"Not for you." Cara wiped the tears off Lucy's face. "That's what makes you special."

"But it's not hard for you! And it's not hard for Daddy! So it doesn't make me special. It's easy. So why am I so hard to love?"

I bit my lip, desperately holding back my own torrent of tears. "Nothing about you is hard to love, Lucy."

Lucy held onto each of us with one of her hands, tugging us both toward her. "I need a hug."

"Of course, sweetheart." I kissed the top of her head.

As Cara and I embraced Lucy, we embraced each other. I could smell her perfume, even more potent than usual, and I felt her light brown hair tickling my cheek.

Slowly, Lucy's distress mellowed in our arms.

And I just knew.

I couldn't let Cara go so easily.

Lisbeth be damned.

Once Lucy had settled and I got her set up in front of the television with all the snacks her heart could desire, I found Cara sitting at the foot of the front door, trying hard to polish out a scuff made by the sole of Lucy's slipper.

"Don't worry about that, Cara."

"Oh, I don't mind."

"Seriously, you've done more than enough."

Cara dropped the rag she was using into her lap and sighed. "Is she doing okay?"

"For now. I'm expecting it'll be a long night."

Cara looked up at me with a trembling gaze. "I'm sorry."

I frowned. "Why are you sorry?"

"I feel like I got too involved or —"

"No, no, don't be sorry. Not at all." I sat down beside her and touched her arm. "You were great. This would have gone way worse without you. Trust me."

She smiled meekly. "I'm sad to hear it could have been any more difficult."

I nodded. It could always be worse when it came to Lisbeth. But that didn't matter now. I had other things on my mind. "Cara, I need to ask you something. It might be bad timing, but I can't…not say this."

Her eyes widened.

"I want to know if you'd let me take you on a date."

Cara was quiet.

"I know. Whiplash…but —"

Cara threw her arms around me. "Yes."

# Chapter 23

## Cara

"You look uncomfortable," Katie said. "Are you uncomfortable?"

I pulled at the dress that was tight around my waist. "Kind of? This used to fit, I swear —"

"Doesn't matter. Here, try this." Katie held out a cream-colored sweater dress with a turtleneck.

I ran my hand down the soft fabric. It was very much Katie's style. Neutral and loose. "Isn't that a little modest? I still want him to be into me."

"Girl, you've been fucking him for weeks."

"I *was* fucking him. Past tense."

"You don't think you'll hook up tonight? Please. He asked you on a date, Cara. He wants you. Now put it on!" Katie shoved the dress into my hands.

I rolled my eyes but smiled. I was grateful for Katie's support and advice. I had been a wreck ever since he had asked me out, elated he'd changed his mind, yet terrified he might change it back again.

*Focus on the positive, Cara. Don't stress.*

"Where's he taking you?"

I pulled off the ill-fitting dress and slipped on the one Katie had given me. "I don't know. He said it was a surprise."

Katie sighed dreamily and threw herself down onto my bed. "Oh my God, he's totally going to sweep you off your feet, Cara."

I had been trying not to get my hopes up. Doing so was the preamble to having my heart broken. And Wesley had already built my hopes up once. I couldn't afford to fall apart again.

I glanced into the mirror as I smoothed the fabric down my waist.

"Oh, C…you look beautiful."

"Yeah?"

"I mean, you would look beautiful in a trash bag, but…"

"You're overdoing it, Katie."

My sister shook her head. "I'm just being honest with you."

I didn't want to be conceited, but she was right. The cream contrasted with my chestnut hair, made my brown eyes look warmer, and the material hugged my curves in all the right places. And I wanted nothing more than Wesley to admire my body and remember what it did to him.

"He's calling."

I spun around — my phone was buzzing on the bed beside Katie. "Give it to me."

Katie smirked playfully and answered before handing it over. "Hello, this is Cara's phone…hello, Mr. Taves!"

I lunged for the phone, but she rolled away from me just in time.

"Oh, you're running ahead of schedule? You're outside right now?"

We played a game of keep-away that felt desperate. "Give me the phone!" Every time I thought I had it in my grasp, Katie was able to jerk away.

"Yes, I'll let her know." Katie hung up the phone and then held it out to me. "He's outside."

"I got that, jerk." The reality washed over me suddenly. "Oh God, he's here. He's *here*."

Katie ran her hands over my shoulders. "Relax, Cara. This night is all for you, okay? Just remember how fortunate he is to have this time with you."

That seemed like a ridiculous concept. Wesley was a billionaire business mogul. He could have any woman on the face of the earth. Not to mention his drop-dead good looks. So why would he want me?

While I stood frozen in place, Katie pushed my coat and purse into my hands. "Don't keep Wesley Taves waiting, darling."

I took that to heart and nearly sprinted out of my bedroom, shrugging my coat on, and trying not to trip in my high heels. *Deep breaths, Cara. He's lucky you're giving him another chance.*

As soon as I got to the front door and grabbed the handle, I stopped. *Breathe. He wouldn't have asked if he didn't want to do this.*

*If he didn't feel he had something to prove.*

I lifted my head high. The handle felt like it was searing my hand. *Just open the door.*

As I stepped through the front door, I felt like I was moving through a portal. From anxious girl to confident woman. Even if I didn't quite buy it, I could pretend.

And when my eyes landed on Wesley standing on the

sidewalk, holding a humongous bouquet of flowers, I didn't shy away. I smiled, big and bold. "Hi."

"Hi."

We were both quiet as I descended the stairs toward him. He looked edible. Unsurprisingly. He always did. But even more so now. His blonde hair was tousled to perfection and his face was clean-shaven. He had opted for a long black coat with a white scarf hung around his neck, as if we were going to the opera.

I couldn't resist kissing him as soon as he was within my grasp. I grabbed onto the scarf tightly, getting onto my tiptoes, kissing him longingly. Hopefully.

Wesley drew away first. Perfectly taken off guard. He smiled, my lipstick giving his lips an even more flushed look. "Ahem. I suppose you got my message."

I glanced up into the window of my apartment. Katie was peeking through the curtain. However, the moment she saw me looking, she leaped away from the window. "Yes. My…assistant told me you were early."

Wesley chuckled. "Your assistant?"

"Yes."

"Do you often have to beg your assistant to give your phone back?" Wesley cocked an eyebrow.

I blushed, realizing he must have heard me chasing Katie around the room, but managed to laugh. "Well, you know it's so hard to find good help these days."

Wesley smiled and nodded. It felt as though he wanted to speak, but he was trapped in my eyes. Admiring me. "Oh! These are —" He held the forgotten flowers. "These are for you."

I accepted them gingerly into my arms, pressing my face toward the blooms. The scent of fresh, romantic roses. *Perfect.* "Mmm. Thank you. They're beautiful."

"Not nearly as beautiful as you deserve."

Damn, this man could sweet talk. I already felt weak from wanting him. Part of me itched to text Katie and tell her to leave down the fire escape so I could ask him up to my apartment right then and there. I could show him just how much I'd missed him.

"Let's go. We have places to be."

"Do we?"

"Yes."

I inclined my body closer to Wesley's. "And what places are those?"

He smirked. "I knew you'd ask me that." Without another word, he opened the car door. "But I'm afraid you'll just have to be patient, Cara."

I grinned. This night was going to be perfect.

§

Perfection might have been an understatement. As we wound through the streets of the Upper East Side, I imagined all of the posh and expensive places he could be taking me. I wasn't trying to be vain, but when you're with someone who can have whatever they want, the imagination is prone to run wild.

I could barely believe it when our driver stopped right in front of the iconic steps of the Metropolitan Museum of Art. My mouth went dry. "Why are we stopping?"

Wesley smiled at me. "Because this is where we're going."

The driver was suddenly there to open my door, and I had no choice but to accept just how outrageous this all was.

Wesley took my arm and escorted me toward the front doors of the Met.

It didn't look like anyone should be walking up these steps this time of night, darkness looming over the facade. "Isn't it closed on Saturday nights?"

"Yes. Usually. But tonight, we have the place to ourselves."

I let him take me inside in a complete daze where we were met with a docent from the museum who took us back to the American Wing. While the vaulted ceilings of streaming sunlight felt ethereal in the day, there was a magic about visiting at night. There was a magical glow about the place that felt like the sculptures peppering the floor were about to burst to life and begin dancing.

I was so taken, I nearly didn't notice the table for two set squarely in the middle of the room until Wesley pulled me in that direction. A bottle of champagne waited for us.

I blinked as if it would all disappear once I awoke from this dreamlike state. Not the case. "This is…too much."

Wesley pulled out a chair for me. "Not enough, I'd argue."

I sat delicately. I didn't want to upset the universe and see this all taken away from me in an instant.

Wesley sat across from me. "After all, a woman like you deserves much, much more than this."

I looked up at the golden statue of the goddess Diana that the whole room revolved around. "What could be more than this?"

I felt Wesley grab my hand and immediately snapped my attention back to him. His thumb slid all the way to my wrist, feeling the chain of my bracelet.

His thoughtful brown eyes lingered on the butterfly and then looked back to me. "The world, Cara. That's what you deserve."

Only a moment later, a waitperson came to pour our champagne and serve our first course. The dinner was lavish and must have cost a small fortune between the caviar and champagne alone. But I let myself indulge and tried to lean on Wesley's words.

He believed I deserved the world. Maybe I should start believing in that for myself.

The conversation at first was stilted by nerves, both of us thrilled to be there with one another and also terrified to say the wrong thing. I didn't want to reveal how much I cared. After all, before he'd broken my heart, I'd been ready to tell him I loved him.

Once we overcame the nerves, though, it was just…us. Wesley and Cara. The way we bantered, the flirtations, the ease of conversation, even when the subject might not have been the most comfortable.

We avoided the subject of Lisbeth entirely, though. The day before had been traumatic at best. But I had to ask about Lucy, at the very least.

"She should be having the best night of her life. First sleepover with my friend's kids. I was worried she might get nervous and not want to spend the night, but she handled it better than I did," Wesley said anxiously.

"Worrying, are we?"

Wesley sighed but smiled. "Always."

I rubbed my foot on his leg softly. Wesley reached down and grabbed my ankle, squeezing it gently.

My heart raced and my posture stiffened.

Wesley's eyes locked on mine as his hand began to trace the line of my ankle and calf back and forth. "That dress looks fucking incredible on you."

I pulled on my sleeve subconsciously. "Oh, you think so?"

"Absolutely."

"My sister — I mean…my assistant helped me pick it out."

Wesley gave me a wry grin. "Oh, a *sister* assistant, is it?"

I picked up my glass of champagne. "I like to keep

work in the family." I eyed him over the rim of my glass and then took a sip.

Our dinner was mostly finished at this point, so Wesley asked me if I'd like to take a walk through the galleries. How could I say no to a private visit to the Met? Every visit I'd made previously was accompanied by narrowly avoiding stampedes of tourists and trying to peek over shoulders to see pieces of art.

Plus, a little walk through the quiet galleries with Wesley seemed ideal.

To be honest, though, I wasn't looking at much of the art. I was happy to be distracted by Wesley's company. Trading stories and thoughts on the art around us, while we strolled closer and closer together, until Wesley grabbed my hand.

Hand-holding, somehow, was more intimate than all the times we had been in bed together. This felt more purposeful, less impulsive.

We strolled until coming to a stop before a painting. Wesley pointed to it. "What do you think of this one?"

I took in the image: a young child leaning on her mother's lap, looking right at the viewer as the mother sewed. "*Young Mother Sewing* by Mary Cassatt. Well, she really knows how to get the point across with those titles, huh?"

Wesley didn't reply. I glanced up at him. His jaw was tight, expression stoic as he took in the painting and all it meant to him.

I tightened my grip on his hand. "Wesley?"

"Hmm? Sorry." He cleared his throat and dropped his gaze to the floor.

It was like I could read his mind. A mother and a child, seemingly the most implicit relationship in the world. The one thing that seemed to be innate, yet, Wesley had witnessed crumbling again and again. I pulled myself closer to him, tucking our clasped hands near my hip. "Hey. Yesterday was tough."

"Mm-hmm. Yeah. Yeah, it was."

I glanced at the painting once more. The little girl's golden hair and dark eyes invoked Lucy just enough for it to feel like a mirror to life.

"I feel foolish saying I was hoping it wouldn't be that tough."

"Oh, Wesley…you shouldn't feel foolish for that." I could've benefited from my own advice. I held myself accountable for every hope I'd ever had in my life. From the success of the daycare to my unclear relationship with Wesley. But hearing him judge himself for it hurt my heart.

He shook his head. "I just knew better than to let her in like that. And then Lucy was so hurt, I…"

"*You* didn't hurt Lucy. And Lucy isn't thinking that. Lisbeth hurt her. Not you."

Wesley paused, taking in the painting once more, before speaking. "Cara, I know you're very young."

My chest tightened. Was he about to school me on the ways of the world I wasn't yet privy to? Be condescending to me? Make me feel like an immature girl? I wasn't sure I could handle that.

"So this might sound…scary." Wesley breathed in deeply and then turned to me so our bodies were facing one another. He grabbed my hands, as if we were standing before an altar. "I think that Lucy deserves a woman like you in her life. I never thought I'd find someone who I could see fitting into her life that wasn't her real mother. Never that I ever expected Lisbeth to actually step up or change her mind or…"

Wesley went silent, emotion overcoming his ability to speak.

I touched his cheek. He lifted his eyes to mine, big and

brown. And for the first time, fearful. "Don't hide from me anymore, Wesley."

His eyes searched my face in a panic. "I know I've broken your trust once before. But if you'd give me another chance, so that I can give Lucy a chance, too. That'd mean the world to me."

I ghosted my thumb over his cheekbone. "I'd like nothing more."

A look of relief washed over his face. "Really?"

"Really."

Wesley brought his lips close to mine with the intent to kiss me but stopped just short. "You've taken me by surprise, Cara."

"Trust me, no one is more surprised than me that the stranger who saved me from an oncoming car turned out to be…" *A man I'd fall in love with.*

"Turn out to be what?"

He'd already been so vulnerable. It simply wasn't the moment to tell him. We'd have to work up to it again. But I still felt it through my entire body. *I love you.* "That you'd turn out to be so wonderful."

Wesley's lips settled into a smile before he kissed me.

And as his lips teased mine, I thought what I wanted to say over and over.

*I love you, I love you, I love you.*

# Chapter 24

Wesley

After our first date, Cara and I were even closer than we'd been before.

We didn't sleep together that night. I was determined to be respectful and make her truly understand I wanted her for more than just her body.

It was hard. No pun intended. But I managed.

I didn't manage the same restraint the next time I saw her. Or the time after that. Between long workdays and time with Lucy, Cara and I squeezed in as much time together as possible. Except this time, she was not my secret that I saved only for my bed. I took her on dates and showed her off to the world that she was mine. The only person still left in the dark was Lucy.

This was Cara's idea. It was clear she was still unsure about trusting me. I didn't blame her. I was the one who'd turned the tables so suddenly, pulling away after drawing her so close.

"I just don't want her to get hurt. I'm a grown woman, I can handle it. But Lucy doesn't deserve any more of that."

She was right, again astonishing me with a maturity beyond her twenty-four years.

However, after only two weeks, I was getting antsy. I was determined to make Cara mine in every sense possible. And while Lucy had to be left out of it until we were abundantly sure that things were sticking, there were other ways I could get close.

"So, your sister. Katie, right?" I asked softly as we washed the dishes together.

Cara had stayed late for dinner after her shift with Lucy; Lucy was already curled up in the den in front of the television, so we had the privacy of dishwashing to discuss *us*. "Yes. What about her?"

"Well, you two are so close…" I focused on scrubbing a plate under the hot water, trying not to lose my nerve. "I think it's important I meet her sooner than later, don't you think?"

Cara laughed. "You want to meet my sister?"

"Yeah, I think she might have some insight as to why you're such a weirdo."

"Rude!" Cara flicked some water in my direction and I bristled, laughing.

"You know I'm kidding!"

We went back to our chore, heart pounding in my ears, waiting for Cara to acknowledge what I'd said. "Sure, you could meet Katie. She's been dying to meet you. We could grab some dinner this weekend maybe."

"Sure. Sure." That was only the half of it, though. Of course I wanted Cara's sister to like me. But her sister wasn't the one who ultimately had a say in our relationship's permanence at the end of the day. "And maybe your parents, too."

This time Cara stopped and put down the bowl she'd been drying. "Um…"

"I know it's sort of soon. Maybe a little fast. But if you're comfortable, I'd like for them to know about me as soon as possible." I wanted to avoid any surprises. When I met Lisbeth's parents for the first time, we were already engaged. Worse, her parents didn't know anything about me because she hadn't even bothered to mention me to them.

One of the many red flags I had ignored.

Cara considered carefully for a moment before slowly nodding. "Alright. Family dinner's Wednesday night."

§

The dinner table was…quiet.

I might even have said *tense* if I wasn't trying to be optimistic.

In the days leading up to dinner, Cara had prepped me on everything about her family. Both her parents had grown up on Long Island and still lived in the house she'd grown up in. Mom was a teacher and Dad was a landscaper. Katie was a business student and asked a *lot* of questions. Her parents were very loving but always wanted to be in her business, and they would have no qualms about trying to be in mine, too.

While I normally took exception to nosy people, I would put up with most anything if it meant keeping Cara and her family happy.

I decided not to dwell on my nerves and instead think of all the positives. I picked out an outfit that was very presentable but not flashy, made sure to get a couple of nice bottles of wine, and arranged for a dessert to be sent over for after dinner from one of my favorite places in the city.

If things went awry, it wouldn't be because of me.

However, from the moment I stepped foot in the Smith house, it seemed our meeting was doomed.

Katie was the first to greet us. She was taller than Cara and clearly had her finger on the pulse of major fashion trends. She wore a cashmere sweater set and had acrylic nails and extensions that made her look flashy and ready to tear a boardroom apart. It was hard to believe she was Cara's *younger* sister until she opened her mouth.

"Mr. *Taves*! I've been obsessed with you since your interview with *Vanity Fair*. I had it posted on the inside of my locker in middle school."

*Damn, I'm old.*

"Please, call me Wesley."

Katie grinned. "Wesley. Well, since we're basically family, I think we can afford a hug."

I looked askance to Cara. I had never been a hugger on a first meeting, but again, I would do anything to make sure I was endeared to her family. And Katie wanted a hug, so I let her throw her skinny arms around my neck while I patted her back awkwardly.

"Wesley, this is my mom, Linda, and my dad, Stan."

Linda and Stan as a married couple sounded like they would be dear and sweet. But from the cold, thin smiles they gave me, they were anything but.

"Wonderful to meet you both. I've been so excited to meet the people responsible for raising this amazing woman." I took a step toward them, ready for them to also be looking for hugs like Katie but was stopped when Stan stuck out his hand for me to shake.

"Yes, we've been curious to meet you, too, Wes."

I bristled. People I just met didn't call me *Wes*. And not only had Stan just come right out with a nickname on our first encounter, but he'd also done it with passive aggression. *Curious* didn't mean they were excited or happy. It meant they were wary.

In that moment, I should have known they'd already formed an opinion of me.

But I remained chipper. I held out the bottle of wine I'd brought to Stan. "Cara told me you liked pinot noir."

"Oh, well, that's nice, isn't it?" Stan passed the bottle to Linda to examine the label.

Cara wrapped her hand protectively around my bicep. I knew she had meant it to be reassuring, but it just felt like a warning.

This was going to be a long night. And awkward.

And so it proved to be around the dinner table. Conversation was stilted and slow. We exchanged pleasantries while I tried to overshare how much I already knew about the family in an effort to show I was invested. Instead, it ended up coming off as overzealous.

The only person on my side was Katie. In every lull, she asked me a question about MediaDeck. "I've been reading up on your new venture, Readly. Are you looking to compete with Goodreads?"

I chuckled. "It's just an effort for continued competition with Amazon. You know, these conglomerates thrive on all being reflections of each other. We feel we can offer a superior user experience because of our ability to see how other platforms have performed and what their users don't like about their interface."

Cara's nerves seemed to melt away whenever Katie and I spoke, her beautiful smile bringing sunshine to the otherwise gloomy room. "I knew you two would have a lot to talk about."

The moment I felt even slightly settled into the conversation, though, Stan cleared his throat. "I'm just going to come right out with it." He was ready for a challenge, eyes locked in mine. "I've been doing a lot of reading about you, Wes."

I dabbed at my mouth with my napkin and put then put it aside. It was clear we were done with dinner and it was time to move onto the interrogation. "Oh?"

"Yes. There's an awful lot about you on the internet."

I sighed. "Privacy doesn't exist when you're in the Fortune 500, unfortunately."

Stan's eyes hardened on me. If he'd liked me, he might have laughed.

I was on guard, ready to fight, as if I was in a business negotiation and not meeting my girlfriend's parents. Cara must have noticed my edginess. Her hand found mine under the table, her fingers curling around mine. Her touch immediately softened my whole body. I remembered why I was here. I was here for Cara. I was here for Lucy.

*Stay calm, Taves.* "Mr. Smith…I know the circumstances are —"

"Inappropriate." He crossed his arms.

I nodded. "Some may say that. I was going to say…not typical. And I know the difference in age between your daughter and myself might give you some cause for concern."

Linda nearly scoffed. "Some?"

"*Mom.*" Cara was ready with the defense. I squeezed her hand softly. She didn't need to be fighting for me like this. Not with her parents. I knew her heart.

"But I'm very committed to her. She's a wonderful woman. I adore her. My daughter does as well. And —"

"Yes. Your daughter. How old is she again?" Linda looked to Cara for an answer.

"I told you. She's six."

"Yes. Silly me. Six. That's a tricky age for someone to come in and assume the role of mother, don't you think?"

I cleared my throat. "Lucy's mother has not been in the picture since she was still a baby. And —"

"And why is that?"

Cara murmured something under her breath. She was stressed, seeming to have little hope for this to turn around in my favor. My confidence, already on such an unsteady foundation, was starting to tremble. "She wasn't interested in motherhood."

Linda pursed her lips. "Well, it's a very hard job. Especially without a supportive husband."

I took a deep breath. She didn't know what she was talking about, but I didn't want to correct her. "I've shown up tenfold for my daughter —"

"I can't imagine how that's possible with how mammoth your company — uh, what's it called?" Stan's eyes rolled up as he tried to remember.

I gritted my teeth. If he was going to have the audacity to insult me and my work, he may as well know what the hell he was talking about. "MediaDeck."

"*Right…*" He smiled wolfishly. "MediaDeck. And you're launching a new branch of your company in the next quarter, right? Surely, you don't have time to run a company, be a doting father, and give time to a budding relationship?"

Katie suddenly cut in, waving a hand toward parents. "You guys, quit it with the third degree! They seem happy. You're happy, right?"

I glanced at Cara. She wouldn't look at me. I felt my heart break. Was I losing her right here, right now? I would have deserved it, too, after pushing her away the first time.

But I couldn't bear the thought of losing *us* so soon after we'd begun again. "I am. I think we both are."

"Yes," Cara agreed in a tight voice. "Very happy. I wish you could see that."

"Oh, Cara, sweetie. You're so young, when happiness is such as fickle and changing thing." Linda smiled at me saccharinely. "I'm sure you'll agree, Wesley. The older you get, the clearer everything becomes. And the things that made you happy in your twenties don't make you quite so happy anymore as you age." She let out a long sigh. "I just don't think you're ready, Cara."

Cara's body tightened. "I'm not a child, Mom."

"You're more of a child than Wesley is. And I'm sorry, I know some people think age is just a number, but I don't. I don't understand how a man in his forties could be interested in a girl as young as Cara unless he wanted just one thing from her."

That was the kill shot. I was an older man who, in their eyes, only wanted to take advantage of their daughter.

"Could you *please* stop talking about me like I'm not even in the room?" Cara snapped. "And how dare you imply he's taking advantage of me? As if I have no say in the matter?"

Katie hummed in support. "Mm-hmm. That's fucked-up."

"*Katie*," Cara's father admonished.

"I have had a choice at every turn to say no to Wesley. He's never *forced* me to do anything. In fact, I was the one who accepted his professional offers. I've held my own. *That's* why he's interested in me."

God*damn*, I wanted to kiss her fiercely. She was so full of fire and passion. For *me*. I couldn't believe how lucky I was.

"You know what I meant, pumpkin," Linda said, not

even willing to apologize for offending her daughter. I would have to take note for the future. I never wanted to put Lucy in this position.

Cara crossed her arms over her chest and shrunk into her seat.

Stan took the stage now, eyeing me intensely. "You have to admit, Wes, your track record isn't reassuring. What's to say you won't just chew her up and spit her out like you do with most all of your ventures."

"I'm not sure I follow."

"Well, for one, your personal life is kind of dicey from everything we've read," Stan replied with a humorless chuckle. "And while I know you're plenty successful, I also know you haven't achieved that without cracking a few skulls…stepping on a few backs. You get my meaning, don't you?"

I pursed my lips. I hated when people combined my personal and business behaviors. They were two separate worlds. In business, I *had* to be cutthroat. In my personal life, I just hadn't found the right person yet to get serious. I hoped now that I had. "Cara isn't a venture to me, and I'm offended you'd suggest that."

"You tell 'em, Taves," Katie said.

At least I had one of the Smiths on my side. Linda and Stan exchanged a look. Stan cleared his throat. "You've got a daughter. You probably already understand how hard it is to protect her. You'll understand when she's older how that shifts, but I think you'd be reacting the same with her."

"I think I've had enough of everyone talking about me like I'm not here." Cara pushed her chair out from the table. "Come on, Wesley. I think we should go."

"Cara!" Linda's eyes widened, the same luminous amber as her daughter's. "Be reasonable."

"You've made it clear that Wesley isn't welcome here and as long as he isn't welcome, I don't feel welcome, either."

I felt stuck to my seat until Cara shook my shoulder.

"We're leaving."

I got to my feet to follow her. She had a point. They had already made up their mind. If I was to change it, it wouldn't be tonight.

"Cara, if you leave this house right now, you are not welcome back." Stan's voice was gruff and unflinching.

"Daddy!" Katie gasped. "That's unreasonable."

Linda shushed Katie. The young woman looked frantically to me and Cara. She'd done all she could. It was clear the Smith girls were beholden to what their parents wanted for them.

Despite my negative feelings toward Cara's parents, I couldn't stand for her to choose me over them. I was still new in the trajectory of her life. They had been there from the beginning. "Cara, you stay."

Her eyes flashed with fire. "Are you out of your mind?"

I shook my head and then held an open hand up to her parents. "Well, I wish I could say it was lovely to meet you, but it's clear the feeling isn't mutual. So I'll take my leave."

If anyone responded, I didn't hear them. I tuned out the sounds of the house as I walked through the front door. My whole body was buzzing.

"Wesley!"

I turned around. Cara had followed me out, dressed to leave. "Cara, I mean it, you can't follow me."

"They've always told me what I can and can't do. Don't do that to me, too, Wesley. Please."

Who was I to ignore her pleading? Especially when she was choosing me?

Cara blew past me to the car and waited for me to unlock it.

I took one glance back at the house as if it were cursed. And in a sense, it was. Or at least, it seemed to have cursed my relationship with Cara.

What that meant for us, though, I wasn't yet sure.

# Chapter 25

## Cara

The entire drive home was silent. Not even the radio played.

I couldn't make sense of what had just happened. I knew my parents were going to give him a hard time, but I had no idea they weren't even going to give him a chance.

Not even give *me* a chance.

It was clear that any move I made to be my own person somehow offended them if it wasn't in the realm of what they deemed appropriate.

So when they said, "It's him or us," I chose with my heart. My parents needed to understand I was an adult and could make my own life decisions.

I couldn't stand the thought of losing Wesley. Letting him leave would have most certainly been the biggest mistake of my life thus far.

Besides thinking of what just happened back at my parents' house, I couldn't help but worry about Wesley's feelings. Would this affect our relationship? Pull us apart?

Even by the time he parked the car in front of my apartment, his expression hadn't changed. His lips were in a tight line and his hands were locked around the wheel so tightly his knuckles were white.

I'd never had to comfort him in his anger. Only in his sadness. And something told me that pulling him out of this mood would be harder. By trying to comfort him, I was worried I'd somehow insult his masculinity.

Instead of speaking, I touched his shoulder carefully.

Wesley sighed at my touch. Relief.

I caressed his tense muscles. "I'm so sorry."

He didn't speak.

"I didn't know they were going to attack you like that."

Still, nothing.

"Wesley, please say something."

"What would you like me to say, Cara?"

My lower lip trembled. "I don't know. Just something that lets me know you don't hate me."

Wesley lowered his head. "Of course, I don't hate you, Cara. How could I?"

*Thank God.* "I don't know. It feels like I just walked you into an execution without realizing it."

"No, you didn't." He swallowed. "I just don't think you should have chosen me over your parents."

"You don't want me?"

Wesley shook his head, a lock of blonde hair falling onto his forehead. "No, that's not what I said. I just…we haven't known each other that long. They're your parents. You need them. Trust me, I wish I still had people in my life that close to me. I don't think I'm worth throwing all of that away."

"Oh, Wesley…" I unbuckled my seatbelt and slid my hand around his back, pulling my chest toward his over the center console. "I've never made my parents angry in my life. If I'm going to start, I don't think there's a better reason than falling for someone."

Wesley's distraught expression shifted, a small smile on his lips. "You're falling for me?"

I pulled back shyly, not meeting his eyes. "Well. Yeah. A little. Not to scare you."

He touched my waist. "It doesn't scare me at all."

We leaned our foreheads together. Our lips were so close we could kiss, but neither of us moved to do so. A different kind of connection was forming. Deeper. More intimate.

"You shouldn't sacrifice your life for me."

"Wesley, my life is just beginning with you."

A breath caught in his throat.

I closed the space between us with a delicate kiss to his lips. Then another one, longer and deeper. His hands tightened on my body. We had come so close to losing each other. Now it was clear he didn't want to let me go.

I slid my hand down his chest, pulling on the fabric of his shirt to bring him closer to me. I wouldn't let my parents ruin this for us.

"Cara." My name, whispered desperately into my mouth.

I wrapped my arms around him, drawing him as close as possible. We had been tangled together in lust so many times. But this moment was different.

Something deeper was growing between us. No longer just our bodies eager to join together, but our souls seeking one another, having bonded through shared difficulties.

Wesley's hands gripped my hips, trying to pull me onto his lap, but the clunky architecture of the car prevented it. "Can I come upstairs?"

"My apartment's a mess."

Wesley pushed his face into my neck, kissing me,

nipping and sucking, marking me as his. "I don't care. I need you. Need to make love to you."

Fucking was just lust. *Making love* was more. And for him to say it out loud made everything clear.

I was so glad I chose him. I refused to lose Wesley, not after our story had just begun.

"Okay. Come upstairs with me."

It took a few minutes before either of us made a move to leave the car, too caught up in our foreplay. We were reluctant to draw apart.

Finally, though, I pulled away and let myself out of the car. Wesley followed wordlessly at my heels into the apartment building and up the stairs. As I unlocked my door, he stood behind me, hands drifting over my waist, lips caressing the shell of my ear. "It's a bit small."

"I don't care."

As soon as the door opened, Wesley was on me, turning me to him, and claiming my mouth in a passionate kiss.

We stumbled through my studio to the bed, pulling off clothes, kissing and fondling each other until we fell back onto the quilt. It had been on my bed since I was a child. The memory of my mother helping me make the bed, both of us tossing the blanket into the air so it landed unwrinkled, flitted through my mind.

*Shake it off, Cara. Stay in the moment.*

Despite having Wesley many times over, his muscular body never failed to fascinate me. I relished running my hands over his chest, down his firm abs, around his hips to the round cheeks of his ass, welcoming the feel of his warm body up against mine.

Not to mention the way he looked at me. His brown eyes, heavy with lust, called to my soul.

I rubbed my body up and down his length, coating his

cock with my wetness. Wesley grasped my hips, stopping my movements, and kissed me gently. "What's wrong?"

He shook his head. "Nothing." He cupped my face in his hands, running his thumb against my lower lip. "I want to go slow. I want to give you pleasure." He kissed my chin. "Want you to feel —" then my jaw "— everything I do to you." Finally, he reached my mouth. His kiss built in intensity. At first it was sweet, then eventually deep, his tongue dueling with mine for dominance.

As we kissed, Wesley began to nestle inside me, slowly rocking his hips. I moaned into his mouth, tugging his hair with my fingers.

He took his time, just as he said he would, slowly thrusting, inch by inch, then drawing out almost completely before plunging back in. He held on to my hips, controlling the pace.

With each stroke, I felt he was worshipping me. Most other times he'd taken me, it was fast and hard. He'd made me desperate for pleasure, driving me mad with his cock.

This time, however, I wanted it to last as long as possible. Our hips rolled together, and the sounds of our panting breaths and moans of pleasure filled the room. I'd never felt more cherished. More *loved*.

"Does this feel good, sweetheart?"

"Amazing." I wrapped my arms and legs around him. "I want you closer."

He buried himself deep, pulling my knee up to change the angle. I held him tightly, my hips meeting his with each slide.

Our eyes locked, neither of us wanting to break the connection. I was starting to tremble, the pleasure was too great. I felt my eyes begin to fill with tears. I whimpered, "You feel amazing."

I pressed my forehead to his, gasping as our slick bodies moved together.

Wesley wrapped his arms around me, as if he could draw me closer, but there was not an inch of space between us. "Oh God, Cara, I need you."

"I need you, too." My whole body began to shake. I was about to lose myself in him. Completely and utterly.

*"Cara."*

I couldn't control my cry of pleasure. My body detonated like a firework, heat and euphoria bursting through me.

"Fuck, Cara, I'm coming!" Wesley growled, releasing inside me. His cock throbbed, filling me, and expelling every last bit of his seed into my tight center.

I stared up at the ceiling, completely content. It'd never felt like this. And it didn't have anything to do with my orgasm. It was everything to do with the man who had made love to me with everything he had in him.

Suddenly, tears were streaming down my cheeks.

Wesley ran a hand through my hair. "Oh God, have I — did I hurt you?"

"No." I tried to catch my breath. "It's just…you made me feel so special."

Through heavy lids, he smiled. "You deserve nothing less. Are you sure you're okay?"

I nodded. Though he had not said the words, I could feel Wesley's love.

Wesley held me, stroking my hair, and soothed me as I recovered from the onslaught of emotions running through me. I wasn't sure if minutes or hours passed.

My fingers danced through his hair as he held me. "You have to go." It was a statement, not a question.

He sighed. "I wish I didn't have to. I don't want to leave you."

"I'm sure Lucy is ready to see you."

Wesley pushed his face into my hair, breathing deeply. "Soon neither one of us will have to leave."

My heart fluttered. Sooner than later, our lives would completely intersect. Lucy would know about our relationship, I'd probably move in. It would only make sense. My head danced with thought of our inevitable, beautiful future.

Wesley rested his chin on my head. "Can I lay with you just a bit longer?"

"Of course."

He left shortly before midnight. It was a difficult goodbye even though we would see each other the next morning.

The moment I was alone, however, reality hit me.

I had abandoned my parents to risk it all on a man I'd only known a few short weeks.

And whether it went incredibly right or incredibly wrong, one thing was for sure.

It was incredibly *crazy*.

# Chapter 26

### Wesley

"Yeesh. That's rough."

I grimaced. "Tell me about it."

"They really gave her an ultimatum like that?"

"Yep."

"They hate you that much?"

I glared at Jenson across my desk. I gave him an update on the horror story from the night before. Since I had asked Cara out, trying to do things the old-fashioned way, I'd confided in Jenson about our relationship.

"I knew it!" he had shouted. "I knew you wouldn't be able to resist a pretty young woman."

I had to give him credit. Jenson had been my close friend for years. He knew me better than almost anyone.

Naturally, I'd told him about going to meet Cara's parents. He'd been incredibly supportive in the days leading up to it. "They'll love you. You've a great dad, and you're a freaking billionaire — what's not to love?"

Turned out, there was quite a bit about me that the Smiths found unlovable.

First thing in the morning, Jenson had marched into my office demanding a recap. I'd been dreading it, mostly because all in all, the night had been memorable and beautiful. There was something growing between Cara and me. A deep, wonderful thing I could almost call love.

Of course, I wasn't going to tell Jenson all of that. So I gave him the details I had been avoiding replaying in my own brain. Linda and Stan's immediate coolness to me, the interrogation at the dinner table, the way they'd told Cara what she could and could not do with her life, despite her being a grown woman.

"Well, I guess she is pretty young."

"Don't remind me."

Jenson shrugged. "What I mean is, you'd be worried too, right? So would I."

"It's not just worry, Jenson. It's control. They think they can tell Cara what to do. She doesn't even live under their roof anymore. She's a grown woman. She can make her own decisions." I was feeling defensive since her parents had attacked me for trying to manipulate her. Though I was clear on my intentions, there was an inherent power dynamic due to our age difference. I'd lived quite a bit more life than she had. I had more money. I was her employer — hopefully not for much longer, if our relationship kept going in the right direction. We could repeat the old adage "age is just a number" over and over. That didn't mean it was true.

I'd said to her before in the dark and quiet hours of the night how I didn't want her to feel trapped by my life when she was just bursting out of her cocoon. She was just starting her business. She didn't need to be tethered to a man nearly twice her age who already had a child. But

Cara remained adamant. She wanted to be there. And she was willing to work at it, to bridge that gap between us.

I was, too. But the fact remained — there were challenges Cara and I had to overcome. But that didn't mean I didn't deserve a chance to be seen in a positive light.

"So then what happened?"

I smiled softly to myself. "Well, she chose me."

Jenson pounded his fist on my desk, making me jump. "There you go! There he is!"

I flushed. "So we left. And I took her home."

He waggled his eyebrows. "I bet you did."

"Jenson, don't do that."

"What? I'm not doing anything! You just said you took her home. That's totally innocent."

I grabbed a stress ball from the top drawer of my desk and lobbed it at Jenson. He blocked it just in time. "Get your mind out of the gutter, you idiot."

"What? I'm just happy for you, man. It's been too long since you've connected with anyone. Or had anything more than short-term hookups. Happiness suits you."

I rolled my eyes. "Nice try. No matter how much you suck up, I'm a gentleman. I don't' kiss and tell."

"You wound me." Jenson clutched his heart and pretended to be offended.

There was a knock at the door.

"You expecting someone?"

I pushed myself up from my desk with a grunt. "No, but I have a ten o'clock. They might be early." When I opened the door, however, I was not met with my appointment, but a woman with strawberry blonde hair I'd never seen before, her expression so serious she might as well have been at a funeral.

"Mr. Taves?"

"Uh, yes. Can I help you?"

The woman held out a legal envelope to me. "These are legal documents for you."

I took the file from her and she left without another word. I stared down at the envelope, heart pounding. *No… it can't be.*

"What is it?"

I turned around to Jenson, my mouth gaping open. "I don't know. But if I had to guess…"

As soon as our eyes met, Jenson knew what I was thinking. He swallowed thickly, Adam's apple bobbing.

I unwound the thread holding the envelope closed and pulled out the documents as fast as I could, slicing my finger on one of the papers in the process. I didn't even feel the pain through my scattered thoughts.

*Family Court of the State of New York…*

I didn't have to read further. I crumpled the paper in my hand tightly. "Fuck. *Fuck.*"

"Is it custody papers?"

"What the hell do you think?!" I threw the papers down on the desk for him to look at and began to pace around the room.

"Aw, Jesus. Wesley, I'm sorry."

"I knew it. I knew from the moment she said she wanted to visit that she was up to something. I just had this feeling…" I felt sick to my stomach. Lisbeth was attempting to get custody of Lucy. I didn't even care if she was appealing for partial or full. She didn't deserve either. Not to mention, I knew it wasn't what was best for Lucy. If Lisbeth hadn't made it clear from her years of absence, the visit just a few weeks prior had put the nail in the coffin. Lisbeth would always be about Lisbeth, first and foremost.

That wasn't what our daughter — *my daughter* — deserved. She deserved to be the center of our world. Even Lucy knew that Lisbeth would never choose her over her own selfish needs, even if she couldn't say that in so many words.

Jenson sorted through the documents. "Why the hell would she do this after so many years?"

"I don't know. Because she wants to make me suffer? Because she thinks she deserves it? I don't fucking care what her reason is. It's not happening."

"There's no way they'd give her custody, Wes."

"Over my dead body they will." I fumbled to get my phone out of my pocket. My hands were shaking as I tried to pull up her contact.

Jenson stood. "You want me to go?"

I didn't have words to respond, just waved toward the door. I'd apologize for my rudeness later.

Jenson left, closing the door behind him and I finally steadied my hand enough to tap on Lisbeth's number.

As the phone rang, I walked over to the window of my office. My vision was clouded over by rage, red and hot. The spectacular view meant nothing to me in my state.

"Wesley! I wasn't sure when I'd hear from you."

"What the hell is wrong with you?"

Lisbeth sighed. "Can't we ever have a civil conversation?"

"We can be civil when you stop pulling stunts like this. Custody, Lisbeth? Really?"

"She's my daughter, too, Wesley. I want more time with her."

"That's fucking rich." I raked my hand back through my hair so hard I pulled some out by the roots. "Why now? After all this time, why now?"

Lisbeth tsked. "I don't owe you an explanation, Wesley."

"It will come out with the lawyers, though, won't it? You're going to need a really fucking strong case to get the judge to give you the time of day. So lay it all out now. What do you think gives you the right to Lucy *now* when you abandoned her for five years?"

"I did not abandon her!"

I laughed mirthlessly. "You're delusional."

"I wasn't ready to be a mother, Wesley."

"And now you are?"

"Yes."

I felt like I'd been slapped across the face. "You've got to be fucking kidding with that one."

"I know it seems…strange, since I'm a forty-year-old woman. But I wasn't ready five years ago. I had more of my career I wanted to figure out. I felt so stuck when we had Lucy. You were working all the time, and I was losing my mind cooped up in the house with her." She paused. "I'm not proud that I ran away like I did. But I'm ready *now*. And I deserve a second chance."

I resisted throwing everything that had happened during her visit back at her. The way she'd left so suddenly, barely giving Lucy a second look as she waltzed out the doorway with her fiancé. *Yves*… "This is because of Yves, isn't it? You —" It all clicked. "He wants children, doesn't he?"

The hesitation was all I needed to know. "He and Lucy really connected."

"He wants children and you're afraid you're getting too old to give him what he wants, is that it?"

"You're so fucking cruel, you know that?"

"So you might as well have a backup plan, in case you can't become pregnant, is that it?"

"If I were there, I'd slap you across the face."

I went to the desk and picked up the custody papers. "Don't worry, you've already done that."

"I want another chance to be the mother Lucy deserves. Doesn't that count for anything?"

"No. Because, like always, Lisbeth, your reasons are selfish. This time, it's all to do with a man."

"That's why I had Lucy in the first place! For a *man*!"

I froze. "I never pressured you."

"Keep telling yourself that."

"I would never have —"

Lisbeth growled. "It doesn't matter what happened anymore. It's in the past. What matters now is that I'm with the right man."

I no longer loved Lisbeth. But I'd loved what we had, until she ran out on me and her daughter. I had no idea my memory was so…wrong.

"I'll see you in two weeks for mediation. If you refuse, I'll take you to court. Goodbye, Wesley."

Lisbeth hung up first. She always left first. Always the deserter. She was good at that.

The reality of the situation settled over me.

I could lose Lucy to a woman who didn't really want her. Didn't truly *love* her. Not the way a child should be loved. It didn't matter how good a case I had. Courts and lawyers always had more sympathy for *mothers*. Never fathers.

Every time I thought things could work out with my company, my daughter, my girlfriend…*Cara*. Shit, not again. Lisbeth was coming back once more and making it nearly impossible to move on.

I gripped the phone as tight as I could until I snapped.

"*Fuck!*" I threw the phone against the wall as hard as I could.

Lisbeth was about to ruin everything. Again.

# Chapter 27

## Cara

Waking up was hard that morning. I wasn't sure if was the physical activity from the night before or the mental anguish of dealing with my parents.

I had prepared for my parents not to like Wesley. I thought I'd prepared for the worst. But clearly, I didn't know how bad it could get.

I had anticipated my parents being judgmental and disapproving, but not to the extent of telling me I wasn't welcome in their house if I chose Wesley; if I chose what I felt like was turning into love. It was becoming clear to me they wanted a little girl and were not prepared for me to grow into a woman who could make decisions for herself.

But why have children if not to watch them grow and make their own life choices?

I wasn't going to waste my time mourning what could have been last night. Or rather, I didn't have the time. I had to prepare for a meeting with my worst new enemy. Danny Morden.

Since the walk through, we had been back and forth about numbers. Or should I say, he and *Wesley* were going back and forth. It was just through my email and with my signature. I had learned a lot but still needed a bit of hand-holding. And I wanted as much hand-holding as I could get from Wesley.

Now that we had developed our relationship, I loved watching him shift between his personal and professional sides. One second he'd be tenderly kissing my cheek, the next he'd be in a heated phone discussion about Readly. Something about his duality really turned me on.

Anyway, it was time to get up and face the day. I shook off my sleepiness and the nauseous feeling I had from all the drama of the day before, not to mention my upcoming meeting with Danny. I mentally prepared to go about my morning as usual — head to the Taves house, sneak a kiss with Wes, take Lucy to school, and then continue with my day.

On my way to meet Danny, I sent off a text to Wesley:

**Feeling nervous…**

Usually, he was pretty prompt with responses, even if his day was jam-packed. But not this time. I stared at my phone, waiting for the three dots to appear.

Nothing.

My heart dropped into my stomach. Last night had been tough on both of us, that much was obvious. But we had connected so deeply afterward and left things on such a high note, I thought we had risen above the pain. I'd chosen him and he'd chosen me. When he left around midnight and kissed me goodbye, I didn't feel any distance there. In fact, I felt closer to him than ever before.

Maybe I had underestimated what kind of damage my parents' disapproval had done.

Why would a man like Wesley Taves want to get

involved with someone who was still just a girl in her parents' eyes?

I swallowed and shook off the feeling. *Not now, Cara.*

I imagined what Wesley would say if I could have that immediate text back or could get him on the phone. He's smile that lopsided, smug smile and narrow his eyes. "Why're you nervous? You've got all the power. Make him wait."

I did have all the power. The walk through had been such a mess, we'd been able to slash the price of the building by nearly a third. Danny wanted the sale; he wanted the commission. If the paperwork didn't get signed, he didn't win. Of course, I had the power.

So I made him wait. Just as my imagined Wesley instructed me. Usually, I was early to my meetings with Danny, left hanging by his chronic lateness. Today, I'd be the one who was late.

I ambled to the coffee shop near Lucy's school where Danny and I always met, taking in the scenery, window-shopping, stopping to pet dogs. By the time I got there, Danny was already seated, arms over his chest, looking rather displeased.

*Perfect.*

"Sorry to make you wait, Danny."

He looked up at me, aviators perched on his head. "Cara! No matter. I just got here."

*What a freaking liar.*

Danny stood and gave me a kiss on the cheek. "How are your parents?"

I did my best not betray the panic inside me. "Good." *Now who's the liar?* "And yours?"

"Good, they're on vacation, actually. Florida. Lucky bastards. Anyway, let's get started, huh? I got you a coffee."

I sat and eyed the coffee cup. "Mmm. Thank you." I

picked it up and took a sip. Overly sweet and creamy liquid hit my tongue. I nearly gagged but managed to swallow it. "Uh, what is this?"

"Oh, it's a campfire latte. I figured you'd like something sweet like that."

I grimaced. "It's…interesting."

"Good!"

Jesus, Danny could not read a reaction for the life of him. No wonder he was still single even though he had his "illustrious" real estate career and all this money. It was like it had blinded him from being the least bit self-aware.

"Now, let's go through the contract, shall we?"

Danny whipped out a dense document and started gesticulating to places I had to sign and initial.

My body felt hot, and not in a good way. Like I was maybe getting a fever. I was worried I'd start dripping sweat right here in the middle of the café.

I felt the moment the gulp of disgusting latte hit my stomach. Everything began to churn and I could feel the contents of my stomach starting to press upward. A wave of nausea hit me.

"You alright?"

I looked to Danny with alarm. "Huh?"

"You just kinda seemed zoned out."

"I…uh…" *Deep breaths, Cara. It's just a bad latte.* "Sorry, you know, sometimes I get a little bogged down by all the technical speak."

Danny smiled, showing off his canines. An unflattering look. "Oh, I can make it simpler for you if you want. I know it's hard when you don't have Taves here."

If Danny wasn't a family friend, I'd have punched him for that one. Anger like that, though, I usually didn't feel. I was almost always calm and patient — it was necessary when caring for children. Now my temper rose unexpectedly and suddenly, only to drop back down just as quick.

*What's happening to me?*

Danny stared to explain things simpler, but slower. My stomach continued to churn. "You can just show me where to sign. I don't need to…I've already read the contract."

"Okay. Whatever you say, Cara. You're the boss."

I tried not to outwardly cringe at the forced smoothness of his voice. Under the table, I felt the toe of his show rest against my ankle, as if it was an accident. But knowing Danny and knowing what Danny had been wanting of me for a long time, I knew it wasn't an accident.

*Just initial and sign…initial and sign…*

Finally, we got to the signature on the document. I slammed down the pen. Something was not right in my stomach. It was more than just this latte.

I was starting to feel sick.

"Well, now that that's done —" I started to rise from my seat.

Danny grabbed my wrist. "Hey, wait, let's catch up for minute. I have a half hour before my next appointment."

I didn't have the mental fortitude to refuse at this moment. My mind was solely fixated on the way my stomach was churning. I sank back into the chair and tried to train my eyes on Danny's face.

Danny started to talk. Any time he asked a question, I merely answered with a yes or a no.

A wave of bile rushed up my throat. I covered my mouth, thinking for a moment I might projectile vomit across the table and right into Danny's lap. Would that be so bad, if not for my pride?

"Soon, you know, we won't be working together. And maybe we can find a way to meet up as friends…maybe more. What do you say?"

I frowned. "What do you mean?"

"Damn, do I have to spell it out for you?" Danny chuckled. "Alright, fine. You're an attractive girl. I think we should get a drink some time. Be awesome together." He started to reach for my hand across the table. "What do you say?"

Before he could touch me, my stomach flipped once more. *I have to get out of here.* I pulled my hand away from his and leaped to my feet, covering my mouth.

*I think I'm going to be sick.*

Danny called after me as I rushed through the café to the bathroom. I shoved open the door and didn't have time to lock it before I hurled the few contents of my stomach into the toilet.

*This can't be from the latte,* I thought on my third round of puking. *And even though Danny makes me sick, I don't think it's literal.*

When I finally had a moment to catch my breath, throat burning and brain blazing with questions and confusion, it hit me.

*Could I be…pregnant?*

I shook off the thought quickly. I was on birth control. But Wesley and I didn't take any other precautions. And I, admittedly, had forgotten to take my pill a few days here and there, but…

*Shit.*

§

After cleaning up in the bathroom, I hurried back out to fetch my stuff, making an excuse to Danny that a stomach flu was going around Lucy's school (it wasn't) and that I'd be in touch (I wouldn't).

He was less concerned that I was ill and more concerned if I had spread it to him, immediately pulling out a bottle of hand sanitizer. *Jackass.*

I practically sprinted to the nearest drug store. I'd never bought a pregnancy test before, never even suspected. With my few previous partners, we'd always used condoms. With Wesley, we hadn't from the beginning. And once I knew that feeling, there was no way I was going back.

As I walked the test up to the counter, all I could think about was Wesley. How would he react? Should I even tell him? Or should I just…

"Oh, congratulations."

I stared at the cashier. She was a middle-aged woman with red streaks in her hair, wearing an excited smile that faded quickly when she saw my expression.

"I mean…"

I paid for it without speaking. "Do you have a bathroom I can use?"

"Of course, honey." She walked me into the back, to a bathroom that definitely wasn't supposed to be for customer use. I was grateful for her pity, though. Before closing the door behind me, she smiled. "It'll be okay. Either way."

"Thank you."

I locked the door behind me and negotiated the strange task of peeing on a pregnancy test stick.

Once that was done, the waiting began — the longest few minutes of my life. I paced back and forth, trying not to check the timer on my phone, just waited for it to go off.

I couldn't take it any longer, though. I looked at the test. The control was bright pink and next to it…

It was early yet, but there it was. The ghost of a second pink line. I stared and stared. The pink got darker and darker.

And I was…

I was pregnant.

Simple and unceremonious.

One million thoughts popped into my head. How could I afford a baby? What would my mom and dad say? What would Katie say? Most importantly, would Wesley be upset?

What was I supposed to do? And why hadn't I been more careful?

And though my stomach bottomed out in fear, my heart sang with joy, more powerful than my panic. My eyes welled with tears.

Nothing in my life had ever felt more right than knowing I was pregnant with Wesley Taves's baby.

I had to tell him as soon as possible. I needed to know if our love could continue to grow with this…unexpected joy.

Or if I'd have to do it alone.

# Chapter 28

## Wesley

I lingered at work and drove home slowly, even circling the block before I got the courage to finally park. It was already a quarter past seven. I couldn't keep Cara and Lucy waiting any longer.

I knew the second I saw them, though, my heart was going to break.

As soon as I walked into the house, I wished I could have turned around.

I head Lucy's feet scrambling across the floor before I saw her. "Daddy!"

When she emerged from the living room, it took everything in me not to burst into tears. My little girl with her beautiful blonde hair, curious brown eyes, and bold grin with missing teeth…*my little girl.*

What would I do if Lisbeth took her from me? First for just a little bit of time…then completely…

I couldn't lose her.

I dropped to my knees and opened my arms wide for

her. She slammed up against my front, hugging me tight. "Oof! You're getting so big, Luce."

"You're late, Daddy!"

I tried to laugh but couldn't even force out a chuckle.

Over Lucy's shoulder, I spied Cara stepping tentatively into the hall. I looked away as quick as she appeared, burying my face in Lucy's hair. At least Lucy was still here in my arms. I would fight Lisbeth. I already had my lawyers working on my case to keep custody of Lucy. There was *nothing* more important to me.

Even Cara. I cared for her so deeply, but Lucy came first.

Lucy started to wriggle, but I held tighter. "Why are you trying to get away from me?"

"Because you're squishing me!"

I lessened the intensity of my hug but didn't let her go. "Come on up, kiddo." I hoisted her onto my hip. "I missed you today."

"Daddy, you're being mushy."

"Mushy?"

"Yeah, you're laying it on thick!"

I laughed. "Where'd you learn that?"

"Cara."

My heart dropped as I finally looked across the hallway at Cara.

Something was off about her usually bright expression. Her smile was tinged with sadness. Our connection had deepened so significantly the night before, I wondered if she already saw past my cheerful guise, straight into my heart.

Maybe she already knew what was coming.

"Cara's very mushy, Daddy." Lucy leaned her head onto my shoulder.

I locked eyes with Cara. As if I didn't already know. "Is she?"

Cara smiled bigger and folded her hands in front of her, like she was unsure what to do with herself. The gesture made her look so young and vulnerable.

I didn't want to break her heart. But I knew I had to. The heart most important to me would always be Lucy's. She was an inherent part of me that I could not lose. Cara was not expendable to me by any means, but there was a reason I had avoided dating and serious relationships over the years. I knew it would be complicated as a single father. Like the universe was telling me I could not hold these two things at once.

I could only have one love in my life. Lucy.

And knowing I had to break Cara's heart broke mine, too.

I kissed the side of Lucy's head and finally put her down, relishing the way her hands still gripped at my suit jacket. "Hey, honey, could you run off and —"

"I know. Cara already told me that when you came home, I'd need to go play on the iPad with my headphones on."

I frowned, looking form Lucy to Cara. "Did she?" Jesus, maybe she really was reading my mind.

"I hope that's okay." Cara's voice was nervous. Like it used to be when we were merely boss and employee.

I knew what I had to do, but I wanted at least one more moment of basking in the warmth of her love. Maybe that was a selfish thing to wish for. "Of course. Go on, Luce."

Lucy skipped into the living room, leaving Cara and me alone.

I waited for her to speak first. After all, she had called this meeting.

"I have something to tell you."

"Yeah. Me too."

"Should we go sit?" She gestured into the kitchen.

"Sure, sure."

We went into the kitchen and sat at the table. I could smell something baking in the oven. One of her many delicious dishes. God, she was so sweet. She had given Lucy and me so much. I couldn't stand hurting her like this, especially after what we had shared the night before. But even if I remained in her life, she would likely get hurt in the process.

It was best to stop before we became even more entangled.

Cara folded her hands on the table. I couldn't believe how far away she felt. Just last night, in her bed, I had felt our souls become one. "Um, this isn't easy, but —"

"Can I go first?" I hadn't meant to interrupt, but I couldn't hold back. If she was about to say she loved me or something similar, I couldn't handle hurting her after such a revelation.

Her eyebrows jumped. "Oh. Okay."

"I'm sorry, I didn't meant to interrupt you, I just —" I reached across the table and wrapped my hands around hers. "This isn't easy for me to say."

Cara stared at me expectantly, her eyes questioning.

"Today I was served custody papers from Lisbeth. She wants to revisit our custody agreement."

Cara gasped, shock on her face. "Oh my God."

I nodded. "It's…I'm a wreck over it, honestly."

"Wesley, I'm so sorry."

*Oh God, don't be nice to me. Don't be nice when I'm going to do what I'm about to do. Rip off the Band-Aid, Wesley.* "You know that Lucy is my world."

Cara's concern turned to caution. Her back straightened. Preparing for the blow.

"Of course, I know that."

"And I need to make sure nothing gets in the way of her being with me. Even Lisbeth."

"Yes."

"If Lisbeth even got a whiff of something happening between us —"

She retracted her hands from mine and put them in her lap. Her eyes hardened. "I understand."

"Trust me when I tell you, I had no intention of doing this again."

"I believe you." Her lower lip was trembling.

"But between Lisbeth and dinner last night —"

"I'm sorry about my parents' behavior, but please don't end things because of that."

I pulled my chair closer to her. All I wanted to do was wrap my arms around her, kiss the hurt away, apologize for even suggesting we call it quits. But the damage had already been done. "It's not them. But you shouldn't have to choose me over them."

"You didn't want me to?"

"That's not what I said, Cara."

"Then why are you —"

"I know what it's like. To be a parent and want what's best for my daughter. That's not a connection you should sever. Not ever."

Cara looked away. "Don't act like I'm not mature enough to know what I want."

"I…that's not what I meant. I just shouldn't have let you leave with me."

"*Let* me?" Her chest was heaving with deep, angry breaths. "You don't control my decisions."

"No. I don't. And I never meant —"

She reached out suddenly, unable to contain herself, cupping her hands around my face and pulling closer to me. "Then let me be here with you. Let me support you. Don't push me away, Wesley." Then she kissed me.

Her lips melted my entire body. I remembered the night before, lying together, picturing my life with her. Her family's disapproval had been so far from my mind. I had believed that as long as she wanted me, we could overcome anything.

Turns out, that wasn't the case.

When the kiss broke, Cara lingered near my face. Waiting for me to say something, to change my mind.

But I couldn't.

I tenderly removed her hands from my face and put them in her lap. "I'm not completely deserting you. I'm still going to help you with the daycare. And perhaps we can revisit *us*…later. Me and you. If you want. But right now, I need to put all of my energy into Lucy. And you have to put your energy into your work. So for now, let's say your two months are up."

Cara's jaw dropped. Her body recoiled and she looked like she was in pain, as if I'd slapped her across the face. Her mouth opened and shut a few times as she searched for words she could not find.

"I'm so sorry."

Cara put her hand over her mouth, eyes shutting tightly, and tears began to stream down her face.

"Cara, please, believe me when I tell you this is the last thing I —"

"I knew you'd do it again."

I stopped. "What?"

Her jaw tightened and her hands balled into fists. "You broke my heart once because of Lisbeth. I knew it was only a matter of time before you'd do it again." She tilted her head back, taking deep breaths in an attempt to abate the tears . "And to think I…"

Silence.

"To think you what, Cara?"

She shook her head.

"Cara —"

Abruptly, she stood up, the chair skittering behind her and falling with a crash. She tore off to the front door.

I followed in hot pursuit. I couldn't let her go like this. But how could I *ever* let her go? There would have been no good way. I didn't want to let her go at all.

But wanting and needing are two different things.

"Cara, please wait!"

She threw open the front door, bounded down the steps, and into her car. I made it to her passenger side window before she was able to pull away.

"Cara! Don't leave like this!" I knocked on the window desperately. "Please talk to me!"

The window whirred downward. Cara's eyes were facing squarely forward.

"Cara, don't think for a second this isn't difficult for me."

She blinked. "I find that hard to believe." Then she looked at me. Her expression was cold. Full of disdain. "I should have known better. All you do is use people up, and once you've taken them for all they have to offer, you spit them out."

I couldn't believe my ears. *Is that what she really thinks of me?*

"Get away from my car."

If she had been saying it to anyone else, I would have thought she was amazing. Strong, gutsy, determined. But her anger directed at me was visceral, painful. It tore me apart. I stepped back from the window.

Stunned, I watched the car drive off down the street at a pace much too fast for a residential area.

And that was it. Cara was gone.

I had no idea if I would ever see her again.

"Daddy!"

I turned around. Lucy was standing in the doorway, headphones on, iPad in her arms.

"Why are you outside, Daddy?"

"I'm…I was just…"

"Where's Cara?"

I took a deep breath. I had another heart to break. And I wouldn't even have the chance to tend to my own broken heart until much later, after Lucy was in bed.

Would our lives ever be whole again?

# Chapter 29

## Cara

Katie rubbed my back as we waited. "Do you think it'd be weird if I went and played with one of the bead mazes?"

I glanced over at the low table with wires bent in different configurations, beads hanging from them to be moved all around. "It's meant for kids, Katie."

"So? A bit of nostalgia never killed anyone."

I tried to smile.

"I thought you'd find that funny."

In better circumstances, I would have. But I had been crying for nearly two days straight. From the moment Wesley told me things were over, I'd lost it. I didn't even have the chance to tell him that our connection had created something unexpected, yet beautiful. He'd already decided I wasn't worth his time.

So I made the impulsive decision that he didn't deserve to know about our baby.

I regretted it from the moment I left, wondering if that

piece of information would have made him change his mind.

But I wanted him to need me in his life simply for *me*. It was clear that I was not enough.

I could respect his need to focus on Lucy. I could respect the notion that we should take some time apart. However, I couldn't respect him breaking my heart again. After everything — all the vulnerability, after what had gone down with my parents, after the connection we had shared.

He just decided on his own to be done.

That was Wesley Taves. I realized that now. Money could make a person feel like they controlled you. Didn't matter how good of a father he was, or how much he encouraged you, or how giving of a lover he was in bed.

A billionaire would always be a billionaire. And I was just a silly girl, not worth his effort.

"Cara Smith?"

Katie and I looked up to the nurse calling my name. She wore a hijab and a bright smile. "You can come back now."

I got to my feet nervously. Katie held my hand tight and squeezed. I could hear her without her having to speak: *It's going to be fine.*

And by God, I had to believe that.

I told Katie immediately after leaving the Taves house. She was over at my apartment almost immediately and had not left since. It was like a very sad slumber party. She was the one who'd encouraged me to make an appointment with an OB to confirm everything.

"You need to verify the rapid test and find out your next steps, Cara."

Perhaps I didn't have medical evidence, but from the

moment my stomach churned, I *knew*. My body knew. It was making room for something amazing.

I wasn't ready for a baby in the grander sense. Emotionally, though, I had always believed that a baby was the greatest representation of love. And from the way my heart broke when Wesley ended things, I knew that I loved him.

This baby would be born from love. I knew that much. That was enough justification that I was ready for it.

The nurse led us back to the examination room. From there it was a blur of questions and samples, of polite conversation and nervous laughter. Once she finished up, she left us alone again and said the doctor would be in shortly.

Katie and I sat in silence, me on the examination table, her in a chair nearby, waiting for the doctor arrive.

Then came a knock.

My mouth was dry. "Come in."

Dr. Farina was the highest recommended OB per my insurance. She looked exactly like her picture, except much taller. Dark hair, olive skin, and easy, friendly eyes. "Cara?"

"Yep, that's me."

"Hi, I'm Dr. Farina. And who do you have with you today?"

"Katie. I'm Cara's sister."

Dr. Farina chuckled. "I can tell. Same eyes."

Katie and I exchanged a smile.

"Well, Cara. I'm sure this won't come as a surprise to you. But your urine sample indicates that you're pregnant. We'll send your blood out to the lab to confirm your hCG levels, but for now…" She carefully turned her head, trying to read me. "Congratulations."

I chewed on my lower lip. "Thank you."

"Now, I see on your chart that this was an unplanned

pregnancy. You've been on birth control for some time now?"

"Yeah, since I was sixteen. But I must have missed some pills or…"

Dr. Farina nodded. "Sometimes we slip up. Sometimes the pills don't do their job. Either way, you have options, Cara."

Katie had said the same thing to me the night before. "There are options. You don't have to take this on if you don't want to. But if you do, you won't be alone."

As soon as she said that, I knew. "I don't think we need to discuss options."

The doctor's eyes jumped with a pleasant smile. "Well, that makes my job a whole lot more exciting." She looked down at the chart. "Now, first things first, let's try and get a fetal age."

Dr. Farina went through all the various technical details to try and determine how far along I was — the last time I had unprotected sex, the dates of my last period. Once her questioning was through, she poured over her notes and nodded. "Okay. Good. Well, let's get an ultrasound going and maybe we can get a bit more information."

I nervously laid back as Dr. Farina prepared the ultrasound machine.

"It's too early to do a pelvic ultrasound probably, so we'll do a transvaginal. Is that alright with you?"

"Sure." I stared up at the ceiling. I still couldn't believe this was real. Kids always were in my future. They were in my day-to-day life. I felt like I was meant to be a mother. But the timing was still hard to wrap my head around.

While Dr. Farina prepared me for the ultrasound, Katie stood up and grabbed my hand. "Thank you."

"Of course. But you have to promise to be there for me when it's my turn."

"It would be my honor, Katie."

Once the ultrasound started, the room was silent. Dr. Farina probed and prodded until finally, she smiled. "Okay. There we go. See here —" She flipped the screen around to face us. The screen was blotchy, just black and white shapes. She pointed to one of the blobs. "Here's the embryonic sack. And based on the length, I think you're about five weeks pregnant. No visible heartbeat yet, but that should change by your next appointment."

Like looking at abstract art, I wasn't sure I even knew what I was looking at. But I knew how it made me feel. A smile crept onto my lips. This little blob was going to grow and grow. I would eventually be able to make out the full form of my baby inside me.

The sweet came with a side of bitter. I wished it was Wesley with me instead of my sister. Not that I wasn't grateful Katie was there with me. But I wished I could have told him before everything fell apart. And if things panned out the way I had hoped, Lucy would get to be a big sister. I knew her beautiful heart would welcome that.

"Cara, don't cry."

I wiped tears away from my face. "I can't help it." I looked at Katie. Her eyes were also swimming with tears. "*You* don't cry."

"Well, I can't help it, either, dammit."

The three of us laughed. Dr. Farina was incredibly sweet and helpful as she told me all of my next steps. I left the appointment feeling nervous but empowered. My body was built for this. So was my brain. I'd make an amazing mother, even if I had to work my ass off for the next eighteen years to provide for my baby.

*My baby*. I liked the sound of that.

§

After the appointment, Katie and I went for a walk. We were both quiet and uncertain of what the future held.

"I'm sorry this is so much."

Katie frowned. "Don't be sorry."

I shook my head. "I'm your big sister. I take care of you."

"Oh, stop it, Cara. We take care of each other."

I smiled. "You're so grown up."

"Yeah, because I had a really amazing role model." Katie wrapped her arm around my waist and squeezed. "This is the luckiest baby ever."

My eyes welled with tears. "Katie, you can't say stuff like that, or I'll cry."

"Sorry, Miss Sensitive!"

We laughed even though I had started to cry. Only five weeks pregnant and my emotions were already out of control. I was in for quite an adventure.

"I'm gonna have to go home tonight. Mom and Dad are getting anxious."

I nodded. "That's okay. I think I'll be okay tonight."

"You should come."

I laughed. "You heard what they said. I made my choice."

"Cara, they were talking out of their asses. They never really meant it. And…" Katie shrugged. "Now that Wesley's out of the picture…"

"Don't remind me." I touched my lower stomach. I'd been feeling around the past two days, trying to sense if anything had changed. Not quite yet, but I was sure it would happen soon.

Katie stopped walking and put her hands on my cheeks. "You're coming home with me. I won't let you be alone tonight. And Mom and Dad wouldn't want that, either."

I was so tired from the ups and downs of the past few days I didn't have the energy to argue. However, I did regret going with her when I found myself sitting on the enclosed porch of our childhood home, listening to our parents gloat about my relationship ending with Wesley.

"Oh Cara, honey, you know I'm so sad that you're hurt." Mom glanced at Dad. "But we did warn you."

I glared over my plate of coffee cake that I was eating in small nibbles for fear of turning my stomach. "Wow, you're seriously going to do the whole 'I told you so' thing right now?"

Mom looked away sheepishly. "Well, that's not what I meant, but —"

"Of course it is. I'm sure once you two get a moment alone you're going to congratulate each other on your astuteness." I was done holding back. Maybe they'd been right, but I didn't deserve them delighting in my misery.

Dad waved his hands. "Hey, kiddo. Easy. We just want you to trust us, that's all. We know you better than anyone. We want what's best for you. And often, we *know* what's best for you."

I thought about my own child, still so small and fragile inside me. Sure, I will know them the longest of anyone in the world. But did that mean I would know them better than they would eventually know themselves?

Dad patted the seat between him and Mom. "Come here, sweetheart."

I begrudgingly did so. They leaned into me with a hug. I felt suffocated.

"We're gonna make it all better. Promise." Dad kissed the side of my head.

"You betcha. In fact, when Katie told us about things going sour with Wesley, I rang up Mrs. Morden…" Mom began.

I visibly cringed but didn't respond.

"I know Danny would love to take you out. And we think you should give him a chance. You know, the Mordens are like family." She rubbed my arm encouragingly.

Dad was excited to add his support. "Yes, Danny would know how to take care of you, Cara."

I thought about our meeting a couple days earlier. How utterly done I was with Danny's ongoing attempts at flirtation. I couldn't even fathom going out with someone while still so freshly heartbroken *and* newly pregnant — even though that was still a secret.

Danny, however, was a pro at putting his foot in his mouth. It wouldn't take much for him to show his true colors on a date. Then I could come home, say it was awful, and I'd never have to hear about Danny Morden, the perfect golden child, ever again.

"Okay. Yeah…maybe you're right. Maybe I should give him a chance."

Mom and Dad gasped excitedly. I bet my mother was already planning the wedding in her head.

Katie, who had been silent through the majority of the conversation, sighed heavily, interrupting their revel.

"Have something to say, Katie?" Mom asked with a raised eyebrow.

My sister glanced at me. I knew she wanted to argue and tell me not to give in. But I shook my head softly. *No fighting. Not now.* "Nothing. Just tired."

I knew the feeling. I was so tired and turned around that I was numb the rest of the evening. It wasn't until our parents were asleep and Katie and I were curled up in her bed that I was able to explain myself to her.

"Fuck it. If they want me to give Danny Morden a

chance, I'll give him a chance. Then it'll be my chance to say 'I told you so.'"

Katie laughed and pulled me close to her. "Fuck yes, sis."

At least I'd always have her on my side.

# Chapter 30

## Wesley

One of the benefits of being a billionaire is that everyone comes to you, no matter who they are. That included my custody lawyer, Nelson, who had been my divorce and custody lawyer since the moment Lisbeth wanted out of the marriage. Nelson had agreed to come to the townhouse first thing on a Monday morning. I'd decided to take the day off from work so I could think without MediaDeck and Readly hanging over my head. I needed room to think. To strategize.

"You gotta relax, Wesley. I swear to God, I'm getting an ulcer just looking at you." Nelson had an intense Brooklyn accent, born and bred in the area.

"Sorry. I can't help it, I'm scared."

Nelson had a habit of never sitting down. His jumpiness only added to my anxiety. "Don't be nervous. There's no reason to be nervous."

I raised an eyebrow.

"Okay, there's a little reason to be nervous. But we're not bringing a knife to a gun fight or anything."

I pursed my lips. I'd barely been sleeping. The night before meeting with Nelson, I hadn't even been able to lie down. I was exhausted, so it was fortunate I'd already planned to be off work. But it was extremely unusual for me to take any time off, especially with the impending release of Readly.

Readly and MediaDeck were the last things on my list of problems, though. The first was Lucy's custody followed very closely by Cara's heartbreak. Every time I closed my eyes, I saw one of two images. The first was Lucy screaming as Lisbeth snatched her away from me. The other, Cara's eyes as she realized I was about to hurt her. *Again*.

It seemed that wherever I turned, I was hurting someone. Maybe Cara was right. All I did was use and abuse.

Now, at ten in the morning, I was basically a shell of myself. I hadn't shaved in days, sporting the stubbly beginning of a beard, and barely had the energy to don my usual attire. However, I couldn't let the other parents at school drop-off see me in anything but a crisp button up and freshly pressed slacks.

Lucy had been tickled that I was dropping her off at school. She said goodbye to me with a big hug and a kiss. I could have held her in my arms the rest of the day. The rest of her life. But I let her go, trying to hold back the worry from appearing in my eyes. As she skipped off into the school, I held back tears at the idea of losing her.

"You've been Lucy's primary guardian since she was just a baby. Lisbeth left the state after your divorce. There's lots of points against her."

I snapped back to reality. "That's true."

"But…"

The dreaded *but*.

"You're a single dad. And I know as well as anyone a dad is just as good as a mom. But single fathers have harder time in court. Especially with little girls." Nelson wasn't saying anything I didn't already know but hearing him say it confirmed my fear was founded. "And you don't have a girlfriend or anything, right?"

My stomach dropped to the floor. "Um. No."

"Damn. I mean, that's always a toss-up, depending on the judge, but —"

I pushed away the idea that having Cara around would have been better for my case. That would have just been using her. As I had apparently already done plenty. "Hold up. We're going to court?"

Nelson waffled. "Eh, that depends. We'll start with mediation, but if you're resolute and Lisbeth is determined to change the custody agreement, then we might need to go to family court."

"I don't want that."

"Then you might have to get ready to make a few concessions."

"What the hell does that mean?"

Nelson held up his hands defensively. "Woah, woah, woah, easy there, Wes —"

"I'm her *father*. I'm the sole provider. Hell, I pay Lisbeth alimony to live in Miami and screw yachtsman."

"Let's keep that out of the conversation, huh?"

"Why should *I* have to make concessions when my life has been all about our daughter? *My* daughter. Lisbeth chose to leave her. She's made it clear how little she wants to do with her. What kind of credibility does she have?"

Nelson was a remarkably patient man. It's why he worked with people like me and why we paid him the big bucks. No tyrant was too demanding for Nelson. Somehow, he could always neutralize me with an admonishing look. "Wesley. Look at me, kid."

*Kid…please. I'm ten years younger than you.*

"You do a lot for your daughter. That's true. But you've required nannies —"

"I don't have a nanny." *Anymore.* "And besides, what person doesn't require childcare?"

"— and your days are long. You run a multi-billion-dollar corporation. In anyone's eyes, that complicates your ability to be a father to your child."

My life had been dedicated to crafting my empire. That was, until Lucy was born. But by that point, I already had the empire to run. I couldn't just abandon it. Besides, I had to provide for my daughter. And my wife, too…abandoning MediaDeck would have been foolish. Anyone could have seen that.

"*I* know it doesn't." Nelson clicked his tongue, continuing his thought. "People aren't as nuanced as me, though. All I'm saying is that with your long hours and heavy commitments, it's hard for people to believe you can be a committed father figure." He touched his heart. "Not me. Some people."

I remained quiet the rest of our meeting, listening to Nelson lay out our game plan for the custody mediation that was only a week away. I'd have to trust him.

But any optimism I'd managed to cling to was fading.

§

Lucy scraped her fork around the plate. It grated on my nerves. Usually when I was exhausted, I might get snippy with her, ask her to be quieter. But I was so beyond that point. I was just staring at her fork pushing the food around on her plate.

"Daddy, when is Cara coming back?"

I hadn't managed to tell her the truth. I just couldn't. Things were already so fucked-up. I rubbed my eyes tiredly. "Um…well, sweetie, she was only going to be with us for two months, so that time is up now."

"Does that mean she's *not* coming back?"

"Not…not necessarily…" The thought of Cara never coming back, never seeing her bright smile, her freckled nose scrunching as she laughed, her chestnut hair falling over her shoulders, broke my heart. The thought of *Lucy* never getting to see her again…

Utterly destroyed me.

Lucy dropped her fork and pouted her lower lip. "I miss her."

Between my sleepless nights and the stress that had inundated my every moment over the past few days, I felt tears pricking at my eyes.

"Could you tell her that I miss her? Would that make her come back?"

I took a deep breath. *Don't cry. Don't you fucking cry. This is your fault. You don't get to cry.*

"Daddy?"

A tear slid down my face. *Shit.* I slapped it away.

"Did I do something wrong?"

"God, no, Lucy."

"Why are you crying?"

She'd seen. It wasn't worth pretending she hadn't. I was already telling her so many lies. Why gaslight her to believe her own eyes were deceiving her? "Because I'm sad, Luce."

"Because you miss Cara, too?"

I broke down, covering my face. I needed sleep. I needed everything to be okay. I needed Lucy to be mine. And…I needed Cara. Her lightness, her positivity, the potential for a life with *more*.

That all left with her. And it was my fault.

I felt Lucy's little hands on my knee.

"I'm sorry." I wiped my tears away quickly. "I'm sorry for getting upset, I'm just — I don't know why I'm —"

"It's okay to cry, Daddy."

I looked at my little girl. Our eyes reflecting back at one another. A piece of me. The best pieces of me.

"You don't need a reason to cry. Sometimes you just have to cry."

I wrapped Lucy's face in my hands and kissed her forehead. "You're so smart."

"No, silly, it's just true." She didn't look away from my tear-stained face. Who was this brave little girl looking back at me? She was growing up so fast, but still seeing the world as big and beautiful.

Who could have taught her that but Cara?

"I miss her, Lucy. I miss her a lot."

"Well, then we should tell her."

I sighed. "I wish it were that easy. But I think I might have hurt her feelings."

"Then you apologize."

"Well, sometimes people don't accept apologies."

Lucy shrugged. "They never will if you don't try."

I chuckled. "You're really smart."

She leaned into my chest, hugging me with all her might.

Lucy didn't yet understand the way the world worked. How deeply people could hurt each other and how we protected ourselves from that hurt. And though Cara was a kind and compassionate person, I knew I had abused her trust. I would be setting myself up for failure by apologizing now.

"I love you, Daddy."

I buried my face in her hair. Lucy had no idea that we

were at risk of losing each other. And I intended to keep it that way.

"I love you too, Lucy. So much."

For now, though, this was my battle to fight. Alone.

## Chapter 31

### Cara

I hadn't realized the place Danny had asked me to meet him was a nightclub, not a restaurant. So when I met him at the bar, he gave me a strange look when I asked for club soda.

"You in AA or something?"

I held back a glare. "No, my stomach is just really unsettled. I'm hoping this will help."

Danny ordered a whiskey cocktail and started to talk a mile a minute, not even waiting for me to respond. He simply wouldn't shut up.

He was lucky I was there. Not just because it was basically against my will, but because ever since I had found out I was pregnant, I was being plagued with nausea and fatigue beyond my comprehension. However, I'd been staying with my folks, and if they even got a whiff of me canceling, I never would have heard the end of it.

"You can make it through an hour of drinks," Katie had said before I left the house. Though it was frustrating to be around my parents 24/7, Katie's constant support was necessary for my mental health. Plus, it didn't hurt to have all my meals and laundry taken care of while I was grappling with all these emotions and physical inconveniences. "Then," Katie added with a sly smile, "you never have to see him again."

I repeated those two things to myself the entire way there, as a mantra.

Danny swirled his drink around in his glass. "So... daycare owner. How's that title feel?"

He leaned closer to me and I got a whiff of his cologne, which smelled like a fir tree sprayed with chemicals. I held my breath so my stomach wouldn't turn. *You can make it through an hour of drinks.* "Pretty damn good."

"I'd say you earned it with all the back and forth we've done over the past few months." He waggled his eyebrows as if he'd made a suggestive joke.

*Then you never have to see him again.* "Um. Yeah. I guess I owe you a big thank you."

"You guess?"

"I mean I *do*." God, this guy didn't let anything past him when it suited him. "A major thank you. All the time you put into finding properties for me and vouching for me with the owners, that means a lot. Especially since I'm pretty green in the industry."

Danny laughed and nodded. "Well, with Wesley Taves on your side, you can't be that green."

My heart squeezed at the mention of his name. Almost my every waking thought was about Wes and Lucy. It would alternate between pain and worry. He'd broken my heart — again — and I hated him for it. But I couldn't bear the thought of him losing Lucy. He was an amazing father and Lisbeth was certainly just looking for a nice ornament to her new life in Miami. And I'd say that was a generous evaluation.

Even if my heart hated Wesley for what he'd done to me, I didn't want him to suffer.

However, I *definitely* didn't want to talk about him. Especially not with Danny Morden. "Um, yes, he's definitely been a great help in developing my business skills. Negotiations and evaluations and —"

"And I'm sure some other things, huh?" He knocked back his drink.

I blinked. "I'm not sure I know what you're implying."

Danny's mouth split into an ugly smile. "Come on, Cara. I know you're young, but you're not that innocent, are you?"

"Let me rephrase. I *don't like* what you're implying."

Danny raised a hand. "Forgive me. I know you're a good girl. It's just hard to believe that even a man like Wesley Taves would be able to resist a sweet little thing like you."

*A sweet little thing? This guy can't be for real.*

"Not to mention, I don't think I could blame you for being interested in a billionaire. Even if he is old enough to be your father."

"Wesley is *not* old enough to be my father." *Okay, maybe if he was a teen dad, but come on.*

"A little defensive, are we?" Danny gestured to the bartender for another drink. "Listen, I wouldn't blame you if you had a crush on the guy. He's in good shape. And money talks, even I know that."

I couldn't help but laugh. Danny probably thought I found him funny, but I really only saw him as the punch line of bad joke. "Danny, what are we doing here?"

"What do you mean?"

"You didn't come here to talk to me about Mr. Taves, did you?"

"I thought we were calling him *Wesley.*"

I huffed and crossed my arms across my chest. I'd made sure to wear a loose shirt that didn't show off my curves and very little makeup. But I had to look like I tried at least a little. "Whatever. You know what I mean."

Danny tilted his head to the side, so much gel in his hair that not a single lock moved. "No, you're right. We're not here for that."

I felt his hand brush up against my knee.

"You're telling me you haven't noticed how I've been trying to flirt with you?"

I tightened my hands around the cup of club soda. "I don't flirt with people I work with."

"*Please.* We both know that's not true. You've been playing hard to get for months now. I was surprised the way you finally agreed to meet was through our parents."

*Playing hard to get? That's rich.*

His hand slid up my knee to my thigh and his grip intensified. "Look, I know tension when I feel it."

I smacked his hand away. "Don't touch me." It was reflexive. I hadn't meant to be so harsh, but I couldn't help it. More than ever, my body was only meant for me and people I invited to touch me.

And that was not Danny Morden.

"Ohhh, you're feisty. I like that."

Suddenly, he grabbed me by the waist and pulled me closer to him.

"I'm serious, Danny. Don't fucking touch me." I shoved him off, accidentally clipping his chin with my knuckles.

Danny flinched away, rubbing his chin with his hand.

"I'm sorry. I didn't mean to hurt you. I just really don't want to be touched."

He licked his lower lip and laughed darkly. "I get it."

"Look, Danny, I'm giving this date a try because my parents asked me to. It's not…there's nothing here, in my opinion. I don't mean to be rude or anything, but I don't want to lead you on."

Danny narrowed his eyes. "You don't want to lead me on? What the fuck do you think you've been doing the past three months? Hell, even longer."

I felt the blood rushing from my face. "Excuse me?"

Danny grabbed my bar stool and pulled it toward him, entrapping me on both sides with his arms, one on the bar and the other on the back of my chair. "Listen to me, Cara. With all the shenanigans you and your *friend*, Mr. Taves, have been pulling, the sellers are pissed. I think they might back out if someone points them in the right direction."

"I've already signed the contract, the building is mine."

He shrugged. "Anything can be undone if you're quick enough." Lowering his head toward my shoulder, I heard him breathe me in like a predator stalking his prey. "Lucky for you, I've got a lot of sway with them. That can be in your favor if you do things my way."

"Are you threatening me?"

"Threatening? Never, Cara." He grasped my chin. It took everything in me not to slap his hand away. "I'm just saying you should stay on my good side so things work in your favor. You know what I mean? I can be a very persuasive guy when the time comes."

I was too focused on his beady eyes to notice his hand starting to slide under my skirt. It wasn't until his fingers brushed the inside of my thigh that I realized how in over my head I was.

# Chapter 32

## Wesley

Jenson had been after me to go out for dinner since I got news that Lisbeth was filing for custody. I had managed to wave off his invitations, citing I had to take care of Lucy. That is, until he and his wife made plans for our kids to go out for pizza and a movie and presented the plan without giving me an option to decline.

Much to my chagrin, however, dinner ended with him begging me to go with him to a new, trendy bar.

"The movie's not ending for another hour. Let's get a drink and then pick up the kids."

It was either waiting around outside the theater for the movie to end or get a drink. "Fucking hell. Fine."

The bar was actually a nightclub, and it *was* trendy. Much too trendy for my forty-two-year-old ass. I felt extremely out of place among all the twenty somethings vying for a spot at the bar.

"Man, it's too crowded. Let's just call it."

Jenson waved me off. "Don't be such an old fart."

The hostess took one look and recognized me, and that did the trick — soon we were seated at a high top for two. We didn't even have to order. People just seemed to know what we liked. People think the star treatment somehow makes you feel special. It really doesn't. It just makes you think people don't want to talk to you, don't' want to get to know you, don't think you're capable of changing your order ever. So now that the entirety of Manhattan knew that I liked an old-fashioned with an extra twist, that's what I was doomed to drink for eternity.

I would much rather have had straight vodka to quell my nerves.

Jenson eyed me over his old-fashioned. "What do you think?"

"Hate it."

"Come on, Wes."

"What do you want me to say?"

Jenson was quiet. He couldn't do anything right in my eyes at this moment, even though he was the best fucking friend I had and was trying so hard to help. "It doesn't have to be this hard."

I frowned. "What the hell are you talking about?"

"I don't know, it feels like you're forcing yourself to suffer. And you don't need to do that."

I laughed. "You really think I'm choosing this."

"I think your circumstances suck and I don't blame you for feeling them really deeply. But I also think you're making it worse for yourself on purpose. Because of self-loathing."

"Wow, self-loathing. Where'd you hear all that? Your therapist?"

Jenson nodded. "I think you'd really like her."

"No thanks."

"I'm just saying. You didn't have to cut Cara out because —"

I grunted. "We're not talking about this." I'd made Cara off-limits for subjects Jenson and I could talk about. Lucy, fine. Lisbeth, *fine*. But I couldn't hear Cara's name without my pulse skyrocketing.

"Yes, we are. You're so committed to your suffering since Lisbeth left that it's just plain sad."

"Seriously?"

Jenson took a big swig of his drink. "Yes, seriously. And I've enabled that. I'm tired of enabling it. You're Wesley *fucking* Taves. You've worked really hard. You're a good dad. You deserve happiness. But the moment you get even a whiff of it, you run the other way."

I shook my head. "This is fucking rich."

"Don't pretend like I'm not right. Cara was *good* for you and for Lucy. And if you had her on your side for your custody fight, to show Lucy has a female figure in her day-to-day life —"

"The woman I fucked for two weeks and then dated for two more? My kid's nanny? You really think that will give me any credibility? You're fucking insane."

Jenson inhaled and shut his eyes. "Don't talk to me like that when I'm trying to help."

I looked away guiltily. "Sorry."

"It wouldn't hurt. And depriving yourself of happiness deprives Lucy of it, too. You know I'm right. That's why you're getting so mad."

Jenson continued to ramble, but I couldn't listen to him lecture me any longer. He was infuriating because he was correct. I was committed to my suffering. It had become a part of me many years ago. Losing my family early in life, losing many friendships and relationships through the years due to being a workaholic. Losing my wife. Life had shown me that was how I had to be to protect my heart.

In the midst of my musings, I saw her. At the bar.

*Fuck.*

"It's Cara."

"And another thi— What?" Jenson followed my gaze. "Holy shit. Who's that guy?"

I hadn't even noticed she was with someone through my shock. "That's Danny *fucking* Morden."

"Who?"

"Her realtor. Their families know each other. She hates him but her parents are always trying to get her to go out with him and…" I knew right away something was off. Call it a gut feeling. But there was no way I would believe Cara was there of her own volition.

"Well, she looks miserable."

Jenson was right. Cara was leaning away from Danny, trying her best to avoid his closeness as he spoke.

"Go talk to her."

"No, I can't."

"I think she'd be happy to see you."

"No, she's…" I was about to look away when my eyes landed on her wrist. She was still wearing the bracelet I gave her. I could spot the butterfly from a mile away. My lips curled into a smile.

That very moment, Cara yelled, shoving Danny away from her. "Stop!"

It echoed through the bar. But New York being New York, many people pretended like they didn't hear it. Or the music was just too loud.

I got to my feet without a second thought and went directly over to them, forcing myself in front of Cara. "What the fuck is going on?"

Cara touched my arm. "Wesley! What are you —"

"Mr. Taves, what a surprise! We were just talking about you." Danny tried to smile, but his eyes betrayed his nervousness. He was not happy to see me. And he seemed drunk.

"I heard her say 'stop.' I think the whole bar can see how uncomfortable you're making her."

Danny snorted. "Okay, I see what's going on here."

Cara's hand tightened on my arm. "Wesley, please don't."

Her touch only emboldened me. "I don't know what you see, but what I see is a man trying to take advantage of a woman who clearly would rather be anywhere but here with him."

Danny's pupils dilated. "You want a fucking fight, Taves?"

"That won't be necessary." Without a second thought, I clocked him, my fist cutting a sharp line across his chin. Danny's grunt of pain resounded through the bar, followed by gasps from the other patrons. *That'll show him.*

"You're a fucking lunatic."

"Yeah, well, at least I'm not a fucking predator." I turned around to Cara. She looked up at me with shocked eyes, her mouth gaping open. Part of me wanted to take her with me, out of the bar, and protect her even further from this piece of shit. But I couldn't bring myself to do it. "Sorry."

Before she could answer, I rushed out of the bar. I needed the fresh air.

A hand landed on my shoulder. I jumped, nearly knocking Jenson to the ground.

"Woah, you okay man? It's just me."

"Sorry, I'm just…" I wasn't able to form coherent thoughts. My mind was still on Cara and what I'd done to

Danny. My knuckles were pulsing. I could feel a bruise forming as I opened and contracted my hand.

Jenson touched my back. "That was intense. Let's get you home."

"Yeah…that'd be good."

We only made it halfway down the block before I heard Cara calling out after me. "Wesley, wait!"

I turned around to see her running toward me, her shoes clicking against the sidewalk. I should have rushed to meet her, but I was too ashamed, so I stayed glued to my spot.

Cara slowed a few feet in front of me. "I wanted to say thank you."

I shook my head, glancing back at Jenson.

My friend nodded as if reading my mind. "I'll be in the car."

"Thanks." I turned back to Cara.

"You didn't have to do that."

I lowered my gaze to the ground. "Of course, I did. He was taking advantage of you. I always knew he was a scumbag."

"I just mean…you don't owe me anything, you know? I can take care of myself."

"You really think I would have just sat there and let that happen? After everything we've been through?" I focused my eyes on Cara's. It was like sinking into warm honey. Like coming home after our week apart. I had missed her immensely. And seeing her again just reminded me how much I adored her.

How much I needed her.

"We're not together anymore, Wesley. You don't have to stake your claim or —"

"You think that's how I think of you? Like my property?" I shook my head and took a step closer to her. "I wouldn't care if you never spoke to me again or if you hated my guts. For the rest of my life, if I know you're in trouble, I'm going to fucking do something about it, Cara."

Cara inhaled shakily as she looked up at me. "I don't hate you. Even though you broke my heart, I don't hate you. I can't."

She was so close to me, I could smell her. That beautiful, summery perfume alleviating the chill of March. "I regret letting you go."

"It was for the best."

"It wasn't. I miss you. Lucy misses you, I…" I touched her cheek, half expecting her to flinch away. She didn't. "It was a mistake."

For a prolonged moment, we looked into each other's eyes. I leaned forward slightly to kiss her and then decided against it. It was all too much, the moment too heated and adrenaline-filled to make any sort of rational decisions. I retracted my hand from her face and looked down the block to the entrance of the bar. "Let me take you home."

Cara shook her head. "I'm staying with my parents. They'd be furious if they saw me with you. Especially since…" She gestured between us sadly. "You know."

"Who cares what they think?" It came out angrier than I had meant it, but I couldn't help it. Their little girl was a woman. I couldn't believe they hadn't yet forfeited their right to controlling her.

"You do! At least you did last week when you broke up with me."

"I told you, it was a mistake."

Cara laughed bitterly. "Still. Besides, you were right. I can't lose them right now. I need people to be there for me now, more than ever. And family won't leave me behind."

"You have plenty of people on your side. I'm still here.

I'm still your business partner; you know I'm good for the monetary support."

Cara looked away, a breeze flipping some of her chestnut hair out of her eyes. "I'm not talking about the daycare."

I stared hard at her. "Then what are you talking about?"

She hesitated. My mind ran a mile a minute, wondering what she could possibly say. Was she sick? Was something wrong? "I'm pregnant, Wesley."

## Chapter 33

### Cara

Wesley's jaw hung open. I hadn't intended to tell him when I decided to run after him. It felt impossible to avoid revealing the truth. It just slipped out.

But now that I'd said it, his silence was making me regret it.

"It's yours, of course." *As if that weren't obvious.*

Wesley's expression didn't change, as if he was too stunned to speak.

"I know that must be a lot to take in." I wrung my hands nervously. "I'm going to keep it. I don't expect anything from you, so there's no pressure for you to participate or…yeah. I just felt you should know."

His eyes grew sad. "You don't want me to be a part of our child's life?"

"No, no. I'm just saying that you don't have to. I know it's a lot and this wasn't planned. You already have Lucy and Lisbeth and your business and you don't need another thing on your plate, so —"

"A thing? It's not *a thing*." Wesley started to smile. "You're having my baby, Cara."

"Right, but you asked me to leave. So I understand if you don't want to have anything to do with me. With us."

"No! Of course, I —" He grabbed me by the arms, eyes shining with tears. "You seriously want to have my baby? Even if we weren't together, you'd go through with it?"

I flushed. "I know it's crazy, but it just feels right."

Wesley beamed, shaking his head in disbelief. "I don't even know what to say."

"You don't have to say anything. You can think it over. Sleep on it, you know?"

"No, I don't have to. You have no idea how happy I am."

I couldn't' believe my ears. "Really?"

"Yes, I can't imagine anything more wonderful. More perfect." Wesley ran his hands through my hair and kissed my forehead. "I love you, Cara."

My whole body went numb. *Love? He loves me?* I simultaneously wanted to jump for joy and also burst into tears. How could he continue giving me whiplash like this? Making me feel so high, only to drop me so low, again and again. "It's not just me now, Wesley. It's a baby, too. You can't just say things on a whim."

"It's not a whim. Of course, I mean it. I can't stop thinking about you, ever since you left last week, you're always on my mind. Even before that. I haven't been sure about many things in my life, but my feelings for you…" He swallowed. "For our baby. Those feelings are clear." Wesley nodded determinedly. "I love you."

I couldn't say it back, though I felt it deep in my bones. In my belly, where the fragile product of our love was growing. I couldn't say it back because I no longer trusted Wesley like I once had. "I don't want you to leave."

"I won't."

"But you did."

"I know."

"So I came back and you said you wouldn't do it again. You left me before. What's to say you won't do it again?"

Wesley's eyes searched my face. "I'll prove it."

"How?"

"You don't think my word is good?"

My broken heart crumbled even more. I shut my eyes. "Not anymore."

Wesley sighed. "Don't tell me you'd rather do this alone?"

"No, but I know I can. And I've learned so much about what I'm capable of since meeting you. I can run a business. I can be a mother. I've grown so much. How do I know you won't try and control me? Control my business and my life?"

"Is that how you see me? A controlling monster?"

"I didn't say *monster.*"

"Why would you think I'd want control over you?"

"Because you're Wesley Taves. You want control over everything."

He frowned, the joy dissipating from his face as he was faced with this new truth that I now believed. He couldn't fight it. He'd earned the reputation by trying to control things because of his ex-wife.

"If you love me, like you said, you'll love me for the woman I'm becoming. Not just the woman I am."

"I do…I promise, I do."

"Don't promise. Prove it."

Wesley gave a small nod and couldn't help smiling. "You're a good negotiator."

"I had a good teacher."

Wesley dropped his hands from my arms and stood up straight and proud. "Alright. If that's what I have to do, that's what I'll do. I know you don't believe me. That's alright. I haven't earned it. But I will."

His steadfastness was stirring, but his word no longer meant anything. He had to work for it. I was ready to make him prove it.

"I want you with me at mediation for Lucy's custody. I'm not going to hide you anymore."

I raised my eyebrows.

"Think about it. Please." His eyes dropped to my middle for a split second, but I noticed. He was already imagining our future together. Our baby growing inside me, the next year of trying to make a family out of all this mess we'd created.

I nodded slowly. "I'll think about it."

"Okay. Good. Please let me know when you get home. I want to make sure you're safe."

"I will."

Wesley gave me a lingering kiss on the cheek before we parted. If I could have wrapped my arms around him and begged him to take me home, I would have. But I couldn't. Not yet.

He had to work for that privilege.

§

The next morning, when I came down for breakfast, there was hell to pay.

Mom cornered me the moment I hit the bottom step. "I just got off the phone with Mrs. Morden."

*Shit. I should have done damage control last night.* "Mom, can I at least have some breakfast before you interrogate me?"

I would not be so lucky. She followed me into the

kitchen, yammering in my ear. "She told me Danny has a broken nose because of your *friend*, Wesley Taves."

"Yeesh. A broken nose?"

She put her hands on her hips. "You don't sound concerned about this at all."

"I'm not." I couldn't believe I had just said that, but it was the truth.

"Cara! What's wrong with you?" Dad suddenly interjected, looking up from the paper as he sat at the kitchen table.

"What's wrong with *me*?" I looked between the two of them. "Did Mrs. Morden tell you *why* Wes punched Danny? Or did he conveniently leave that out when he gave her a play-by-play of the evening?"

Mom crossed her arms over her chest. "It doesn't matter. That's an unacceptable way to treat someone. I don't care why he did it; jealousy is an incredibly ugly thing."

"Even when a man is sexually harassing someone?"

They both gasped. Dad was incredulous. "You don't mean to suggest —"

"I'm not suggesting. I'm *telling* you. Danny was a complete creep. He wouldn't stop touching me even when I asked him to stop several times. Wesley just happened to see and did what I couldn't do myself."

"Oh really, Cara, I can't imagine it could have been that bad."

I spun around to my mom. "Do you hear yourself? How you're defending him? I was fucking there! He was touching me and reaching under my skirt. I asked him to stop and he didn't."

Mom and Dad were quiet.

"So whose word are you going to trust? Mrs. Morden's or mine?"

Mom shook her head. "I'm just in shock, Cara. He's always been such a sweet boy. And that's all I want for you. All we want."

I was ready to back down, worrying I had been too harsh. But when I looked into the doorway of the kitchen, Katie was standing there, having been woken up by the commotion. Even with bedhead, she looked elegant. And she nodded at me. *Keep going.*

No way I was going to let her down. Or myself, for that matter.

"I don't care what you want any more. I'm a grown-ass woman You don't control me."

Dad gasped. "We aren't trying to control you."

"Like hell you aren't. Telling me who I can and can't date, dictating what I should do with my life and career. You'd have to be blind not to see the strings you've put on me. I'm like your little puppet and you want me to dance any direction you want. Be a good girl. Well I'm fucking tired of it."

"Cara! Language!"

"No! Fuck that!" I could not be stopped. "I'm an adult, a business owner, and I'm going to date and love whoever I goddamn please, whether you like it or not. Did you raise me just to control me? Because if so, I don't want any part of this family anymore."

Mom started to come toward me, her hands wanting to soothe my anger, but I wouldn't let her, bitterly pushing her off. "Cara, we love you. We just want what's best."

"Well, *I* know what's best for me. From now on, you can consult *me* about what's best. I'm not going to let you tell me how to live my life anymore, especially when you've proven that your judgment is so wrong."

The room was silent.

"Danny Morden is a piece of shit."

Still, silence. Filled with anger and hurt.

I had never felt so powerful in my life.

"I'm going to go after what I want." I started for the door, Katie smiling at me with pride. But before I passed her, I decided that a little more salt to the wound was just what the doctor ordered. "And one other thing. I'm pregnant."

Dad paled and Mom gasped, clutching her hand to her heart.

"And it belongs to Wesley Taves. If I'm not welcome here, that's just fine. But I've made my choice. My life, first and foremost. Not *your idea* of what's best for my life."

Katie grinned. "Fuck yes, sis."

"Katherine, stay *out* of this!" In his rage, Dad had crumpled the newspaper in his hands. It was comical.

I held up my hand. "I'll be leaving now. If you want to be a part of my life — and your grandchild's life — you know where to find me."

And with that, I left without so much as a backward glance.

## Chapter 34

### Wesley

When the doorbell rang, I had no idea who to expect. Probably an Amazon delivery or a politician.

Cara was probably the last person on the list. Though it was clear she wasn't wearing any makeup or had done much with her hair, she was stunning as ever. And already glowing. "Cara, what a surprise."

"Did you mean it?" she blurted.

I stepped out onto the front step, closing the door behind me. "What?"

"You really want me at the mediation?"

"Yes. Of course, I meant it."

She inhaled sharply and then nodded. "Then I'll be there."

I gaped. I hadn't expected her to answer me so soon. Just the night before as she walked away from me, I'd prepared for it to be the last time I'd ever see her. Now, she was agreeing to be a part of one of the biggest, most stressful parts of my life thus far. "Are you sure?"

"Are you backing out?"

"No, no. Of course not." I couldn't keep myself from smiling. "How are you feeling?"

Cara's eyes widened. She glanced down at her frame, looking no different than it had before, but knowing that soon it would change. And if she would let me be a part of her life, I couldn't wait to see her body grow with our child. "Oh, I'm okay."

"Good." I wanted to offer her all the help I could give. *One thing at a time, Wes. Lucy first. Then everything else.*

Cara peered over my shoulder, trying to see through the thin crack in the door. "Is Lucy home?"

"She is. Do you want to see her?"

Her lips curved upward. "I've missed her."

My heart swelled. "She's missed you."

Suddenly, she stepped back. "It's…I should wait. Until things are more settled."

I wanted to refute her, but I understood. Our lives were all hanging in the balance. We had both recently accepted a life without each other, only to find ourselves cosmically drawn together once again. As adults, we could handle the whiplash. But Lucy was just a child. She needed to be protected.

Cara looked back at her car, the hazards blinking. "I should go."

"I'll text you the details for Monday."

"Okay."

It took everything in me not to pull her right into my arms and kiss her with everything in me. "Thank you. You have no idea how much this means to me."

Cara shook her head. "No. I think I do."

To my surprise, she took my hand, pulled herself close to me, and kissed my cheek. "I'll see you Monday."

As she drew away, I tightened my hand around hers.

"Wait a second." I pulled her back into my embrace and kissed her.

I could feel a smile creep onto her lips before she pushed me away. "Monday."

"Monday."

Cara backed away from me slowly, and with a final nod, hurried down the steps and back into her car.

I watched her drive off, leaning on the stone banister to catch my breath.

Cara Smith was something else. And goddamn, I was ready to let the world know she was mine.

§

"Wesley, we should get started."

I shook my head. "She'll be here."

I was waiting in front of the elevator that dropped us off at Nelson's office. Lisbeth and Yves were already set up in the conference room. I had tried to keep Yves out of it. It was very unusual for anyone but parents to be involved in custody mediations. But Lisbeth had refused to do it without him.

So I had refused to do it without Cara.

"Your *nanny*?" Lisbeth's tone was full of disdain.

"No. My girlfriend."

Fire burned in her eyes. "You said she was your nanny."

"She was. Now, she's my girlfriend."

Lisbeth snarled like a caged wolf. "How?"

I smiled wryly. "It's really quite simple. I'd be happy to explain it to you if you're too naive to understand."

She glared over at her lawyer. "Are you hearing this?"

The mediator, Tina, gave her a look just as cutting. "Let's wait until mediation officially begins, shall we?"

At least someone could put Lisbeth in her place.

Cara would show up. She'd told me so herself.

Even when it was a quarter past nine and then a half hour, I believed she would show up.

"We can't keep them waiting. It's not good precedent to —"

Nelson was interrupted by the elevator dinging. My heart leaped into my throat.

The doors slid open and there she was. *Cara*. I couldn't hold back my smile when I saw her.

"Sorry I'm late!" She hurried out of the elevator, trying to straighten her black skirt. "There was a crash on the Brooklyn Bridge, so I had to be rerouted."

I cut her off, touching her shoulders. "It's alright, you're here now."

Cara took a deep breath and smiled at me.

"Thank you."

"You're welcome."

This was just the first step in a long line of things I had planned to do to prove myself to Cara. I could be a good partner. A good father to her child. *Our* child. But I had to let her in when times were tough.

And things could not have been tougher than right now.

"Okay, lovebirds, let's get started then. Look alive." Nelson hustled us into the conference room where Lisbeth was whispering angrily with her lawyer.

She immediately snapped her attention to me. "You've kept us waiting a half hour."

"That's my fault. I'm so sorry. But I appreciate you waiting for me." Cara sat in the chair I pulled out for her carefully. I couldn't help but think about the precious cargo she was carrying. "I wouldn't have wanted to miss this for anything."

Lisbeth's lips twisted into a scowl, but she said nothing.

"Alright, then let's get started on the mediation, shall

we?" Nelson shuffled some papers and gave me a look. *You ready?*

I took a deep breath. I didn't know if I'd ever be ready.

Under the table, I felt Cara's hand brush against mine. I glanced at her, immediately calmed by her smile.

I had this.

*We* had this.

I looked back to Nelson and then to Tina, giving her a curt nod. "Whenever you're ready."

And so the mediation began. It started and was stopped quickly. Lisbeth's first point of contention was, no surprise, Cara.

"I'm just fascinated that a woman who has been in our daughter's life for three months is somehow a much better option for her than me."

I shook my head. "It's not that Cara is better for Lucy than you. It's that I'm better for Lucy than you."

Nelson held up his hand. "Easy, Wes."

Cutting comment like this were just a part of the territory when it came to the two of us. Our divorce had been so contentious we couldn't even be in the same room, with our lawyers running back and forth to the mediator until we finally reached an agreement.

"It's curious you've decided now to make a bid for custody." Tina raised an eyebrow at Lisbeth. "What do you think has changed about your living circumstances that make it suitable for a child?"

Lisbeth shifted uncomfortably in her seat and looked to Yves. "Well, Lucy has always been one of my biggest regrets."

I couldn't help but respond. "That much is clear."

If kicking me wasn't immature, I'm sure Lisbeth would have done just that. "What I mean is, the way I've handled it was regrettable. I don't regret having Lucy."

"I'm afraid I don't believe you."

Cara's hand which had not left mine from the beginning of the session, squeezed mine hard. *Stay calm.*

I could do that. For her.

"You don't have to. You've never believed anything I've said. Why start now?"

"What's that supposed to mean?"

Tina held up her hand. "Okay, let's keep things civil, shall we?"

"When I told you I didn't want children, you didn't believe me. When I told you I couldn't handle the baby, you didn't believe me. When I told you I wanted to go back to work, you didn't believe me. What choice did I have but to leave?"

"I never made you go through with the pregnancy. Let's stop that narrative right now."

Lisbeth threw up her hands. "It's not like I had a choice when it made you so happy."

I knew she was shooting herself in the foot right here, talking about how awful the idea of having a baby had been to her. But now, it was about so much more than Lucy. It was about us. What had really gone wrong. I needed to know. So I didn't fuck it all up again.

With Cara, I was going to get it right.

"So you had Lucy because it made me happy? That's it?"

Lisbeth narrowed her eyes. She could see my ploy to get her to give in. And she wasn't going to fall into that. "I grew into the idea."

"Of course. Don't you remember decorating the nursery? Telling our friends and family?" A swell of emotion came up through me. "When we found out we were having a girl? Don't you remember?"

She looked away from me. "Yes, I remember all of that."

"Was leaving our daughter the only way for you to get what you wanted?"

"Leaving *you* was the only way!" Lisbeth's whole body was tense. Yves was playing Cara's role across the table, his hand on her back, rubbing softly. "You got to go on, as if nothing had changed. You went back to work; you were out of the house all day. And to add insult to injury, she looks exactly like you. I was stuck!"

I paused. Perhaps I wasn't there for her like I should have been. Maybe I could have been a better partner.

"You were so focused on Lucy you forgot about me."

"Someone had to be focused on her. From day one, I was there. I've been there the whole time for her." I swallowed. "Lisbeth, I'm sorry that I wasn't the husband you needed. But you could have divorced me and still been her mother. You didn't need to cast her aside, too. You might not realize how much damage that's done, but I do. I see it every day. I've seen how much she has yearned for a mother. Having Cara around, even for such a short time, has completely changed her life."

Lisbeth looked at me, lips pursed tight in an effort not to cry.

"She's needed you ever since you left. You might be ready now, but she's been ready this whole time, Lisbeth. And now you've waited so long that you're a stranger to her."

"Then help me not be a stranger. Give me time with her."

"I'm her father. I'm protecting her. And while I want her to have a relationship with you, you haven't done enough to have it look the way you want it to."

Lisbeth's face broke, hiding her face in her hands. For

once, she looked human. She started to cry. Yves and her lawyer tended to her while the rest of us sat in silence. I looked to Cara. She smiled sympathetically and touched my arm. *It's okay*, she seemed to say.

I nodded. I cupped her hand in mine. *This* was Lucy's home. And mine. This woman. A stranger only three months ago was now my whole life. I trusted her more than I ever trusted Lisbeth in all our years together.

"I don't want to be a stranger anymore, Wesley. Please let me have more time with her."

"More time is something I can allow. But it will happen where she's safe with people who make her feel safe. She won't be schlepped back and forth between Miami and New York. This is her home. And you can meet her where she's at, not the other way around."

Yves leaned into Lisbeth, whispering something in her ear. She nodded solemnly. "You're right. This was…sudden."

*Does that mean what I think it does?* I held back on any internal celebration. If I denied her, she could easily take this to court.

"I just want to be in her life."

"You can be. In a way that's best for Lucy."

Lisbeth eyed Cara. "Three months is all it takes for her to be better at this than me?"

I smiled. "She chose Lucy every day."

"You paid her to be there."

Cara interjected. "I would have chosen her either way."

*Breathe, Wesley. Don't lose it now.*

Lisbeth looked between us and then shook her head. "Fine." Without another word, she stood and gathered her purse and coat. "I'll be in touch to figure out a better arrangement."

Yves followed at her heels. I almost felt bad he was beholden to her every emotional whim. But better him than me.

I stood to meet her at the door before she left. "And I'll be more than agreeable." I held out my hand to her. A promise. "I'm good on my word. You know that."

She couldn't begrudge me on that point, at the very least. Lisbeth took my hand in hers. No hug, no kiss. We could be amicable. It didn't mean we had to be friends. Yves took my hand next.

Then, without another word, they left.

As soon as the door shut behind them, I couldn't help letting a cheer burst out of me.

# Chapter 35

## Cara

The moment the door closed, Wesley let out a cheer. I leaped up to join him, embracing him. His lawyer, who I'd only just met, threw his arms around us. We did our best not to scream too loud in our happiness.

Lucy was his. Maybe someday, ours.

After working through logistic details with his lawyer and the mediator, we collected our things and headed for the elevator.

"I'm sure you two have a lot to talk about." His lawyer patted him on the back. "Take your time. Take a breath. You earned it."

Wesley shook his hand. "Thank you. Thank you so much."

"Don't thank me. You two did all the work." The lawyer winked.

The elevator dinged open and Wes and I stepped inside. He pressed the button for the ground floor and the doors rolled shut.

Leaving us in a thick, desperate silence.

Our hands had not unlocked from the moment I arrived.

"Thank you."

I looked up at him. "You're welcome."

"I couldn't have done that without you."

"Yes, you could have."

"No. I really couldn't have." Wesley lifted my hand and kissed the back of it.

There was still so much unsaid, so many things we had to talk about. But for now, we could enjoy in this victory.

"How are you feeling?"

I chuckled. "Why does that feel like a loaded question?"

"Because it is." His eyes dropped to my midsection and then darted back up. "You're pregnant, after all."

Just hearing him say it made me smile. "I've been feeling horrible."

Wesley laughed. "You seem awfully happy about it."

"Because I am. Is that crazy?"

He shook his head and planted a kiss to my forehead. "Not at all. That's exactly how I hoped you'd feel."

The elevator beeped as we descended, floor after floor. Wesley wrapped his arms around me and held me close to his chest. "I'm awfully happy about it, too."

God, he knew all the right things to say. I clung to him, burying my face in his chest.

"I love you, Cara. You don't have to say it back, but I want you to know that I —"

"I love you, too."

Our eyes met.

I repeated the words carefully, attempting to see if I truly believed it. "I love you, too."

I really did.

Just then, the doors slid open at the ground floor.

But something in Wesley's eyes told me we weren't just going to walk out of the building as though nothing important had just happened.

He pulled on my hand. "Come on."

We left the bank of elevators and quickly darted into a hall off the main lobby where there was a single occupancy bathroom. Wesley pulled me into it, locked the door behind us, and pushed me up against the wall, kissing me fiercely.

"Sorry," he whispered against my lips and continued to kiss me.

"Why are you sorry? Don't be sorry."

"I don't want you to think this is all you are to me. You're so much more, Cara. But I just had to touch you, feel you against me."

I let my lips hover over his as I took in his words.

"You're the love of my life. Mother of my child. Both of my children, really."

Wesley's hand slid down to my waist. Elation filled my body. I never thought I'd get to feel him touching me like this again. I thought we were done for good.

But here we were. Savoring thoughts of our future.

"I'm here for you. I'm going to prove it every day."

I put my hand on his, feeling the nonexistent bump of my belly. "I can't wait."

Wesley smiled and then pecked my lips. "What about your parents?"

"I told them they could go fuck themselves."

He laughed loudly. "Who is this woman in front of me?"

I took a deep breath and smiled. "She is her own woman. Utterly and entirely."

Wesley lifted his chin, sizing me up. "Yes. She is." He put his lips to my ear. "And she's amazing."

His lips trailed down my jaw, to my neck, each kiss accompanied by another compliment. "Wonderful…incredible…perfect." I could have listened to him praise me all day.

For once in my life, I believed those words. I was every one of those words. All because I had chosen myself and my life over what those around me wanted.

I guided Wesley's hands down my body to the hem of my skirt.

"Are you sure?"

"Yes."

"Here?"

"Now."

Wesley's fingers traveled up my thighs and caught on my panties. He pulled them down delicately and then slipped his fingers between my lower lips. Just a slight brush over my clit and my body jerked to life. "Oh, fuck."

"You're so sensitive now, baby. And so wet for me."

I had read that pregnancy could heighten the libido. I just hadn't expected it so early and so soon.

But I wasn't about to complain. Wesley's hands felt like heaven as he finger-fucked me while he kissed and nipped at my neck. I raked my fingers through his blonde hair, pulling my body as close as possible to his. I wasn't about to lose him again.

I moaned into his shoulder as my pleasure grew, warmth blooming through my belly. I had to muffle my volume for fear of people hearing us.

Finally, I couldn't take it anymore. "I want you inside me. Oh God, Wes, I want you to fuck me."

"Yeah?"

"Yes. Now."

Wesley spun me around to the granite countertop at one end of the bathroom, a huge mirror decorating the wall behind the sink. It was a shock to see us beside each other. We didn't even have so much as a picture of the two of us together. Now, here we were in the mirror.

It was an image I hadn't expected to look so right.

Wesley pushed his nose into my hair, meeting my eyes in the mirror, clearly admiring the image as well. "What do you think? Don't we look good together?"

Blonde and brunette, brown eyes of different qualities, his tall and toned body, my diminutive, curvy figure. We were a perfect match, even if some people might not agree.

I knew the truth. "*Perfect* together."

"I'm glad you think so." Wesley unzipped his pants as I pulled up my skirt. He nudged my legs apart while his cock pushed into my core. I gasped. "Look at me."

I looked into the mirror, our eyes meeting again.

"Watch."

I kept my gaze on his as he slid his cock deeper inside me. I watched the relief and pleasure spread over his face, mouth opening, eyelids lowering. A beautiful sight.

"See what you do to me?"

I nodded, licking my lips as he began to lazily thrust into me.

"Your beautiful body. Your everything." Wesley put one hand to my belly. "I can't wait to watch you grow heavy with my child."

I groaned. The thought made me even wetter.

His hands slid up to my tits. He thumbed my nipples through my shirt, and I pushed them further into his palms, groaning. "These, too."

I laughed.

"I'll take good care of you in every…way…possible."

His last three words were punctuated by hard strokes inside me.

I dropped my hands to the edge of the counter, holding on tightly as he quickened his thrusts. "Mmm…Wes. You feel so good."

"Mmm. That's all I care about, sweetheart." Wesley was watching me closely in the mirror, memorizing all of the ways he was affecting me. "I want to make you feel good for the rest of my life."

I gasped and wrapped an arm around the back of his neck. "Faster."

He complied, groaning into my ear with every pulse of his hips.

We didn't speak for a few moments, allowing our euphoria to build. But we watched each other in the mirror, our breaths coming together, in sync with each other's bodies.

"Oh Wesley…" My orgasm was building, stronger than ever. I touched my stomach. There was a flare of even more pleasure, if that were even possible. "Wes —"

"Fuck, yes, baby. I've got you."

I shook my head, unable to speak, and grabbed his hand, pressing it right against my low belly. Wesley's eyes widened, the implied placement of his hand reminding him of just how close we had become. "I love you."

He moaned and his hips bucked harder.

"I love you so much I'm having your baby."

The intensity on his face broke into desperation, a fierce growl flying from his mouth.

I turned my face to his. "How does that make you feel?"

His lips parted to speak, but instead, he kissed me hard and came. The grunt of release rumbled against me so hard I could feel it in my pelvis. I came just a moment after him, my pussy clenching around him over and over. If he hadn't done the job already, he certainly would have then with the deluge of cum he spilled into me.

I would look forward to that for the rest of my life.

"My God, Cara." Wesley pressed his forehead to mine, trying to catch his breath.

I reached back and grabbed his backside. "Don't leave me."

"I won't."

But I wasn't just talking about him physically leaving my body. It was all of it. I didn't want him to leave me again after I'd taken so many risks to be here. "Don't leave me."

Wesley caught my meaning that time and kissed me. "Never again, Cara. No matter what."

§

Wesley and I both went to school pickup that afternoon to get Lucy. He went in to get her and I waited in the car. As I sat there, watching all the parents and children reuniting after the day apart, I was struck with excitement for my future child. I was already developing that sort of relationship with Lucy, but I couldn't wait to bond with my baby that way, too.

Of course, we had a long way to go, the baby being a mere peanut in my belly, but I was never averse to daydreaming.

How would I balance a baby and a new business? Well, now that Wesley was by my side, nothing felt impossible.

Nothing at all.

I spotted Wesley and Lucy walking out of school, hand in hand. My heart swelled. That was my family right there. I didn't know exactly what the future held for me and Wesley, but I knew we could handle anything together.

And Lucy…Lucy was mine, too.

"I have a surprise for you!" I heard Wesley cry as he got closer to the car. He came up behind Lucy and wrapped his hands around her eyes.

"Daddy, I can't see!"

"That's the point!" They walked over to the car and came to my door. "Okay, keep your eyes closed…" Wesley smiled at me through the window and then opened the door.

Lucy was very committed to following the rules. "Can I look now?"

He laughed. "Yes. Open them."

Lucy opened her big brown eyes and looked up at me. "Cara?! Is that really you?"

"Of course, it is!" I started to climb out of the car, but Lucy beat me to it, leaping right into my lap.

"I missed you! I missed you so much! I kept asking Daddy when you'd be back and he said you might be gone forever!"

MY eyes filled with tears as she buried her head in my shoulder. I stroked her soft blonde hair. "Not gone forever. Not ever again."

"You promise?"

I glanced at Wesley and then nodded. "I promise."

Wesley had to prove his commitment to me. But I had to prove mine to Lucy.

And I had no doubt both of us would be able to do so.

## Chapter 36

Wesley

From the moment Cara and I reunited, I didn't leave her side. Well, as long as I wasn't at work. She moved in with Lucy and me almost immediately, our lives intermingling without any hiccups.

Lucy was thrilled she was going to be a big sister, not to mention having Cara as a maternal figure in her everyday life, permanently. She didn't even let the whiplash of Cara's departure and return get in the way of her joy.

We didn't tell Lucy about the drama Lisbeth had created. It didn't make sense to. Besides, Lisbeth and I were actually communicating with civility for the first time since our divorce. Lisbeth wanted Lucy to be the flower girl at her wedding and while I told her I'd consider it, I was most likely going to say yes. That would be a special way to usher in their relationship. As long as Lisbeth stayed respectful of Lucy's needs and kept her at the center, we would be able to make things work.

There were a few matters that were…complicated.

One being that piece of shit Danny Morden, who threatened to pull the contract out from under Cara. A quick phone call from my lawyer shut him up, though. I wasn't about to let him ruin Cara's dreams.

The second, more pressing issue in my eyes, was the topic of Cara's parents.

It took a while for them to come around, but Cara was resolute.

"I'm not calling them. I've got too much on my plate. Plus, I did nothing wrong."

This was true. Her body was adjusting to pregnancy and with that came bouts of morning sickness, fatigue, and shifting moods. On top of that, she had the beginnings of her new business. And perhaps most importantly, Stan and Linda needed to realize she wasn't a little girl anymore.

She would wait for them to come to her.

That's when I knew she really was coming into her own.

And eventually, they did. The phone call lasted hours, Cara's parents arguing while she remained stalwart and strong.

I left her alone for most of the conversation but couldn't help standing by the bedroom door and listening for a moment.

"I've made my decision. It's my life and my child. You should be happy that I'm not going at this alone. And I'm going to choose *my* family over everything else, always."

*Her family*. The words had me overcome with emotion. Cara had dedicated herself to Lucy. To me. I would do everything in my power to dedicate myself to her.

When the phone call ended, Cara came out of the bedroom looking tired and bedraggled, but with wonderful news. "They want to see you."

Which is how we ended up piled into the car headed out of Brooklyn to Oceanside.

"Will they like me?" Lucy asked timidly from the backseat.

I glanced at her in the rearview. She had picked out her outfit and done a marvelous job. Pink and frilly, her hair tied back in a bow.

Cara spoke first, turning to face Lucy. "Of course, they will." She reached into the backseat and squeezed Lucy's knee. "How could they not love someone as cute as you?"

Lucy shrugged and glanced out her window. "I don't know. Not everyone likes everybody."

Cara pursed her lips, looking to me.

"You know, Lucy, Cara's mommy and daddy are just as nice as Cara." I couldn't tell her the truth. That they scared the shit out of me. However, even though they might not have been nice to me when I met them, I doubted they would pull the same act with a little girl. "If you're uncomfortable, you just tell one of us and we'll help, okay?"

Cara sighed from the passenger seat and rested her hand on her stomach. Now nearing three months pregnant she was *just* starting to show. Not that anyone could tell except for me. It was only when the fabric of her clothing was pulled very taut that an outside eye could tell.

It was just for me and her.

When we pulled up to the Smith house, I immediately felt a fight or flight response. I didn't want to walk into my demise yet again. "Alright." I smacked my hands against the steering wheel. *Showtime, Taves.* "Let's do this, huh?"

Cara smiled at me and grabbed my hand.

*I needed that.*

"There they are!"

We all looked to the front door where Stan, Linda, and

Katie all stood. Katie was the happiest, followed by Linda who managed a polite smile. Stan trailed behind in the welcome department, looking stoic and cold.

It didn't matter what they thought of me. I knew what Cara believed. I could see it right on her wrist; the bracelet I'd given her. She never took it off. On top of her constant reassurance, that was a sign.

And I couldn't imagine a person in this whole world that wouldn't be charmed by Lucy Taves.

Cara got out first and Lucy followed before either of us could fetch her. I watched as Cara and Lucy walked hand in hand up the walk toward Cara's family. Just as expected, they were all enchanted by Lucy. Even Stan cracked a smile.

*Deep breath. You can do this.*

I finally got out of the car and followed my girls up the walk. Stan's face returned to stone when he laid eyes on me, but Linda made up for it. "Wesley, we're so happy you all could make it." She embraced me and kissed my cheek. She was making an effort. For Cara's sake. I could appreciate that.

"We've been looking forward to this all week. Haven't we, Luce?" I nudged my daughter, who was being a bit bashful, leaning into Cara's leg.

Lucy nodded adamantly.

"So this is Lucy, hmm?" Linda bent down. "I've heard so many wonderful things about you. Would you like to come inside with me?"

Katie grinned. "There may or may not be something for you in the living room."

Lucy's ears perked at the suggestion of a present. "Alright. That sounds nice."

"Of course, it does! Come with me. I'm your Aunt

Katie. I'm like the cool, fun aunt." Katie held her hand out to Lucy.

Lucy looked up at me and then to Cara.

Cara let go of her hand and pushed her toward Katie. "Go ahead, honey. I promise, she won't bite."

At Cara's encouragement, Lucy accepted Katie's invitation.

Katie led Lucy inside. "You'll have to tell me where you got that dress. Does it come in my size?"

Lucy giggled so loud I could hear it even after she disappeared inside. "No, definitely not!"

Thank God for Katie.

Left alone with Stan and Linda, the air was tense.

Stan cleared his throat. "Wesley, I think you and I should talk in private. Man to man."

Cara touched my back softly. She had been very clear that if anything was making me uncomfortable, we would leave. But I'd been looking forward to getting a chance to talk with Stan since this meeting was arranged.

I could finally let him know my true thoughts, uninhibited by fear.

"I'd love to, Stan. You lead the way."

Cara pulled on my arm before I followed Stan inside. "We'll be in the living room if you need anything."

I smiled and kissed her cheek. In these few weeks together, I'd realized that Cara and I were more similar than different. She was a protector like me. She just did it differently. Softly with her words and her love. I would have to take some notes from her book on that.

I followed Stan through the kitchen and onto the glass enclosed porch. It was a sunny, early spring day. The porch was filled with greenery that was happy to be soaking in some rays.

"Take a seat."

I did as I was told, sitting on the wicker loveseat across from Stan.

"We're not…pleased, you know. Linda is better at hiding it than me, but this whole situation is not how we would have wanted it to go."

I nodded. "I'm sorry to hear that. But as a father myself, I understand why you feel that way." I had resolved before coming here to be as agreeable as possible. I would take any of his abuses for Cara's sake.

It didn't mean it was easy, though.

"Yes, and now that you two are having a child…" Stan cleared his throat. "I am happy to know that Cara isn't doing it without the father. And I'll admit we were very impulsive the last time we saw you. I'm not proud of how I handled myself. My daughters are my world. You understand that."

"Of course."

"And just because Cara loves who she loves…" Stan nearly rolled his eyes as he said that, unsure how I could possibly be the man for her. "I'm not going to sever ties with her or my grandchild. But I'm still not sure about you."

"Is there anything that would make you sure of me?"

Stan held his hands out. "Maybe. Maybe not. Jury's out."

*Maybe.* I could live with maybe. That meant there was a chance that one day, they might be sure of me. "Well, Stan, you don't have to like me. I wish you did, but you don't have to. That's your prerogative." I cleared my throat. "However, I'm committed to Cara. To her well-being. To her goals. To our child. I have no question that I can support her however she needs. Financially and emotionally."

"But what about your daughter? She'll always come first, won't she?"

"Yes." No question. "But that's a mutual feeling. I know Cara would put Lucy before me if she had to. That's just something we both have come to understand."

Stan frowned. "Hmm."

"Stan, I love her very much."

"So will you be marrying her? You have a child on the way, after all."

I held back a laugh. "I've offered. Cara doesn't want to rush. You can ask her yourself."

"It's good to know you're willing to step up."

"I am. I've never been one to back down from what I want."

Stan smiled. *A smile! I've done it!* "Okay. I respect that. I still want to get to know you some more, of course. I'm not sure about you, but this conversation has given me a bit more confidence in what you can offer my daughter."

"Of course."

"Cara's a special girl."

"Trust me, I know."

Stan was silent for a moment, his lips tightening. "I admit, I don't think I was ready to have her find someone so soon and move on from me being the man in her life."

I smiled softly. We both had daughters and understood how precious they are, but we were of different schools of parenting. Stan had beliefs that his daughters would eventually grow up and find husbands and he would need to pass the baton. It was protectiveness. I could understand that. But in that moment, I resolved that I would never make Lucy feel she owed me her allegiance that way. Besides, who knew who she would grow up to be? "Having girls is scary, isn't it?"

Stan's eyebrows jumped. "Now that you mention it,

yeah. Yes, it is. I thought that feeling would go away one day, but it doesn't. Something to think about."

We were both quiet, sizing each other up. It seemed that for now we had come to an agreement. I was on a trial basis. Stan could change his mind about me at any moment. But for now, we were civil. Amicable, even.

The door to the porch burst open and Lucy rushed in, holding up her gift. "Look Daddy, look what they got me!" Lucy brought the gift closer. A pair of binoculars. "So I can watch the animals. Like squirrels and birds and —"

"Well, that's just about the nicest gift you've ever gotten, don't' you think?"

Lucy nodded enthusiastically.

I looked over at Stan. "Did you say thank you?"

She followed my gaze and then bashfully looked back at me.

"Go on."

Lucy, being a brave girl, walked over toward Stan, binoculars to her chest. "Thank you for my present."

All of Stan's walls fell. "You know, if your daddy is okay with it, you could call me Grandpa. If you want."

Lucy grinned and nodded. "I'd like that." She threw her arms around him, and Stan drew her up into his lap in a tight hug.

"Oh, I've missed this…"

"It's nice, isn't it?"

Stan glanced at me from over Lucy's shoulder. "Yeah. The best."

Cara, Katie, and Linda joined us only a moment later. Cara smiled when she saw Stan and Lucy, and then her eyes found mine, full of concern.

I smiled. I could give her the details later; all she needed to know right now was that everything was okay.

We were going to be okay.

We spent the rest of the afternoon on the porch drinking coffee and eating a spread of Linda's delectable baked goods, watching Lucy as she peered out the windows with her new binoculars.

Cara stayed by my side the whole time, fielding questions without hesitation, her hand in mine. Every question her family had about our life together had her smiling.

By the end of our visit, I felt the warmth of the Smith household. I could see where Cara's boundless love came from. Just thinking that Lucy and our unborn child were going to have this much love in their lives had me beaming from ear to ear.

And if *I* even got a fraction of the love in this room? Well, I was going to live a beautiful life — with Cara by my side.

# Epilogue

## Cara

*One year later…*

I couldn't believe the day was finally here. The opening of Little Wings Daycare. Everything was arranged to perfection, from the infant room to the indoor playground upstairs. So many people had turned out for our opening day. Members of the community, future students with their parents, and investors we had collected over the past year.

Not to mention the most important people of all: my family.

Henry, my little bundle of joy, was in a wrap on my chest. It was his near permanent spot since his birth. I took him everywhere with me. Building walk throughs, business meetings, coffee and dinner dates with my family. He was an extremely well-behaved baby, too, and was a beginner babbler, which made for lots of cute, nonsensical conversations.

Lucy, now seven and in second grade, was playing happy hostess. She was undaunted by anyone, talking to parents and entertaining their little ones, showing off her skills as a big sister. From the moment Henry was born, Lucy took the job very seriously. She wanted to know all the ins and outs of taking care of a baby and had become very adept at diaper changes. However, most of the time she spent with Henry was reading books about animals to him or entertaining him with stuffed animals.

Motherhood was the best thing that ever happened to me. And the hardest. But thankfully, my family was always there to lend a helping hand.

Katie was there keeping a close eye on Lucy so I could focus on making sure the event ran smoothly. Katie was in her final year of business school and had just accepted a job at an up-and-coming fashion brand in the city. She still had big dreams of starting her own business, but with Wesley's guidance, had decided to start slow so she could really hone her focus.

"Everything alright?"

I turned around to find my mother and father. They had been helping out with final preparations all week and had arrived at the daycare early that morning, even before I got there.

"I think so. Do you think people are enjoying themselves?"

Mom smiled. "Oh, definitely. I mean, this is just a parent's dream."

I scanned the first floor. It was colorful, safe, and spacious, led by a team of amazing caretakers and educators I'd hired over the past few months. "That was the goal."

"Well, you did it, kiddo. We're so proud of you." Dad wrapped his arm around me.

Henry cooed at my chest, starting to stir from his post-feeding nap.

"Are you just waking up, sweet pea?" Mom nuzzled Henry's nose with hers and gave him a kiss, at which he giggled.

As my parents doted over my baby, I had to pause and take a moment to reflect on how far we'd come. Throughout the past year, things between my parents and Wesley had softened. But it wasn't until Henry was born that they finally accepted that I was living my own life.

At my bedside in the hospital, marveling at the little life Wes and I had created, Mom had burst into tears, completely inconsolable.

"I'm just so happy…and so sorry…"

Wesley and I were both dazed with exhaustion from the forty-eight hours of labor and delivery and had looked to Dad for an explanation.

My dad was not a crier, but I saw tears in his eyes, too. "We owe you an apology for…everything."

Mom reached out to Wesley and embraced him. "You've just taken such good care of her. And you love her so much. It's obvious. I don't know why we didn't see it before."

Wesley had been an amazing partner throughout my pregnancy. There was nothing that fazed him. From late night cravings to mood swings to swollen feet, there was nothing he wouldn't do for me. Including my unrelenting horniness.

"We should have trusted you." My father ran his hand over my hair.

That apology gave me the extra boost I needed to make it to where I was now. Even the sleeplessness of a newborn couldn't hold me back. At first, I thought I'd have to postpone opening the daycare at least a few months so I could get a grasp on motherhood, but knowing how many people believed in me, exhaustion wasn't going to get in my way.

Of course, the most important person present at opening day of Little Wings was the man who'd made it all possible: Wesley Taves.

He was chatting with his new business partner, Caspar Steele. The two were teaming up on MediaDeck's new venture now that Readly was up and running and Wesley's paternity leave was coming to an end.

As if he felt his eyes on me, he looked across the room and gave me an easy smile. A year and a baby in, and Wesley still made me feel butterflies in my stomach.

It was hard to believe that just a little over a year ago, none of this seemed possible. I was going about building a business haplessly and all alone. Still trying to learn the ropes.

And then I met him.

I never imagined life could be this amazing, but Wesley Taves showed me a world of possibility. His daughter — our daughter — chose to love me. There was no love more powerful than that.

Wesley gave Caspar a tap on the shoulder, nodding toward me, before crossing the room to me. "How're you doing?"

"Good."

"This is all so amazing, Wesley," Mom said, squeezing Wesley's arm.

Dad followed up with a hearty pat to his back. "You should be proud."

Wesley beamed. Though Wesley had always been confident in his own right, getting my parents' acceptance had given him a completely different kind of confidence. "Thank you. You ready for a speech?"

I sighed. "Ready as I'll ever be."

"Oh, you're ready." Wesley kissed my forehead and guided me toward the front of the room. "Just do it as you practiced."

Wesley had said that a speech was a necessity for an event like this. I tried to get out of it, but Wesley wasn't backing down. A speech would be happening, whether I liked it or not.

At the front of the room, the sea of people looked even bigger. How was I going to get all their attention?

"Excuse me!" Wesley held up his hand. "Could we cut the music?"

The music playing under the event stopped and everyone quieted down.

"Floor is yours, baby." Wesley winked at me and gave Henry's hand a squeeze before stepping off to the side.

I cleared my throat. *Now or never, Cara.* "Good morning, everyone! Thank you for being here."

I glanced around at all of the faces. *Focus on the people you did this for.* I found Lucy and Katie in the crowd. My parents. Then Wesley. I tightened my hands around Henry. With all of them, I could do anything. "It has been my dream for years to open a daycare that's able to provide high-quality care to all children, regardless of income. Little Wings is a place for all children. To learn, to grow, to love." I touched the butterfly on my wrist. That's what Little Wings was named for. It gave me a burst of confidence. "I'm happy to announce that an 'anonymous donor' has initiated our ongoing scholarship fund with an incredibly generous donation of five hundred thousand dollars."

The crowd gasped and applauded.

Wesley had insisted I not name him, which I thought was silly, but I left him anonymous as he wished.

"Registration is open for the upcoming session of —"

Wesley suddenly cut me off, stepping up beside me. "Sorry to cut in, but I do have an addendum."

I tried my best not to glare. He'd just hyped me up to make this big speech and now he was interrupting? *Some habits die hard, I guess.* Wesley had become much better at letting me take the reins when it came to Little Wings, so I was shocked he was stepping in like this.

"I can't imagine someone better to run a daycare than Cara Smith. Not just because she's mother to my children and a great roommate…"

The crowd chuckled.

"Wesley, what are you doing?" I whispered.

Wesley smiled at me, an unreadable emotion in his eyes.

I felt a tug on my dress. I turned around to find Lucy standing next to me. "Lucy?"

"Cara, will you marry my daddy?"

I blinked. The words weren't connecting in my head. "W-what?"

Lucy laughed. "Would you marry my —"

"I heard you, I'm just…"

The crowd gasped again, however, this time I wasn't sure why. I whipped around to Wesley, but he was no longer standing beside me.

He was down on one knee, holding a small red box. "Cara…"

I gasped, covering my mouth with my hand. Henry stirred restlessly against my chest so I rocked him side to side, praying to God he wouldn't start squalling.

"I love you. You're brilliant. You're courageous. You're an amazing mother. You said you didn't want to rush things. But I can't wait another moment without you as my wife. Will you marry me?"

Lucy wrapped her arms around my waist and looked

up at me. I smiled down at her, tearing up as I ran my hand through her blonde hair, just like her father's and brother's. I glanced over at my parents and Katie, all of them looking proud and knowing, as if they were aware this was going to happen.

Everyone was saying yes.

Now it was my turn.

I looked into Wesley's deep brown eyes. "Yes. Of course, I'll marry you!"

The entire room exploded with excited cheers, scaring Henry so bad he started to cry, but I comforted him quickly. Nothing could get in the way of my joy and gratitude toward the universe for giving me this gift.

Wesley opened the box, revealing a ring covered in sparkling diamonds.

"I helped Daddy pick it out."

Wesley slid the ring onto my finger. It fit perfect and looked right at home on my hand. "Oh, Lucy, you did a wonderful job." I hugged her tight to my side. "I love you so much."

Then I looked to Wesley who had risen to his feet. "And you…"

Wesley smirked. "What about me?"

I took his face in my hands. "Kiss me, Taves."

He didn't waste another second, planting his lips on mine to another chorus of celebration from the crowd.

With Henry at my chest, Lucy at my hip, and Wesley's arms around me, there was nowhere on earth I'd rather be.

I couldn't wait for the magnificent love that awaited us.

## THE END

Did you like *Nanny for the Protector*? Then you'll LOVE *Bossy: Daddy's Best Friend Romance*.

\* \* \*

**Finding out last night's one-night stand is today's new boss is troublesome.**
**Realizing that he is your daddy's best friend is scandalous.**

You're not supposed to spend your first day on the job being hoisted onto bathroom sinks.

Or let Mr. Tall, Dark and Sexy claim every inch of your soul.

No fraternizing with the boss huh?

Well, I tried calling it off.

Until I saw the way he held his beautiful daughter.

My heart melted.

My guard crumbled.

No way I'm letting go of Mr. Perfect now.

But what happens when my daddy finds out I love his best friend?

\* \* \*

**Start reading Bossy NOW!**

## Bossy Sneak Peek

### *Logan*

I pinched the spot between my brows, zeroing in on my work and tuning out the conversation coming from the front seat. *The wheels on the bus go round and round, round and round, round and round.* The kids' voices on the tablet sang over and over.

I sighed, then hummed under my breath to tune out all sounds and read through the note I was taking. How did the word "round" get in there? I backspaced and retyped.

"All day long!" Charlotte cheered next to me.

A smile twitched my cheek, and I reached out to ruffle her hair.

"Daddy," my four-year-old yelled and batted my hand off. "You'll mess up my hair."

I glanced at the two pigtails she'd given her Aunt Claire strict directions on how to fix that morning. Her red hair was so curly and soft that the ribbons were already coming undone. I definitely wouldn't be the one to tell her that.

"Sorry, Muffin."

"It's okay, Daddy." She tapped my arm. "You can touch my hair later, okay?"

I stifled my laughter. "Okay."

I went back to my laptop. Where was I? Oh, yeah. Trying to catch up with work while I was on my way to Hannibal, Missouri, in a car with my friend, sister, and daughter. Not the quietest bunch. I blew out a breath as my office email pinged with updates.

"*French fries!* I should be back at the museum," I bit out.

"If you're going to say a cuss word, just say *the word*," Claire, my younger sister, twisted in the front passenger seat to eyeball me.

My gaze slid to Charlotte. She was already sucked into another video. I looked back up at my sister, and her grin told me everything. She knew I'd have hell to pay with Lacey if Charlotte picked up a bad word from me. And Charlotte could pick up everything. So fast. Too fast. I refrained from touching her hair. She used to be so tiny, and now she had pigtails, fancy jackets, and sneakers. Soon, she'll be putting on nail polish.

"I can even help." Claire's eyes twinkled mischievously. "A cuss word is f—"

"Claire!" I growled and covered both of Charlotte's ears. "Stop."

"Fish!" My sister beamed.

Charlotte whined and shook her head. Her ribbons came free, and her hair poured down her face. Eyes widening, I leaned away from the crime scene. If she even suspected I had a hand in her pigtails coming loose, we wouldn't make it to Hannibal in one piece. Thankfully, she was so lost in Cocomelon that she tucked the strands behind her ears and continued watching.

Claire's laughter pulled my eyes up. "Lucky."

"Tell me why I invited you again?" I eyed her before going back to my laptop.

A couple of months ago, my Aunt Grace's lawyer informed me she'd left her estate to me. While I was sad she was gone and I missed her, traveling to a new city to settle an estate wasn't in my plans and didn't fit into my tight schedule. But the man insisted that I couldn't handle it over the phone. Now, here I was, tucked in an SUV, on the way to Hannibal while heaven knew what was happening back at the museum.

A work email pinged, and I clicked on it. A new art consignment just arrived, and they were offloading it onto the premises. A sigh left me. I should be there. What if they didn't handle it properly? What if—

"You'd feel a lot better if you just turn off the laptop and take in the countryside," my friend slash art director at the museum, Chris, threw over his shoulder. He'd turned chauffeur for this trip. "There's a lot to see."

"Chris is right. Look up, bro," Claire put in.

I eyed them both and took a second to glimpse out the window. Endless fields of grass and sunshine held no appeal to me, except when they were slapped onto a canvas and priced very highly. *No, thanks.*

"Or...you can look at this as a break. Remember one of those? When you stop working and just relax?" Claire said.

"Like you're one to tell me. I dragged you away from work. When last did you use your sick days?"

"Um, hello? Do you know what being sick means?" Claire returned. "You're running on fumes, old man."

"I'm thirty-seven!"

"Yikes. The only thing I heard was 'get off my lawn!'" Claire said in a fake feeble voice.

Chris guffawed. "Yeah, I heard that, too."

"Idiot, you're only two years behind me."

"Daddy said a bad word," Charlotte murmured.

I facepalmed, and Chris and Claire shared a fist bump.

"You're enjoying this, right?" I said above their laughter. "You guys are the worst."

When Claire coughed herself out of a laughing fit, she said, "Relax, Logan. Enjoy this. Like a normal person would enjoy a mini-vacation."

"Vacation," Charlotte repeated.

"Yes, Charlie." Chris glanced back at Charlotte. "Tell your dad he needs more vacations."

"Vacation!" Charlotte threw both hands up.

Soon enough, all of them chorused "vacation" over and over. I sighed and leaned back, struggling hard to keep from smiling. I wouldn't have made it halfway to Hannibal if it wasn't for them.

When they'd calmed, I resumed perusing my emails. More popped in, some from art shows inviting me to check out their work. I gritted my teeth. If only Justin hadn't chosen this critical time to quit.

"What is it?" Chris voiced.

I looked up to meet his eyes in the rearview mirror. "What?"

"You're grumbling like a grizzly bear," Claire said, her voice high and teasing, but I could hear the worry underneath.

"Nothing."

"Justin's resignation?" Chris guessed.

I gave in. "This is the height of the season. Many art shows. Pieces to peruse. The worst time for a seasoned curator to quit."

"You have a new one starting next week."

"True," I bit out.

I was never one to complain. Whatever came my way, I fixed it with an immediacy that left heads spinning. Maybe the journey to Hannibal, and knowing I was far from the museum when I should be there, rose my hackles.

"Daddy, what is that?" Charlotte's voice pulled me out of my thoughts.

I followed the line of her chubby fingers.

"It's a tour bus, Muffin." I read the inscription on the side. Something about Mark Twain.

"What's a *too* bus?"

"Tour bus. It takes you around town and shows you exciting places."

"Daddy, I want one."

I laughed, collecting her hand in mine. "Sure, Muffin." I was banking on her forgetting in the next fifteen minutes, and I was half-right. Before we turned the corner, she pressed her face against the window and pointed at more sights, asking what they were. Chris, Claire, and I took turns answering.

It'd been a while since I was in Hannibal. A slight twinge of regret passed through me. Over the past few years, I'd grown very busy and didn't visit Aunt Grace as much. But we always spoke over the phone. How fleeting life was.

And apparently, reflection time was fleeting as Charlotte grabbed my hand, drawing my attention to her. I quickly set my laptop to the side and focused on my daughter. Her wide eyes, bright smile, and curious questions lightened my mood.

Lacey said the trip would be good for Charlotte. I knew it was partly because she was busy with her wedding preparations, but I was glad to have Charlotte to myself for a whole weekend. I was usually so busy I barely had enough time with her. Ribbons out of the way, I ruffled her hair, and she leaned into me, her tiny hand resting against my arm. My heart squeezed. I kissed the top of her head.

Even though the romance between her mom and me ended as quickly as it began, she was the greatest gift I never knew I needed.

"I love you, Muffin."

"Love you, too, Daddy."

Claire glanced back at us. I half excepted her to roll her eyes, but she smiled softly. She enjoyed teasing me, but she was the sweetest aunt when Charlotte was involved.

"Alright, we're here." Chris pulled the car to a stop and got out.

Back home, I had rented an Airbnb for us and sent Chris the address. With Charlotte's hand in mine, I got out, and we walked to stand before the stately home with vines running up the sides.

"Looks like something from the nineteenth century," Claire noted.

"It is," I started. "It has a fascinating history. It's—"

"Daddy! Let's see!" Charlotte tore from my side and ran past the fence, the walkway, and onto the porch. "Open it."

I smiled, shaking my head. "The history can wait, then."

The interior was nothing like the outside. It was all polished wood and shiny surfaces.

"Fancy." Chris walked past me, taking our luggage upstairs.

"I'm staying in the bigger room!" Claire yelled, running up the stairs behind him.

"Not on your life." Chris sped up.

Shaking my head, I walked into the living room, then the kitchen before going upstairs. The master bedroom was for me. Thank goodness Chris and Claire stayed away from it with their bickering. But my little Muffin couldn't care less. She was jumping on the bed, her hair flying around her face.

"Charlotte." I channeled my "dad voice." "No jumping on the bed."

She collapsed on her back and groaned. "Then what do we do?"

I pushed aside the curtain covering the bay windows and took in the gardens, the park, and the gently flowing river. Charlotte appeared next to me.

"Daddy, can we go down to the water?"

I looked down at my daughter. She was so excited she could barely stand in place. "Sure thing, Muffin."

"Yippee!" she yelled and sped out of the room, announcing our new plans.

Soon, we were all winding through the park, curving between locals and taking in the sights. I forced my head away from work and focused on Charlotte running close to the water, holding onto the metal bars and waving at the ducks.

"How are you feeling?" My sister walked astride me, thumping her shoulder against mine.

I raised both shoulders. "Good." I looked between her and Chris. They always seemed to be working out new ways to torment me, and right now, suspicion sat firmly in my gut.

Instead of teasing, they just smiled.

Even worse. "Whatever you both are up to, I'm not falling for it." Not waiting for their answers, I went down to the water and joined Charlotte for a couple of minutes.

She drifted on, and I kept close.

"What's happening there?" She pointed ahead.

I squinted. Seemed a lot of folks walking beside us were all drifting in that direction. "It seems to be a market of sorts." Overly bubbly request coming in *one, two...*

"Can we go?"

I laughed. "Of course, Muffin."

She started ahead, and I followed behind, glued to her skipping form.

I could relax. This could be a vacation.

**Start reading Bossy NOW!**

Printed in Great Britain
by Amazon